The Dead

The Wilds Book Three

Donna Augustine

Chapter One

Survivor or victim. That was how I'd always divided people. Some people thought they weren't exclusive to each other. Personally, I'd always found it hard to be both at the same time, and I'd determined from a very young age which category I was going to be in. It took me a long time to climb out of the victim column, but I'd done it.

Turned out the hardest part wasn't getting into the right category, but staying there. I was finding out that it only took one small blip in the span of your life to kick you back onto the wrong list. Like right now, for instance—as I sprang up in bed, my shirt soaked through with liquid fear and my heart pounding like a scared rabbit, not one part of me told the story of a survivor.

My fingers stiffened around the blanket I gripped as if it were my funeral shroud, trying to stop the trembling in my hands. I forced myself to breathe through my nose, even as it felt like it was an eighth of the size needed to do the job.

Time to do inventory; I needed my checklist, the one that kept me sane on the mornings when the dreams didn't seem so dreamlike and the stench of death clung to me like I'd bathed in my own destruction.

I was safe in the confines of the Rock, in a house that was smack in the middle of a walled community—walls I used to hate but whose brick seemed to comfort me on mornings like this. A quick look around showed that there weren't any Dark Walkers in my bedroom. The sounds of chimes weren't tinkling on the air and nothing was trying to steal my life or my magic.

I was alone, like I had been every day for the last two weeks, since we'd returned with Tiffy. The panic started to chip away from a body frozen in fear and my shoulders sagged. I sank deeper into the bed as my inventory, once again, drove out imaginary threats.

The fact that I had a whole day before I'd be facing my nocturnal stalkers again gave me solace. By then, the memories would've faded, bleached away by a beautiful sunny day, and my tired body wouldn't care about last night's battle.

I got out of bed, trying to think of the positives, like how at least I hadn't screamed this time and called attention to my sad state. Seeing Dax appear in my doorway ready to slay my enemies and not finding a foe almost made me wish the dreams *were* real. It was hard to look tough, like nothing bothered you, when you were screaming like a stuck pig.

Dax would stand in the doorway and assess the non-threat, not saying anything. I'd sit there, without an excuse. Finally, I'd nod and he'd back out of the room, not knowing what to do with the invisible monsters any more than I did.

He'd been hanging around later in the mornings than he used to. It didn't take a huge mental leap to figure out why. For someone who prided themselves on being independent, I still hadn't told him he didn't need to hang around in some roundabout way. I would today…if the right moment arose. Or tomorrow. It wasn't like there was a pressing need to tell him right away. Why bring up an awkward discussion for no reason?

Bookie, on the other hand, had no qualms about discussing it. I'd had the unfortunate opportunity to startle him when he'd come by predawn last week with a hankering for some of Tank's jerky stash.

I'd been forced to confess my sad state of affairs as he interrogated me worse than Ms. Edith had when I'd lived in the Cement Giant, that hellhole that was only a mound of rubble now.

I'd told him it wasn't a big deal, but blowing Bookie off when he caught scent of an unanswered question was like trying to rip a half-read book from his bare hands. He wasn't called Bookie for nothing.

I'd tried to tell him it

3

only happened once in a blue moon, but the skepticism in his eyes and the unsaid words told me he hadn't bought it.

Then he'd gone on to explain how the human brain can only handle so much—even mine—and he wasn't surprised that the recent occurrences had caused this.

He'd told me that in the Glory Years, way back before the Bloody Death ravaged the world, they'd had these people called therapists. They'd believed it was a good thing to talk stuff out. I would've thought he was making the whole thing up if Bookie wasn't such an expert on that time.

He'd sworn up and down that it worked. He'd even suggested that I try it on him. Of course, I explained he was crazy. There was only one thing that was going to fix me—killing every Dark Walker I could get my hands on. My body might have been weary, but my soul was ready to fight. I dragged myself over to my dresser and pulled out my work clothes for the day, determined to drive away these fears the only way I knew how—my enemies' blood.

***

I got to the trader hole an hour later, with a belly full of Fudge's crispy bacon and none of the watch dogs the wiser, and there were more than one these days. If it wasn't Dax dogging my

4

steps, or Bookie offering to play therapist, Rocky was showing up. I had either the worst timing of anyone alive or they were all keeping tabs on me. Lucky for me, there were some issues with the north side of the Rock's wall that needed Rocky's attention, and a foal had decided to come early, so I'd lost Bookie. Dax must have had something other pressing matter, since he'd already been gone this morning, doing whatever it was he went and did. Of course, I would've gotten out of the Rock alone anyway, but them being handed distractions was much less time consuming than me having to spend an hour or two planting fake ones.

I dismounted from Charlie, the horse Rocky had given me because he'd said he owed me for vetting his place—even though I hadn't found a single Dark Walker—and tied his reins to his saddle. I wouldn't tie him to the hitching post, trapping him if he needed to make a quick getaway. As long as everything was calm, he'd wait patiently for me to return. If he needed to leave, then that was what he should do, and I understood. He wouldn't abandon me unless his life depended on it. He was a great horse, even if I hadn't earned him.

I knew there were motives behind the horse and how nice Rocky was being, even without Dax's near constant reminders. Rocky wanted to keep his place free and clear of the Dark Walkers, and to do that, he needed me to stay. Dax had motives too, though. He wanted to keep an eye on me because it was hard to get revenge against an enemy you couldn't see.

If I wanted to get real logical, did motives matter that much anyway? Does anyone ever do anything without something in it for them? Except for maybe Bookie, who seemed to be operating on a higher moral plane than the rest of us. It seemed to me that most relationships were built on give and take.

There I went again, getting too deep. The only way to survive this world at the moment was to keep it all nice and shallow. I could dig through the deep muck of ulterior motives after I had a safe place to burrow in, and that wasn't now. It might never be if I didn't handle business. I gave Charlie a pat on the neck, told him I'd be back as soon as I could, and walked into Bert's Trader Hole.

Bert, owner and bartender of the establishment, squinted, setting loose a whole new layer of wrinkles on an already well-etched face. This was my third time here this week, and I wondered if he'd found the fresh grave in the woods, about a half a mile away.

Not that he'd say anything if he did. He knew who my people were. People in these parts were well aware of the Rock, along with the man who ran it. Even if they hadn't heard of Rocky—which was as likely as finding fresh month-old bread—they'd all heard of Dax. He'd been busy making sure everyone who hadn't known him before did now, in addition to what would happen if you crossed him.

Dax's motives were pretty obvious. It was good business to let everyone know it was in their best interest to keep their mouths shut about our presence in the area, since there were oodles of Dark Walkers sniffing around. I wasn't completely positive that was the only reason, though, as it was hard to be a hundred percent sure, since Dax hadn't sat down and written out his agenda for me. I didn't take it personally because I didn't want to have to return the favor and spell out exactly what I was doing every day. It was more of a guessing game between us. Either way, his tour of intimidation turned out to be pretty helpful.

Still, I'd make sure the next grave was buried a little farther out this time. When people looked at you as if death just strolled through the door, it was even ickier than the looks I'd gotten because I was a Plaguer. I was starting to think that maybe in this life, I was meant to be the walking and talking reminder of death. The Grim Reaper in the flesh. There were worse things to be, I figured—like dead.

Ignoring the owner's look while wondering if I should trade in one of my knives for a sickle, I found the darkest seat in the place and tucked myself into the corner where it would be hard to see my face. My crazy red hair was piled up under a hat I'd borrowed from Rocky. With my black

7

leather pants, fashionably broken in to just the right degree and in all the right places, I almost blended—to strangers, at least.

Bert's steps were slow as he approached my table and his lines were crinkling deeper than ever, but I got my whiskey. I flipped him a Newco coin and his bent fingers caught it with the ease of long practice.

Even though we weren't in Newco anymore, their coins were the easiest commerce unless you wanted to tote around oil or gas. The coins were another thing I'd gotten from Rocky. Apparently Dark Walker spotting not only entitled me to a horse, but it paid a healthy wage, which I was more than willing to part with for a sip of the strong stuff.

I leaned back and waited, whiskey in hand. The first sip burned going down, and from the taste of it, I figured it was strong enough to kill any of the germs living in the grime that clung to the glass.

I hoped my prey wouldn't take all day so that I'd have fewer questions to field on my return. The longer I was gone, the more they always seemed to have.

As if I'd conjured him, a single Dark Walker strolled through the door. Or maybe magic had nothing to do with it. It had been getting easier and easier to find my targets lately. Still, it was mighty nice of him to oblige me this way.

My watchers were sure to notice me missing by noon and I was running out of excuses; not that they ever believed any of the ones I'd offered up. Still, I tried. The way I figured it, when you were trying to dupe someone, it was insulting to not do it as well as you could. Otherwise it was like implying you didn't care enough to even consider them.

As far as actually believing me, it didn't really matter. The bottom line was I was a grown woman. Whether they wanted to treat me like one or not wasn't my problem. It was theirs. I was doing what I had to do for me. Right now, that was drinking whiskey and watching my soon-to-be victim.

The Dark Walker moved about Bert's alone. A single scout, he probably wasn't meant for any real conflict. They wouldn't send a single Dark Walker after me and have any hopes of success, not after parties of them had gone missing. They wouldn't be that stupid.

The six-foot scout, masquerading as a human, squinted and surveyed the clientele, which consisted of me and a handful of drunks at a table across the room. He was definitely looking for me; all the Dark Walkers were. No wonder I was having nightmares. I'd never be truly free until they left me alone.

If I knew what they wanted, maybe I could get some leverage. Why Ms. Edith, my tormentor for so many years when I'd been imprisoned at the Cement Giant, had called me the key. Or maybe I'd still be in the same boat I was now. Didn't make a difference. I was done sitting idly by, while

9

each one I let walk away alive could be the one who pulled the trigger on me tomorrow.

No, there would be no more waiting. Every Dark Walker I saw now was going to be a dead one. I didn't know how many there were, but I'd chip away at their numbers. I'd keep going until either they were all gone or I was, and I'd like to see the Dark Walker that could kill me. It was going to be one hell of a fight.

As if it sensed my ill will, its squinty gaze glanced over to my corner. Even in the shadows, I knew it made me, knew it had found what it was looking for. The gloves I wore were a telltale sign for anyone paying attention, which wasn't as often as you'd think. Even in the Wilds, people liked to walk around in their own little bubbles, and boy, did some of them get pissed if you tried to pop them. But not this one. He was here doing a job.

It walked over to the bar and ordered a drink. I watched it throw back a single shot. It shuddered slightly, and I could tell it didn't like the taste of whiskey.

I bided my time and kept my hands on the roughened wood table, instead of reaching for a knife. My instincts were to attack it now, gut the thing before it had a chance of slipping away, but Bert's had too many witnesses. I wasn't sure if even Rocky or Dax could keep me from getting banned from the local holes if I started murdering creatures inside the joints. Then it would be back to waiting in the bushes. I hated sitting in the bushes with the ticks. In the end, that was really what kept me seated. Damn bugs bothered me.

The Dark Walker didn't order a second whiskey and headed out, confirming my suspicions it wasn't here to do the dirty work. It was a scout. There was only one reason they'd send out a single scout. Their numbers weren't as good as I'd feared. Otherwise, they'd be sending groups. That was what I would do.

I let it leave before I pulled my hat down low and rose to follow it, registering a grunt from Bert as I left. I pushed open the door that had just slammed shut behind it. It took a minute for my eyes to readjust to the morning sunlight, but I found it walking quickly toward the hitching post. It leaned down and started unwinding the reins while his pinto waited.

They always rode horses, just like the locals. No trucks out here to tip off the innocent. They never dressed overly nice and never too poorly. Everything was meant to blend. I recognized the effort only as someone who'd put the same concentration into the task would.

I walked up but stopped a good eight feet away, just the perfect amount of space to throw my knife but still remain out of reach.

"What happened? You come all this way and don't even say hello?" I asked,

11

toying with it as it had its back to me.

It was hard not to have a little fun with them after I'd done this so many times. I mean, they did want to kill me and all. It wasn't like I started the fight.

They could at least provide me with some amusement if they were going to hunt me. Fair is fair, even in the Wilds. Maybe more so in the Wilds, where it wasn't an eye for an eye as much as if you started a fight, you better finish it, because otherwise your opponent would scorch the ground you stood upon.

The Dark Walker turned just as I pulled my hat off, blazing red hair a touch darker than it naturally was from the coffee rinse I used. I wanted to make sure there was no question about who I was.

The reins dropped from his hands and I caught sight of the tremble. So he'd heard the stories. Knew his buddies were disappearing. Good. This was exactly the reaction I wanted. The more unsettled, the easier it was to steer them. A panicked animal ran. A calm one thought about where it was running.

But even unsettled, he still kept to the game. "I don't know what you're speaking of. I'm just trying to get my horse and leave, lady. I just stopped in here for a quick drink on my way back to my farm." He turned back to his horse, but not before I caught him looking at the gloves on my hands.

"Yep, that's there, too." I tugged off the black fingerless glove on my right hand and held it up for him so he could get a clear shot of the scar if he wanted. "It used to be a 'P,' but I'm sure you know that."

As if he couldn't stop himself, he glanced over his shoulder and his eyes shot to the top of my hand. He dragged his stare away and shook his head. "I don't know what you're talking about."

As soon he looked away from me again, I was on him, my knife at his throat. I might've been small, but my aim, especially when I picked a target, was always true thanks to my magic, which was nearly burning a hole through my chest at the moment. Seemed the more I used it, the more it wanted to be used, burning hotter every time.

He grabbed my arm, but it didn't budge and it wouldn't. He outweighed me by near double, but strength had nothing to do with this. I'd pictured my knife at his throat, and that was exactly where it would stay until I no longer wanted it there.

"The more you struggle, the quicker you die." I kept the pressure of the knife even, breaking his skin enough to scare him into stillness but not so much to nick his artery and kill him. Not yet, anyway. I'd gotten this part down to a science. "We're going to walk forward into the trees over to your right," I told him.

"If I don't?" he asked, his voice raspy as he tried to conserve the air he used to breathe while my knife restricted it.

13

"Then you'll die here, instead of maybe living another day." I might not have been willing to kill him in the middle of Bert's, but he was going to die today.

"From what I hear, I'm dead anyway."

I heard a thread of hope in that sentence and used it to my advantage. I pressed the knife firmer to his neck. "Should I take that as you are choosing to die here? You walk a bit, you might figure out a way to get this knife off your throat. Maybe I'm the one that dies?" Not likely, but you always had to throw them a carrot, grease the wheels, so to speak.

He moved forward toward the trees, like they all did when they saw a possibility of clinging to life. I would've done the same; that was how come I knew it would work. When it came to death, nothing in this world really wanted to die. Not the plants, animals, people, or even the monsters.

We got to the place I would normally stop but encouraged him on farther. After the evil eye Bert had been throwing my way, I figured a little more distance from the hole might be a good call. I kept him moving for another half a mile. I pulled my knife away and gave him a shove.

This was the part that always got sticky, but maybe if I just did it enough, I would figure out a winning tactic one of these times. Don't they say practice makes perfect? No one ever heard them say practice makes you a great big failure. *No*

14

one ever said that. I didn't know who exactly "they" were, but they really knew their shit, because stuff they said had been around a long frigging time.

Although when they said every cloud had a silver lining, they didn't bother to elaborate that it was often lightning. I'd realized their wisdom left some leeway for interpretation.

Still, I was putting my faith in practice as I watched his eyes shoot everywhere and the panic set in full force, hoping this wasn't going to go bad like all the other times. "Now, you're going to tell me exactly what you things are and why your people want me."

"I don't know what you're talking about. I'm a simple farmer." He raised his hands in surrender, palms up, displaying a damning lack of calluses for the farmer he claimed to be.

"Is it possible to cut through all the bullshit and you just tell me what I want to know?" They always denied it until the end. One of these times, I was going to get something original.

"I'm a farmer." He was shaking his head emphatically, and I could smell the sickly sweet odor that always clung to the Dark Walkers grow stronger, ruining the nice forest bouquet of pine trees. They always smelled the worst right before they—

And there he went, trying to shoot around me to get back to his horse, right on schedule.

I hit his back with

15

the force of someone much heavier and we landed on the ground with a thud. Flipping him over, I was going to try and reason with him one last time, but with the wrestling, things got messy and targets were found. Less than a few seconds later, I was staring down at another dead Dark Walker.

I climbed off his still body, and a stray piece of his flesh hanging from my shirt caught my eye and led to a self-appraisal. "Just once, could it not end with me covered in black, goopy blood and guts? How am I supposed to lie convincingly when I look like this?" I demanded of the dead creature. Even if he'd been alive, the gaping wound in his chest probably would've prevented an answer.

I grabbed a couple of leaves and tried to wipe off the worst of the mess that had somehow ended up on my pants.

Cursing the entire way, I went and grabbed my shovel, one of the many I had stashed around the various holes, while debating whether I needed to move him out a little farther or if I could dig his grave where I'd killed him.

Chapter Two

I stopped both horses about a twenty-minute brisk walk away from the Rock and unhooked the Dark Walker's horse from mine. "Stay here. I'll send someone out to find you soon, okay?"

The pinto didn't give any notice it understood me, but all the horses I'd brought to this pasture seemed to like the area, so I figured he'd catch on too and graze for a while. It was far enough that no one from the Rock would be lingering around to see what I was doing, but still technically Rock territory. You had to have a pretty big set of balls or a death wish to take anything off the Rock's territory.

I pressed my knees inward and Charlie moved us forward, knowing the way to get home on his own and just waiting for the go-ahead. I took the extra time to start working on my lies, which I was behind schedule on, since my mind kept wandering back to the look Bert gave me. I usually had my story straight before I rode back into the Rock.

The large gate, a huge, rusted metal affair, started grinding open at my approach. I waved hello to Carmine, who stood behind the wheel that operated the monstrosity as I passed into the security of the walls.

The metal gears were grinding closed behind me as Dax came into view, stepping right into my current path toward the stables and Charlie's lunch.

There was something about his presence that always kicked my heartbeat up a gear. It didn't matter what the circumstances were, fight brewing or not. He could be dressed in dark work pants and a snug T, like he was now, or covered in mud for all it mattered. His pale eyes would fix upon me, a startling contrast to the rest of his dark features, and I'd feel like I'd just gotten a jolt of energy. Sometimes I wondered if it was his magic mingling with my own that caused it, because no human had ever made me feel so strongly.

Maybe it was just him. People reacted differently to Dax, in one way or another. Some liked him more, some less. Others, which were the good majority, feared him.

Even now, after being here for weeks and him not laying hands on a single soul, I watched as people changed their direction,

18

giving him plenty of space where he stood in the middle of the road.

When I looked at him, I got it. Not that I was scared around him, but why others might be. Sometimes I wondered if people sensed what lay beneath, as if their survival instincts knew on some level that something wasn't as it seemed. He didn't help the matter with the hard expression he wore. He had the look of someone who'd killed his fair share and might be killing some more real soon.

Unfortunately, according to Bert's reaction, so did I. Maybe that was why I wasn't scared of him. I'd realized since I'd been in the Wilds that sometimes death was just part of the day. It didn't necessarily make you a bad person; sometimes it just meant someone else had to die so that you could live.

And there was something nice about knowing the toughest beast in the Wilds had your back.

Maybe that's all it was, his beastly magic. Dax was unsettling enough. If I dug too deep into my psyche over our connection, I might not like what I found. I'd decided a while ago that I needed to lower my expectations to just needing enough to get by. That concept had recently expanded to not dwelling on why I might need it either.

Wandering around in the mess of my thoughts was more than my mental stability could handle at the moment. That kind of

19

stuff could lead to some ugly revelations I wasn't particularly in the mood to acknowledge.

Dax stepped forward and grabbed Charlie's bridle. "Let me help you to the stables." It was a little too pushy to be a true offer.

"Sure," I replied in the same tone I'd use to say *lovely morning*, as if I didn't know a lecture was about to come either before or after the what, where, and when questions.

I didn't like to play stupid, but there were times when stupid was the only smart choice. Any acknowledgement that I knew what he was up to could be construed as admitting guilt. I wasn't planning on admitting anything. Not until there were no other options. It wasn't anyone else's business what I did, not even his. What did he take me for? One of those people who paid someone to listen to them?

Instead of thinking about all this stupid shit as we neared the barn, I needed to get a story in place. No one was going to accuse me of having boring lies.

We entered the stables too quickly to come up with anything good. Dax looked at Pete, the stable master, then back to me. He couldn't possibly know I was bringing all the horses, could he? Dax kept staring, his eyes narrowing as I sat there playing stupid, according to plan.

Shit, he did know that, too. A soft sigh escaped, carrying my ploy of stupidity with it, letting it dissipate on the air of the guilty. I tilted my head toward the open stable door. It was the loudest acknowledgment he was going to get, and even that was much louder than what I'd planned. I wasn't sure why all my good intentions of lying and keeping secrets blew apart once he got involved.

His own sigh, tinted more with condemnation, joined my own. His hands tensed on the reins he still held. "Pete, I heard there's a loose horse roaming that same pasture to the east again, just waiting for someone to walk right up to it and bring it back here."

Pete, blissfully unaware of all the negative air floating around him, scratched his peppered beard. "Another one? And tame? Not a wild?" The scratching didn't stop but migrated to his almost bald scalp. "That's the third one this week. Can't imagine where they're all coming from."

"Yeah, *real* strange," Dax said, and I wished Pete would shut up. We all knew how many horses had been found and no one needed him to keep count for us. Big know-it-all.

Dax jerked a thumb toward the door as Pete neared us. "Why don't you go try and round it up? I'll help her stable Charlie."

Pete walked out of the stables as he muttered something about strange times and foolish people.

"Where'd you go this time?" Dax asked as soon as it was just us in the   stables.

21

I turned to drop off the horse, taking the opportunity to break the stare-down I'd somehow entered into without consent. If I just looked away, it would be a loss.

His hands caught my waist before my feet hit the ground and then I had an old wooden barn wall behind me, and him blocking the way out.

I was already amped up from the recent kill. His magical overflow, as I'd come to call the weird energy he couldn't seem to keep to himself like a polite magic person should, was spilling all over the damn place in agitating waves.

"Can't you keep that stuff to yourself?" I hated the way it made my skin flush and my breathing weird. The closer he got, the worse it was, too.

"What stuff?"

"Your magic stuff. Can't you turn it down?" If I could, he should be able to. I didn't go around stoking up the burning in my chest all willy-nilly with no regard to others' sensitivities.

"I'm not doing anything." Then he was looking at my neck and his fingers were grazing the skin under my jaw, making the air heavier and my breathing that much worse.

I barely felt his touch before he was removing his hand and flicking something to the ground. "You need to clean up better in the stream before you come back. There was a rotting   chunk of flesh on your neck."

His arms crossed as he stood there, and somehow I'd ended up back in the stare-down. My eyes shot to the door of the barn; I wondered if I was quick enough to scoot past him if I set my magic to aim for there.

Then all I saw was his chest as he repositioned. I looked up at his face, having limited options. "Clearly, you already know. What's left to talk about?" It wasn't the brilliant lie I'd planned on coming up with, but he had a way of kicking me into defensive mode. Next time I needed to make sure I had my lie planned out *before* I got back.

"I. Want. Specifics."

"I. Went. Hunting." Nope, from his expression, that wasn't specific enough.

"Again."

It was strange how that one word sounded so much heavier than anything he'd said yet.

"Yes." I tried to take a step to the side as he mirrored me.

He planted his hand by the side of my head, blocking the path to my right. "Even after I told you not to?"

"If you recall, I didn't agree to not go anymore." I didn't elaborate on how I didn't have to do *anything* he said. I figured that part was implied. He was a smart man. He'd figure it out.

"This place is already hot. The more you kill, the more you're luring them

23

here. What don't you understand about that?" He wasn't screaming, but that meant nothing.

"Mama didn't raise no fool." Technically, Mama didn't really raise me, but I didn't think I should be penalized for something out of my control. It was a good saying and I was using it.

"What?" he said, not understanding where that came from. Seriously, he needed to read more.

Since he didn't quite understand what I was saying, I'd have to spell it out for him. "My point is I get it, but am I supposed to sit on my hands and wait for you to tell me what to do?" It wasn't like I was stupid. I got the basic logic. I just didn't care for how he wanted to do things.

It was the same fight we'd been having for the past week and a half and it was heading in the same predictable direction. It was like my entire existence was stuck on repeat, just like that busted-up CD player Bookie had found in the last ruin, some place he'd said used to be called Atlanta. Same lyrics, over and over and over.

"Yes, that's exactly what you're supposed to do, because you're fucking up my plans." His forehead was going to touch mine soon if he didn't back up.

"What about my plans?" I asked, refusing to stand there meekly and be dictated to.

"What plans? You don't have plans. You have killing sprees," he shot back as we fought for dominance of the space.

"Exactly! Kill them all. That's my plan and it's better than doing nothing." Damn, it was getting warm in here. It was like he lit my magic on fire somehow, and hell if I knew why.

If I didn't know better and magic wasn't involved, I'd say it was just like the scenes I'd read about in my sexy book, right before the girl and the guy got together. Except Dax didn't want me like that. He'd already turned me down once, and the one time he'd kissed me, he acted like it was a mistake.

So of course I didn't want him, because hell if I'd ever want someone who didn't want me. Nope. This was just some weird magic commingling.

He could say he wasn't doing anything, but I knew he felt it too. I saw the tension in the line of his neck. I knew he was breathing harder, even as he must have noticed my own breathing the way he was staring at my lips.

He pushed off the wall and took a few steps back away from me as if it were getting to him, too. Good. Maybe he'd stop doing it.

"I can't fucking believe I'm over a barrel for the first time in my life by an eighteen-year-old twit who thinks she knows best."

I pushed off the wall, getting mad at the same dig about my age. "Why are you so obsessed with my age? Eighteen, eighteen,

eighteen. I'm sick of hearing it. I know how old I am and it isn't that young. Half the women out here are married with kids by eighteen. I'm an adult and can make my own choices."

"They didn't live your life."

He didn't mention the first chunk of my life had been wasted in the Cement Giant, but I knew exactly what he meant. "You're just mad because you'll never be the man Moobie is."

He was standing by the barn door, his profile to me. He turned his head, tilting it in my direction, and I prepared for the bullet he was loading up. "No one will be the man Moobie is because Moobie isn't the man he is. Moobie doesn't exist. He's made up."

My hands shot to my hips. "See, now why'd you have to go and say that? We were having a normal discussion and you have to go and throw that in my face? I'm not crazy. I know Moobie isn't real."

"I don't know what I'm supposed to do with you. I don't. I give up. You win. Go fucking kill whatever you want and take care of your own damn horse." I watched as he walked out of the barn, leaving a vacuum of heat where there'd just been an inferno.

"Now was that so hard?" I yelled after him as my hand went to the spot on my neck he'd touched earlier. Shit. I'd thought that was wetness from my shirt before he'd removed the chunk off me. I reached down and grabbed a handful of hay and wiped the leftover blood off, wondering if there was a mirror in here somewhere, but thinking of what Pete normally looked like, I highly doubted it.

"You didn't get it all," Bookie said as he walked in the stables, grabbed another handful of hay, and walked over to help me clean off a spot an inch over.

"Thanks."

"Yep."

I knew that tone. "Not you, too," I said as I undid Charlie's saddle and started pulling it from his back.

Bookie took the weight from me and ushered me aside. "It's dangerous."

I stepped out of his way. "I've got it under control."

He nodded in a brusque, very un-Bookie-like manner. "Fudge made lunch," he said, switching topics and then helping me wipe down Charlie and get him settled in his stall without saying anything else.

I stared over Charlie's back, but no matter what position Bookie was in, his big hazel eyes wouldn't meet mine. It was almost worse than when Dax wouldn't *stop* staring at me. I tossed down my brush and rested my arms on Charlie. "Bookie, I'm doing what I feel I have to. I thought you understood that?"

Another nod as he finished his side and left the stall. I followed him out.

"I don't know what you think, but I'm not doing anything crazy out there." Crazy for me, anyway, but we all lived in a prison of our own realities. In my reality, killing a few Dark Walkers a week was the only thing keeping me sane.

He shut the stall and finally spoke. "I don't understand why you won't let me come with you. Why do you always disappear? You shouldn't go out there alone. Not even the toughest here go out alone."

"That's not true. Some people go out of the walls alone all the time."

"Who? Rocky and Dax? Dal, you can't compare them to you."

Yes, actually, I could. But then I'd have to tell Bookie what I'd become, how easily I killed. Was I ready to let him see me like that? Could I walk into Bert's and shrug off the looks of dread I got if Bookie was beside me and seeing the same thing? How would Bookie look at me after watching me carve up a Dark Walker as easily as a warm stick of butter? No remorse, no fear, just letting my baser instincts take hold.

I walked out of the barn, hoping to leave the conversation back with the dirty hay.

Bookie walked along beside me, silent for a while until both of our houses, side by side, came into view.

"I worry when you go out there alone," he said as we turned onto the walk to the house he lived in with Fudge and Tiffy.

"I'm sorry." I didn't use that word often, but what else could I say under this kind of pressure? This *worrying about you* shit was way worse than Dax getting upset about his plans being ruined or a Dark Walker trying to kill me.

"But you're still going to do it tomorrow."

"I… Well…" Who was I kidding? Of course I was. This was why I had to think of my lies ahead of time, so I didn't get stuck in these uncomfortable conversations. "Doesn't mean I'm not sorry for it," I said as a last-ditch effort.

"That's exactly what it means."

"I'm doing what I have to do and you'll still forgive me." I waited a minute, hoping he'd agree. All I got was silence. "Right?"

"Of course I will. I'll always be there for you Dal. Don't you know that?"

"Yeah, I do."

Bookie paused right before opening the door to the house. "By the way, Fudge knows you slipped out again."

"How?"

"Sorry," he said, getting me back as he made an exaggerated cringe face and then slipped into the house too fast for me to argue with him.

Tank, Dax's right-hand man, was already there seated at the table beside Tiffy, both of them scoffing down more than their fair share of what looked like lasagna.

I didn't see Tank as often now since he'd been dating Carmine. He said he was home every night, but I never saw him go to bed and I never saw him get up in the morning. I wasn't sure what would happen when we moved back to the farm. Would she come with us? I couldn't imagine Tank leaving Dax's side. It would be like stripping the spots off a pinto.

Unless we never got back to the farm.

"Heard you had a busy morning," Tank said as I sat down across from him.

"Didn't see you come in last night," I shot back.

"Dal, Dal, Dal…" Tiffy said. "You must be careful out there. You don't have friends like I do." For a four-year-old, she sure knew how to beat someone with the inadvertent I-told-you-sos. There was no doubt anymore to the people in the know that Tiffy's friends were real, and she never missed an opportunity to rub it in.

"People around here make an awful big deal about going for a walk," I said, shooting a look at Bookie to hold the rest of the details to himself if he valued his life.

Fudge walked in and laid another tray on the table. The second her hands were free, they started fluttering around like I'd seen her do quite often, especially after she heard something she didn't like.

"What is that thing you do, Fudge?"

"It's called the sign of the cross," Bookie said as he reached for some pasta. "It's one of her religious things."

"What's it do?" I

30

asked, wondering if I should give it a try.

"It's to make me feel better when you're being crazy. Now eat," she said. "You're still too skinny, even with all the food you take in."

I didn't argue when it would only delay the eating process. Lasagna was a special item we didn't see much of, and it was a calling like a siren's song to my growling belly.

I'd made it through a plate and a half of lasagna when Tiffy started giving me the eye. I knew the eye. It might have been wrong to dread talking to a four-year-old, but this one could say some scary shit.

She sat there as poised as someone in their thirties and crossed her arms, giving me a knowing smile. "Dal, I want to show you my new doll."

Oh no. I knew the doll ploy. When she broke out the doll ploy, it was serious business and there was no way of getting out of it. Might as well go listen now and get this over with. "Sure, Tiffy, let's go see the doll."

She smiled and got up from the table, and I followed her chipper step with my own footfalls of doom.

When she closed the bedroom door, it sounded like someone hammering the final nail in my coffin.

"I talked with my friends," she said as she sat on the bed and reached for a doll that was resting on her pillow.

I let out a string of swears, not caring how old she was. After all, I felt like I was the one who needed protecting. "I thought

31

you weren't going to speak to them anymore?"

"I don't remember ever agreeing to that," she said as she straightened out the ruffled pink dress the doll was wearing.

Of course she didn't. Wait, didn't I just use almost those exact words in the barn earlier with Dax? "Were you—"

"Nope."

"Tiffy?"

"No proof, no crime." Her little shoulder shrugged, as if dropping the invisible crime's weight with effortless ease from settling upon her shoulders.

"You're off the hook for now, but don't do that again, okay?" It wasn't like I hadn't done some of my own eavesdropping in the past. A girl had to do what a girl had to do out here. "What did you talk about with your friends?"

"They said to not worry. I can't get the Bloody Death."

"Why not?" I remembered Dax telling me about how he'd found her, alone in a house full of victims of the disease, so I had my own suspicions. Was Tiffy a Plaguer like me and we just didn't know it? "Tiffy, you ever see visions? Images of the people you meet doing things that they aren't currently doing?"

"No."

Okay, not a Plaguer. So why couldn't she get the Bloody Death? "Did   they tell you why?"

32

"No." She reached over, grabbed a brush sitting on her bedside table, and started brushing the doll's hair. "This is the new doll."

"She's beautiful," I said, not actually looking at the doll. "Did they say anything else?"

"No, and you barely looked at her." She held the doll in front of my face so it was unavoidable. "Look at her."

"Oh, so pretty!" I forced myself to stare at the face for a whole second before I kicked back into question mode. "That's all they said?"

"Yes." She turned her doll this way and that. "I think she needs a blue dress like mine. Can you sew me one?"

"Uh…" I could kill no problem. But sew? I didn't know how to sew.

"It needs ruffles, like this. See?" She was pointing to the trim of her own dress.

"Maybe we should ask Fudge. It'll come out much better that way."

I was halfway to the door before she nodded.

33

Chapter Three

Another morning gripping the blankets after another bad night. The good nights were getting sparser and sparser. I kicked into inventory mode almost instinctually now, checking off the list: no chimes, no sickly sweet smells, and the walls of my room were white, not cement.

As I listened for noises, the house was too quiet. I wasn't just missing monsters but a man who might want to meddle with my plans for the day. Dax could say whatever he wanted about giving up, but that man had never quit anything in his life. I wasn't trusting those words for a second.

I scrambled out of bed before Dax could spontaneously appear, like he often seemed to do. A quick stop in the bathroom and a mad grab for clothes and I was out the door.

The aroma of bacon and sausage permeated the air around Fudge's house, but I forced myself to keep walking as I spotted Dax through the window, sitting at her table eating. Not even bacon was enough to bet my morning freedom on.

But that left me with one big problem. Where was I going to get breakfast? Where did people eat around here if it wasn't for Fudge's food? I'd never had this problem before, and the idea of killing on an empty stomach wasn't appealing.

I tilted my head back, trying to catch a whiff of food on the air, but the only thing I could smell led me back to Fudge's.

The food back at the house was all uncooked. I didn't know what to do with the stuff the way they gave it to me, all raw. Our icebox acted as additional storage for Fudge.

I stepped onto Main Street, a block from Rocky's office, and heard Susan, the woman in charge of administration, calling my name. She was walking with Angel, who handled the wall guards and security. They were heading in my direction and I stopped and waited for them to catch up to me.

"You heading to breakfast?" Angel asked.

"Yeah." I was smack in the center of town. I looked about the place trying to catch a whiff of bacon and eggs in the air. It had to be close. "But where is it?"

"It's in the house behind the town hall," Susan said as she looped her arm into mine and tugged me along with them. "Fudge isn't cooking today?"

"She is, but I thought I'd check out what everyone else does for a change."

"I'm glad you came by. I've got a stash of books I think you'd *really* enjoy."

"Really?"

"Yeah. I'll drop them off at your house in the next couple of days. I have to get some back from Carmine first. They're really good books, so I'd make sure your stack of candles is high."

Tapping on glass drew my attention, and Rocky was standing in his office window, staring at me and waving me in.

"Looks like he wants to talk to you," Susan said.

"Yeah, I better go see what's up. I'll catch up with you guys in a couple of minutes?"

Susan turned to Angel, before the corner of her mouth quirked up and she said to me, "In case you don't make it, come by Carmine's house tonight. We're trying out some new recipes for blushes and lip gloss."

"Are you sure that's okay?"

"Of course! Why wouldn't it be?"

Yeah, why wouldn't it be, I thought. No one here cared that I'd had the

Bloody Death. Lately, it seemed like I was the only one who remembered. I nodded and they headed off to breakfast without me.

I crossed the street, passing some locals all with smiles and waves, or at the very least nods. I knew all their names, and not one of them ran in the other direction or looked scared. Even at the farm, it had never been like this.

Walking toward the town hall to see what Rocky wanted, I realized I didn't dread seeing people. I didn't fear looking at them, wondering if they'd look back, and if they did, what expression they'd be wearing.

I stopped with my hand on the door and really took a look around at the bustling community, filled with people who liked me. This was exactly what I'd always wanted and it had snuck up on me. My dreams for tomorrow were here, today, and they had come in the last place I'd ever expected to find them.

Sure, there were still problems. I had Dark Walkers looming outside these walls hunting me. But I also woke up in a place where I was greeted with smiles and a welcome. I was living a life I'd only dreamed of a year ago.

I swung the door open to Rocky's office, and he looked up from where he was sitting behind his wooden desk, nothing too ornamental but solid and strong. It fit him. Even the warm hue of the wood reminded me a bit of the deeper red shades of his hair.

"I like when you smile," he said, matching my expression. He had a warm smile, but I was more interested in the heaping plate of food sitting in front of him at the moment, my mouth already watering from the smell of bacon. I was pretty sure his booty had come from the place I'd been heading.

"Did you want something?" I asked, hoping whatever it was would be quick before the food grew cold or the serving trays grew empty. I might be on the small side, but I could hold my own in the breakfast department.

"You hungry?" he asked.

I took a few steps toward the door. "Starving, so I'm going to head on out if you—"

"Stay and share mine," he said, and was dragging a chair beside his before I could say yes. He opened up a drawer and pulled out a fork. "Here. By the time you get over there now, there'll be a line and you'll get crumbs. They always bring me too much, anyway."

Eat off the same plate as him? I'd shared food with the girls back at the Cement Giant all the time, but something seemed so...intimate about it. But I was hungry and it did look good.

"Maybe I should just go get—"

"Don't be silly. Sit."

38

He sat back down in his chair, picking up a piece of bacon and taking a healthy bite of it, his face displaying just how good it tasted before he said, "Cooked perfectly today."

Maybe people ate off the same plate all the time? How would I know? I sat, took the fork, and started digging in.

"This is good, thanks," I said. Not as good as Fudge's, but she was a tough act to follow, so I didn't hold it against them. Still better than what I would've made.

"So, now that Tiffy's back, what are your plans? Give any thought to it?" he asked, his arm brushing mine as he stabbed a piece of sausage.

"No, not really," I said, scooping up a nice heap of eggs, preferring to eat rather than talk.

"If you're planning on staying for a while, there are a couple of empty houses. It's probably hard to live with Tank and Dax."

I shook my head. "Tank isn't there much. He's always over at Carmine's house lately, so it's not as crowded as you'd think with just the two of us over there," I told him as he was eating a piece of sausage. "What's wrong? You get a piece of gristle? Spit it out."

"No. It's fine," he said, but looked like he'd just swallowed something very unpleasant.

Personally, I would've spit it out. I didn't like swallowing gristle, but   to each his own.

"I really think your position in the community deserves certain benefits, like your own residence."

I ate some more eggs as I figured out the best way to lay out the hard truth on him. This was going to need another bite of bacon, too.

After three bites, I was ready. "The thing is, Rocky, I haven't actually done anything yet," I said as I heard the outer door open and hoped it was going to provide an interruption from this current conversation. It wasn't like I wanted to tell Rocky how to run his place, but he needed to get a little better on resource allocation if what I'd seen was any example. As much as I liked Charlie and the salary, a house all to myself was going to eat up more resources. He needed to stop being so loose with the town resources.

"Maybe she likes her current residence?" Dax asked as he stepped into the open doorway, not offering up a distraction but making the conversation tougher by joining in. How far away could this guy hear from? Was anywhere safe? And how was I supposed to get out of the Rock today?

Dax stepped farther into the room, and I'd never seen someone smile and yet somehow look mad at the same time.

He stopped beside me and picked up the fork I'd been using to stab a piece of sausage off the plate. "Sorry to break up your morning breakfast here," Dax said, "but, Dal, we've got to run." He plucked the sausage off the fork and popped it into his mouth. Maybe eating off the same plate really wasn't a big deal. Now *three* of us were eating from the same dish.

"Sure." I nodded as I stood. Dax hadn't mentioned any plans to me but I'd avoided him since the barn yesterday. Still, I wasn't surprised. Dax hadn't bugged me to sit in the bushes and stare at Dark Walkers for weeks. Since there was no way I was going to be able to lose them both at this point, my day's agenda had been officially cleared.

"Thanks for breakfast," I said to Rocky as I stood.

Rocky grabbed my arm before I took more than a step away and then leaned over and kissed my cheek. "Have a good day." Nothing but smiles while I was reeling from the weird move. Why the hell was he kissing my cheek? He'd never kissed my cheek before.

Things had been getting stranger and stranger with these two. I knew they both wanted me for their very own Dark Walker watcher. Was this a new part of their game to see who got to keep the upper hand?

I turned and saw Dax's expression. Oh yeah, just another part of their game. He was way too pissed for it to be anything else. I might hate losing, but I'd never met anyone who hated it more than me until Dax came into my life.

"Don't worry, she'll have a good day," Dax said, "because I'll make sure

41

of it." Rocky's grip was replaced by Dax's arm shuffling me forward.

I didn't know what Rocky's expression was because I didn't have a chance to look back as I was steered out of the office and then the building. We walked past the gate and toward the house. Did he forget something he needed? He didn't have a notebook for me in hand.

"So which hole are we hitting up today?" Maybe it was a new one that I could add to my list. Might be a good idea to expand my range. I'd already heated up the two holes to the west and Bert certainly wasn't very happy.

"None of them," he said, his fake smile long gone by time we got to the house. "What were you doing back there?"

"Eating breakfast?"

"Why?"

"Because he offered and I was hungry." Where was he going with this?

"You're too young."

"To eat?" I asked, shocked at such a bizarre statement. "To eat alone with him? That makes no sense."

"Which is why you shouldn't eat with him."

The looks he was giving me made it seem like he thought I was being the obtuse one. Then he walked off like he hadn't said we had plans this morning.

I shook my head as I

watched him disappear. I really hoped the two of them figured out their issues soon, because this was way too confusing.

But in the meantime, looked like someone had a free morning.

Chapter Four

I was sitting in the darkest corner, glass of whiskey in hand later that morning, still thinking of Dax's words yesterday. He might have told me to stay put this morning but he'd also said he'd given up the day before. Who knew what he wanted anymore?

And even if my hunch was that he wouldn't appreciate my plans for today, this was my life to live. Yeah, sure, I owed him some loyalty, but I didn't owe him my every waking moment. I'd already lost too much time doing what other people told me to do. I hadn't had a choice then. I did now.

Wasn't like he'd told *me* where he was storming off to, or when we were actually going to start going after Dark Walkers. If I waited for him, I'd be a hundred before I killed them. Unlike him, I didn't have those kinds of years to squander.

I wasn't living out the rest of my life like prey. They hunted me? Well, fuck them. I'd hunt them right back, and there wasn't anyone who was going to stop me. I gave as good as I got, maybe better, and that was the way I liked it.

I waved a hand and motioned for Bert to bring me a refill. He looked less than overjoyed to see me again, not even a day later.

By time two Dark Walkers entered the hole, I was almost done with my second whiskey. Good thing too; I had a two-whiskey maximum before I cut myself off from dealing out death. Put on too much of a buzz and you might be catching a deathblow instead of doling one out. There was nothing worse than having to sit here without a drink for hours. You really started to notice the atmosphere with nothing else to do.

I took in the man and woman. They looked like a couple, probably intentionally. This was something new. Maybe the Dark Walkers thought I wouldn't notice them because they were holding hands? They couldn't be that stupid, could they? Although I had noticed how often people overlooked a threat for the stupidest reasons. Maybe if I'd been the romantic type my eyes might have flitted right over them?

The duo surveyed the room, and when the woman's eyes landed on me, I waved a hand in greeting. She turned quickly, as if she didn't know *exactly* who I was.

Yeah, the wave was definitely a two-whiskey move. That was why I never had three. Another whiskey and the wave might've turned into the finger and I wouldn't wait until I got them outside before I pulled out my knife.

The door squealed open as it admitted another body just as the pair was getting settled across the room, and I wondered if I was going to have a trifecta today.

Dax was silhouetted by the bright sun against his back. He stood in the doorway for a moment, and I knew by some crazy intuition, or maybe just the tilt of his head, he'd seen me waving at the Dark Walkers.

A curse slipped out and I slumped back in the chair. I raised my hand to Bert to bring me a third whiskey. Looked like I wouldn't be doling out any death today— might as well have that other drink.

Dax strode over, his pace a little quicker than his normal gait. He swung an empty chair beside me and settled in, side by side, shoulder brushing shoulder. I was already trying to snuff out my keyed-up energy, knowing today's fight wouldn't be happening, at least not at this moment. I didn't need his magical overflow jazzing me up.

"How'd you know which one I was at?" I asked.

"You don't exactly make it hard."

We both fell silent

as Bert delivered my drink. I dug out another coin, but he waved it off now that Dax was sitting beside me.

"Rocky has you on the payroll," Dax said. It wasn't a question, and I was tempted to ask if he had splinters in his seat the way he said it.

"Some people don't have their own oil supplies. By the way, where is this rig?" He never lacked for a constant flow of the stuff, but I'd never seen the place myself.

He leaned forward and threw back my glass of whiskey before answering. "What would be the fun of telling you that?" He inclined his head slightly toward where the couple was at the bar.

It hadn't even been a full inch of movement and yet I knew exactly what he was doing and what the question was. When had we gotten to this strange place where we didn't need words?

He cleared his throat, and it was a silent *are you going to answer me?* Dax question if I'd ever heard one. Technically, I'd never actually heard one, as they were silent, but he had the loudest silence of any person ever born.

I leaned back in my chair, looking everywhere but him, as if I didn't know what he was saying—or not saying.

It should've been easy. I'd spent the majority of my life keeping things way more important than this to myself, but I was

47

fighting the urge to speak. Why wouldn't I just tell him? Why was it that when it came to him, I wanted to give him every little thing he wanted and then that feeling drove me nuts until I did the exact opposite? He turned me into one of those schizophrenic people Bookie had talked about the other day.

Dax leaned forward until I had no choice but to see him, and his eyebrows rose. Now he was practically yelling—still with no sounds, of course—*You're going to sit there and ignore me?*

I pressed my lips together, trying to pretend I had no clue and keep the words in, just to prove to myself I could hold back. *I will not speak. I will not speak...*

He leaned a little closer, and his scent, that perfect blend of the forest and man, drifted to my senses and screwed with me as much as his magic.

That was it. I couldn't take it. "Yes," I blurted out. "Yes, yes, yes."

He leaned back, as if I were a rabid dog that had snapped for no reason. "A nod would have sufficed."

He didn't get it. I didn't want to understand every little goddamn thing he did and said—or didn't say. It was weird. And I didn't like all the touching lately, either. Or the closeness. Like, why was he sitting right next to me? He could've taken the chair across the table. We looked like we were a couple or something, and that wasn't what we were.

He didn't want me

like that, so what was with the act? Once you shoot down a girl who's lying in your bed offering herself up, it's pretty clear that's not the type of relationship you're looking for, so have some dignity and keep a respectable distance.

And now he was intruding on my Dark Walker hunting. It was bullshit. There was no sanctuary left.

"Should I expect this on a regular basis? You told me the other day I could do whatever I wanted." My pent-up frustration found an outlet in the snippiness of my tone.

He leaned back in his chair and kicked his feet up on to the one in front of him, taking his sweet old time in answering. "We both know I didn't mean what I said in the barn."

"And how did we both know that?" I asked, grabbing the imaginary bait even when I could smell the trap a mile away.

"Because I said I gave up. I don't give up on anything I want. Some things take a little longer than others, but I don't give up. Ever." And if the nail hadn't been driven in enough, he had to give it one last blow. "I'd say your career of solitary hunting has come to an end."

"You think so, huh?" I asked, not able to take a statement like that sitting down, especially paired with the relaxed demeanor of someone wholly confident in themselves.

49

"I'd be willing to bet on it."

"We'll see about that."

"Yes, we will."

The couple stepped away from the bar and headed toward the door.

I stood and bent over the table toward him. "I've got some killing to do. You can join me so I'm not so solitary or wait here. But it's happening."

His chair scraped along the floor and I wasn't sure if I was going to be brawling with him or Dark Walkers.

"What the hell. What harm are two more going to do at this point?"

"Glad you're seeing it my way."

I headed for the door with Dax at my back. The second we stepped outside the hole, the Dark Walkers were already running toward their horses. Great. He was already screwing things up just by being here.

"See what you did?" I didn't wait for an answer as I took off after them. Before they could unhitch their mounts, I held my knife at the guy's throat and had him walking into the forest a minute later.

Let Dax take the smaller girl. This was my show. I had to walk the whole way into the forest on my tiptoes just so I could keep the knife at the larger one's neck.

Dax passed me on the way, the squirming female under his arm. "You don't think this is a bit ridiculous?" he asked, looking at the mismatched sizes.

"No. I don't."

50

He rolled his eyes as he dropped the girl to the ground.

Things progressed quicker than normal as the female immediately went on attack as soon as she hit the ground, and the male followed suit.

Ten minutes later, there were two bloody Dark Walkers on the ground. Two more dead, no closer to answers than I was before, and more graves to be dug.

"What exactly has this accomplished other than covering me in grime and blood?" Dax asked, as he leaned against a tree and watched me dig.

After the initial blip, it had gone down the same as it always did. They'd said nothing of value and then they'd died. Only difference was I had someone watching me dig the graves this time around.

"It's two less Dark Walkers, that's what." I flung an extra-large pile of dirt aside.

"Two less of an unknown amount."

His movement caught my eye, and I looked back over to see he'd crossed his ankles. I dug the shovel into the dirt with a bit more gusto. "Two less of a finite amount."

"You don't know that. You know nothing, even after doing this who knows how many times. They could be breeding a thousand a day. This could be the equivalent of pissing in the ocean."

"You didn't have to partake." It didn't matter what he said. I knew they weren't breeding that quickly, or I'd have thousands after me. But he wasn't looking for logic and I didn't particularly care to argue it with him. I kicked the already dead body by my feet. Damn, why wouldn't these things talk?

"Oh no, I did. I needed to see the brilliance of your plan firsthand." He looked down at my barely dug hole. "How long is this going to take? I've got things to do today that might actually help our cause."

"A lot less time if you helped."

"This was your choice. You clean it up."

"I haven't tasted the fruits of your labors either, whatever these mysterious plans might be."

"And you aren't going to know as long as you keep up this shit. You might not mind broadcasting what you're about, but I'm not telling my plans to someone who insists on putting themselves in the line of fire every day."

"Is that the problem? Afraid I'll die and you won't get your vengeance?"

He grabbed the shovel from me, ushering me out of his way with his crowding. "Yes, because every time I've saved your ass in the past was so beneficial to me?" He started digging with a vengeance, and I wasn't sure if I was supposed to answer that question or not.

His attitude seemed to be sinking even quicker than the hole he was digging, but that wasn't my problem. His comment grated a bit, but not enough that I was going to stop him from digging. My plan or not, he'd killed one of them. He could take a turn digging.

It took him a fraction of the time to dig the grave for two than it normally took me. He tossed the shovel aside, jumped out of the hole, and dumped the two bodies inside of it, making even quicker work of burying them.

I looked at the position of the sun and remembered it was Saturday night dinner. There was just enough time to go get cleaned up before the meal started. Perfect timing.

Chapter Five

Saturday night dinner was the biggest event of the week when you lived at the Rock. Somehow, I'd been given a standing invitation even though I hadn't ID'd a single Dark Walker within the walls, or done much of anything to earn my keep. Dax was also invited. I wasn't sure how he'd earned his invite either, but who was I to judge? At least he wasn't on the payroll for doing nothing—or I didn't think he was.

After the day's adventure, I hadn't wasted too much time getting ready back at the house. Dax's magic lately was pumping out at maximum output, to the point I was starting to not feel like I was myself around him anymore. No, it was better I went alone.

The dinner table was set up alongside the lake, close

to where Rocky's house was, ready for its fifteen regulars, plus Dax and I. If the Rock were its own galaxy, these people were the planets orbiting around Rocky.

Susan and Angel were already there with smiles as I approached. I looked about and realized Becca, Dax's ex, hadn't shown again. Susan had told me she was avoiding Dax, not me, but it was the only real awkwardness left.

People started to find their seats. I gave it a moment, waiting to see which ones were left open. There was a certain pecking order, even with something as trivial as how close to the head of the table you sat. Things were going well here and I wasn't looking to throw a rock into the gears.

By time the bodies settled in, two options remained: a chair beside Rocky's place at the head of the table and one farther down. It was an easy choice. I'd let Dax sit beside Rocky and I would stay out of the limelight at the other end of the table. Plus, the seat farther down was between Carmine and Angel, who'd both been motioning me over.

Before I got there, though, Rocky cut across my path.

"Come on, I saved you a seat by me." His hand was on my back and he was steering me toward his seat, the one that had been *saved*.

He sat and tugged at

my hand, pulling me down beside him. But then he didn't let go of it, even after I was seated. The warmth of his palm had me looking down at where we touched, wondering what he was about, and I watched as his fingers then weaved through mine.

Dax had told me a while ago that Rocky wanted to use me. I'd assumed it was for how I could spot Dark Walkers. Or maybe even for sex. I hadn't held it against him, as I'd thought of using him as well. I was eighteen, long past the point when most women in the Wilds experienced their first affair. It was part of living life. Rocky had seemed a fine candidate.

But sitting here at the head of the table with him, his fingers entwined in mine, I realized that Rocky didn't want to use me for sex like the guards in the Cement Giant had used the girls, and he wasn't trying to keep me here to protect his place, either. He was holding my hand. Even I knew that holding hands, sitting beside him at dinner—this was *boyfriend* realm.

Did I want a boyfriend? Could I even have one, considering my situation? I'd ruled out other entanglements, but Rocky wasn't like Bookie. He knew what this world was like, the nasty, dirty underside of it, and had no delusions of a greater good. He would understand what getting involved with me might mean. And if I had to leave him, he'd be able to handle it. He was a grown man with some calluses built up. He'd probably had plenty of girlfriends, too. Nothing idealistic here.

"Have you thought about the house?" he asked me as his thumb started going rogue from the rest of his fingers and doing this circling motion on my skin that felt kind of nice.

"Dal?"

I drew my eyes from where our hands were interlocked, and the movement of his skin on mine, back up to his face. "What house?"

"The house I mentioned the other morning. If you're going to be staying on, I thought it would be more comfortable for you to have your own home. Have some privacy."

"Why would you think she's uncomfortable?" Dax asked as he made his presence at dinner known. I'd been so shocked by the hand-holding and public demonstration that everything beyond had blurred.

Rocky straightened in his chair but his hand remained firm on mine. Until I noticed Dax staring down at our hands. His jaw tensed and I was pulling my hand away before I thought about the action or why I was doing it.

I knew Dax was protective of his resources, of which I was clearly counted, but he was going to have to realize I was allowed to have a life outside of his revenge. But maybe I should sit him down and talk to him after dinner.

Dax, seemingly

57

appeased by my actions, turned to stand behind the man who was sitting on the other side of me, Tyler, who happened to be in charge of the community's plumbing system.

"I'm sure you'd be more comfortable sitting over there," Dax said to him.

Tyler wasn't someone I'd want to anger, as I liked indoor plumbing and all, but Dax didn't have the same qualms as I did. He pissed off anyone he wanted with seeming impunity.

The guy looked disgruntled, but only while he was facing away from Dax. By time he got to his feet, he was smiling and telling him it was no problem. I watched as Tyler took his plate to the lone seat down the table, and hoped I'd still have a working shower by tomorrow and thinking that other house might be looking really good soon if we lost our plumbing because of this.

Dax settled into the seat beside me.

Rocky leaned back in his chair and looked over me to Dax. "I thought we were going to do this civilly?"

"Do what?" I asked. It would be nice to have something other than my own speculations to work from. All I did lately was guess at this and guess at that.

"Nothing," they answered in unison.

"And that *was* civil," Dax said as he leaned back in his chair and watched the platters of food being placed upon the table.

"Kicking people out

of their seats is civil?" Rocky asked as I watched a kid put the steak platter in front of me.

"When I could've dragged him by the neck? Yeah, I'd say so." Dax leaned forward, stabbed a juicy steak, and placed it on my plate before placing one on his own.

He'd handed me food before, usually jerky, so I didn't quite know why exactly it struck me as weird he was serving me, but it did. Had he ever done that at the farm? Not that I could remember, but Fudge had. But it hadn't been like this. No, he was sending Rocky a message that I was his responsibility.

Even if I was his responsibility, which I wasn't, I could still have relationships. I wouldn't lose my magic with my virginity. I was going to have to have a talk with Dax, right after I ate this steak. He really had picked me out a good one. It was bigger than even his.

Rocky leaned in closer to me. "I hope you enjoy the meat. That's from my prime cattle."

Maybe a not-so-subtle reminder that Rocky was actually the provider? Margo had told me once that when you didn't know how to respond, sometimes a simple *thanks* worked. "Thank you," I said, hoping it bought me enough time to get some bites in.

I was just about to pick up the knife and fork when my chair was tugged a few inches away from Rocky and toward Dax.

"You looked a little cramped," Dax said, looking at Rocky as he did.

There was still the same amount of room in between them, except now I was closer to Dax.

"Thanks," I said to Dax, using Margo's advice and hoping it worked, because I was damn hungry and all I really wanted at the moment was to eat.

I moved toward a large serving bowl to get a scoop of mashed potatoes but Rocky's hand cut me off.

"Let me help you with that." He dumped a healthy mound on my plate, nearly double what I would've taken.

This was getting really weird now. Why wasn't I allowed to put food on my plate? But wow, that was a really big mound of potatoes. I never would've had the nerve to take that much, so I certainly wasn't going to complain.

"Thanks," I said, wondering how far I could take this *thanks* plan and how large my servings were going to get.

I leaned closer to the corn, waiting, but somehow they'd lost interest in me and were only looking at each other. Damn, this could've been an epic meal if it had just lasted a little longer. I didn't dare hog the rest of the food the way the table all seemed to be staring down at our end. Didn't they have anything to talk about? Why did they all seem to be trying to listen to us?

Dax, who'd just taken a bite of steak, said to Rocky, "Very good steak, Rocky. Where did you get it? Dal and I would enjoy a meal   like this during the week."

"It's from my private herd."

"Really? I didn't notice one of the cattle missing from the few you have."

I leaned forward, so the most either of them could see was a partial of my profile as I tried to chew on steak like I hadn't just heard Dax say that. I looked down the table. No one else was bothering to pretend ignorance.

"Just butchered. You would know something about fresh meat, wouldn't you?"

I leaned my chin on my hands so it didn't drop open. What the hell was happening here? I knew they both had their squabbles, but this was getting ugly. Rocky was walking a fine line now. Maybe I should lean back or try to break up this conversation?

"You're absolutely correct. The fresher the better. I might do myself a little hunting tonight if the mood strikes," Dax said before I'd gotten past being frozen in indecision.

But I kicked into gear quickly after that last comment. "Hey, Carmine, how's it going with the theatre plans?" I had to nearly scream from where I sat, but it was time for action. It was a popular topic, and I prayed that everyone's interest would shift to the coming theatrics and not the current ones.

Carmine came to my aid, and picked up the thread and ran with it. It took off as one of the people in charge of maintenance said something about how many generators they'd need to find in order to get that movie theater up and running. The conversation drew everyone in, even Dax, who said he knew where there might be some preserved discs.

It was so hard to find media these days that I was impressed with their dedication but thought it was a bit of a long shot. I'd never say that out loud, though. Everybody needed a dream and I hoped this one worked out. Seeing a real live movie like they'd had in the Glory Years was something I'd longed to experience myself.

I had a vague memory of one a long time ago when I was just a child in Newco, still with my parents. I wasn't sure if it was real or something I'd conjured in my own mind out of bored delirium in the Cement Giant.

Before I knew it, dessert was being served. I wasn't sure I'd ever seen such a glorious red as the bowl of strawberries placed on the table. Or maybe they just looked like that because of the mounds of cream against the bright color.

"Your favorite, right?" Rocky asked as he piled up an embarrassing amount into a bowl for me. Okay, I might have to say something about the portions, but I was certain it could wait until tomorrow. Or until I finished the bowl.

My head jerked away from the red and white vision, my taste buds still firing off from the first bite. "Yeah, it is."

"Here, you've got a

little cream on your face," Rocky said as he cupped my cheek, and then his thumb was running over my lower lip. I wasn't sure why you would wipe cream from there, since it was part of the mouth and my tongue would take care of it anyway. Must have fallen into the boyfriend category?

He really wanted to be my boyfriend in every sense of the word. My face tingled where his hand had been as I stared back at him. He was perfect, except his hair was deep auburn and not black and his eyes were a warm brown and not the pale bluish-grey Dax had. And no, I didn't feel the same pull I did when I was with Dax, but that was just Dax's magic at work.

Rocky was a great man, almost the most perfect man I'd ever seen if I'd never met Dax, and I shouldn't hold that against him.

"Why don't I walk you back to your house after dinner?" he asked, and I liked the softness in his eyes when he looked at me, and the width of his shoulders, which looked like a nice place to curl up and rest against for a while.

I knew what he was asking, and I hammered down images of darker hair and lighter eyes because they didn't matter. I nodded. "That would be nice," I said, knowing he'd take that exactly as I meant it.

People got up as they finished and were mingling as they said goodnight. I turned and Dax was standing in front of me, calm as a breezeless evening. Maybe I wouldn't have to talk to him. He seemed to be accepting that I'd made a woman's choice.

Rocky headed over and I motioned for him to give us a moment.

"Sure," Rocky said, smiling like only someone who'd gotten the upper hand could, and I hoped he didn't think this meant I was agreeing to stay here permanently.

He gave my hand a squeeze and walked to the other end of the table. "I'm going to go talk to Tyler for a minute. Let me know when you're ready."

I should've known something was coming but I didn't, not until Dax's arms were wrapped around me, my hands resting on his chest, as my entire body seemed to jolt to life. "What are you doing?"

"What? Don't tell me you only like to play boyfriend with Rocky," he said softly before he pulled me in so that I was snug against him.

His eyes went to my lips as I felt his hand travel up my back until it was cupping the base of my head.

He was inching in slowly, his eyes on my parted lips. Any second now I'd be pushing him away.

I should really pull back, but I didn't move an inch. Maybe once I could breathe better I would. I felt his fingers on the back of my scalp as they threaded in my hair. Any second now, I'd be moving out of his hold.

Then his lips grazed

mine, his tongue peeking in between my lips to slide over my tongue, sending a shock to my nerve endings, as there was a slow, tentative tasting of each other. Our bodies parted slightly, and instead of stepping away, my hand shifted to the back of his neck. I didn't know why my fingers threaded through his hair other than I seemed to always want to touch it when I saw him.

It seemed to trigger something within him. Instead of continuing to pull back, he moved his other hand up and was cupping my head and tilting it, and we were fitting together even closer, the intensity notching up along with the contact.

I felt like I was burning everywhere we touched, and then, suddenly, he pulled back, his arms dropping from me. He stepped back and looked almost as confused as I did for a moment, but his recovery was much quicker.

I watched Dax turn and say to Rocky, "You can go for that walk now."

It hit me then what we'd just done, and in front of everyone.

Rocky looked frozen in place. I could see the words bursting to be said on everyone else's lips.

All I could think was, *I am going to kill him.* The only thing that kept me in place as I watched him walk away was making more of a spectacle of myself.

I turned to the group, who were looking like this was the best theatre available, and said, "What? You never saw two people kiss   before?"

They stopped staring, but I heard a few giggles in the group as they turned away, and I thought I heard someone say, "Not like that," but I wouldn't have sworn to it.

I closed the ten-foot distance between Rocky and me. "Hey, sorry about that. I don't know what came over him."

"I do. Don't worry about it."

His words were exactly what I wanted to hear, but his face didn't show them, and he kept looking away from me.

"You ready?" he asked, and I nodded.

Rocky was polite as we walked, but he didn't so much as reach for my hand, seeming to be lost in his own thoughts.

"Did you want to show me something?" I asked, finding myself trying to break the awkward tension.

"Nah, I'm tired."

I didn't say anything else as he walked me home. I stepped in front of the door and he was gone shortly after.

I waited all night for Dax to come back. Even after I'd given up and went to bed, I was still waiting against my will, listening to every creak of the floorboards and for his familiar footsteps.

When he did finally

come in hours later, it was way past the point I'd normally be asleep. I lay there for a few seconds, telling myself to fight it out with him in the morning. But the image of how Rocky looked after that kiss was still fresh, and I knew sleep was futile.

I climbed out of bed, ready to have it out.

He was walking into the kitchen when I found him. "What was that?"

"I thought you were a grown woman? If I need to explain that to you..." His words trailed off as he walked past me and toward his bedroom.

"That's not what I meant," I said as I followed him.

"He needed to know how misguided he was, and since you seem intent on letting this go on, it was the most efficient way to get the job done."

"It showed him nothing. You just made a spectacle of us." And it didn't seem to bother him one iota, with how calm he was acting.

"Trust me, it showed him. If he didn't get the message, then he didn't want to hear it."

"What message?"

He stopped in the middle of his room and turned to stare at me, and I realized he wasn't anywhere near as calm as I'd thought. "That you aren't interested in him. He's not the one."

"How do you know that?"

"Because you're not."

"You don't know   everything in my head,

67

Dax."

"If he was, you wouldn't melt for me."

"I do no such thing!" I said, even as I was thinking back to the kiss and wondering if that wasn't what I'd just done.

"I think tonight said differently. That's the problem—you're so green you don't even know what you want."

"And you do? Stop trying to control my life. I didn't get out of that place to have someone else try and rule my every move," I said, as he was pulling off his shirt and I decided it was a good time to call it quits for the night.

"Then stop making stupid decisions," I heard him say from the other room.

Chapter Six

I looked through the pile of books Susan had
dropped off this morning. Right smack on top was the
picture of a hilly landscape, the title *Mexico's Wild
Terrain* written in yellow across the front. Mexico. I'd
heard Bookie mention the name. Another country the
Glory Years had wiped off the map.

Susan had come by with them this morning. The
timing seemed a little too convenient, but I'd appreciated
the distraction. After glancing at the *Mexico's Wild
Terrain*, I thought Susan might have oversold her
collection a bit. I'd browse through it, but I doubted its
ability to keep me up all night reading.

I moved Mexico's landscape to the side for future
perusing to find a half-naked man with a woman in his

arms on the cover of the next book. I lifted that one up to get a better look, only to find another cover with a shirtless man standing in the shadows looking all hot and bothered. I dumped the entire bag out and found myself staring down at a collage of half-naked men covering the floor.

Jackpot, baby! I was going to have to kill the next ten Dark Walkers in Susan's honor or something to repay this kind of debt. Maybe come up with a new recipe for lip gloss for her that didn't sting your lips.

I grabbed a book off to the side that had a guy with dark hair and light eyes. He was holding a girl with flaming red hair in his arms like he never wanted to let her go. This looked like a good place to start.

I was trailing a finger over the man's arms on the cover when I heard the doorknob. I shoved all the books into the bag as quickly as my hands could move, having to settle for flipping the top one on its face, since I'd lost Mexico in the shuffle.

Dax stepped in and just stood there for a moment, making me wonder if he'd somehow seen my pile of sexy-time books. No way. I was sure I'd gotten them in the bag in time. I was positive of it. Plus, the tension pouring off him wasn't about sexy-time books. A raised eyebrow and a hint of mockery would be more in line with catching me with these books.

His expression had me glancing over my shoulder and expecting to see a monster or something behind me. Like expected, I didn't find one, and I had a feeling the monster would've been the better-case scenario. Kill 'em and be done, with plenty of reading time left in the day.

"What is it?" The words felt like I'd just swallowed a mouthful of dust or some other distasteful substance. I was the one who was always on the brink of doing something disastrous or needing rescue. I'd been hanging low-key all day. So what was the issue?

He'd been gone since I'd gotten up this morning, but that wasn't enough time for the world to have fallen apart. Or was it? Come to think of it, you didn't need that much time for things to get ugly. I'd seen it firsthand. Shit, it could go bad in a matter of seconds.

He finally unfroze and walked over to the couch, tossing his bag on it. "I had some business to handle, and on my way back here, I heard there's been some outbreaks of the Bloody Death."

It was the only thing he could've said that would wipe out last night's kiss and following fight and make them insignificant. I sat on the floor with my back to the couch, curling my legs underneath me. It was the one thing everyone feared and everyone predicted.

Once there'd been billions of people in the world. There was no way to be sure how many were left, but it was safe to say only a small fraction of that. After the Bloody Death, the numbers had quickly dropped below the magical amount needed to keep an advanced civilization running. Although that was a horrible loss, it was better than mass extinction. Every time there were whispers of another outbreak of the Bloody Death, you never knew how far it would spread, or how many people we would have left. How many could we lose before the human race was doomed to extinction? "How bad?"

"From the information I have, it's hit several different communities. It took out Seaside completely."

"Seaside?"

"It's a community not that far from here. Some said it's already spreading up and down the whole East Coast, but it's hard to know for sure with the way panic starts kicking in."

Even if it were half as bad as that, it was still bad. Would this finally be the end we all feared? I rested an elbow on the couch cushion as my chin went to my hand, trying to hold back the words I didn't want to speak.

I shouldn't have bothered. He said them for me. "That's not a few sporadic cases but the beginnings of a possible wave."

He didn't have a look on his face anymore, and that was almost worse. I let my hair fall in front of my face and didn't bother pushing it away as I imagined the Bloody Death running through this world…or through this place.

I'd never wanted to

come here, but now... It wasn't the farm. It would never be the farm. But it hadn't been so bad, either. Had even turned out to be better than I'd hoped, and I wasn't going to let this happen. As long as I was here, I wouldn't let this place fall. I stood and walked with no real destination as I started putting the pieces together.

"We need to tell Rocky right away. If we can keep everyone within the confines of the walls, limit the exposure to the outside, it'll be okay." I nodded to myself, thinking out the needed steps. "We've got to close up tight. It's the only way to protect everyone. This place is well run. There's probably enough food to be self-sufficient for at least a few months." I needed paper and a pencil so I could start making a list. "After it passes, we should go to the Skinners. They have a cure. Everyone says they never get sick. We've got to get it from them, whatever it takes, and figure out what it is. But first, we need to help keep everyone else safe."

"The Skinners don't have a cure anymore. If everything we've heard is true, only the Dark Walkers do." He was sitting on the couch looking like he was drained while I was just firing up. What was wrong with him?

"No, the Skinner leader will still have some. No way he didn't keep a private stash." I knew I would have, and Dax was more thought out than me, so he had to know that too.

"What are you

thinking?" I asked when I turned to see the blank expression. "I know you and Rocky aren't getting along that well, but we have to help him, them, even if neither of us can get sick."

He was shaking his head. "I'll warn him. That's not it."

"Then what?" And where was a damn pencil when you needed one? If Bookie were here, he'd have one. Bookie would help me make a list and get this organized. He always helped me.

"We're not going to be able to save them. The disease will eventually get in here."

I spun back to Dax from my search for a pencil. "Then we go to the Skinners. I know they have a cure."

"Dal, we're not going to be able to stay here at all. This is going to be a problem."

"We have to. You're not making sense." Where the hell was Bookie? I didn't need nos right now. I needed Bookie's optimism.

"We can't." He crossed the room, coming closer to me, and then stalled, as if he decided it was best to give me space. "The cases are too close. I don't know how many, but someone around here is going to get sick and you're going to get blamed."

I was shaking my head before he finished speaking. "No. You're wrong. I've been here for a while. They know I'm not contagious." They were over it. I'd barbecued with these

74

people. I'd shared shots of whiskey. I even had a bag of sexy books. You didn't share those unless you liked someone. They wouldn't turn on me.

"Dal—"

"You're wrong." I turned away from him, looking for even more space. "You're right about a whole lot of stuff, but about this you're wrong. Very wrong. These people like me. They really like me." I'd seen it in their expressions and heard it in their laughter at my jokes. I was solid with these people. He just didn't understand because he didn't hang out with them the way I did. They were still cautious around him so he didn't see who they were, how they were good people. "It's not like at the farm where they only tolerated me."

He leaned a shoulder against the wall, as if he'd decided that he didn't have the energy to pursue me. "The farm is different. That whole area is. They've seen more of the Bloody Death. These people haven't. There hasn't been an outbreak around here since most of these people were born. Outbreaks change people. I've seen it enough times to know. Once they get scared, they aren't going to be the same."

"But you don't know them, haven't seen their memories like I have. These people are better than most of the people you've met."

"No. They aren't. They're just more sheltered."

"Stop acting like you know everything." Why was he saying these things to me? Was he trying to drive a wedge between these people and me? He'd dragged me here when I hadn't wanted to come and I'd made the best of it. It was almost starting to feel like I belonged, and now he wanted to yank me from here.

"We're going to have to leave."

"Is this about Rocky? Is that why you want to leave?"

"Dal—"

"No. I'm not leaving without a reason. We couldn't stay at the farm, and I understand that, but there's no reason we can't stay here. You're just trying to make me want to leave. That's why you don't want me to go to the Skinners, because it's too close and I'll come back here. You want me to go chasing after the people you want to get." I shook my head and crossed my arms. He wasn't dragging me out of here because of some crazy notion. He'd have to kill me first.

I thought those words would make him angry, but he didn't look mad. I wasn't sure what I saw there as he said, "Blame me if you want, but it'll be easier for you if we leave now."

"You need to have a little more faith in people. They're not going to blame me."

"For your sake, Dal, I hope I'm wrong."

He was staring at me like the weight of the world was about to hit my shoulders and I didn't see the crash coming from above.

"Stop doing that. Looking like that, like you feel bad for me. I don't need you to. Everything is good here."

"I hope you are right. I've never wanted to be wrong as much as I do right now." He walked out the door.

Chapter Seven

It was still dark out but the birds were chirping when Dax stepped into my room. He didn't need to knock, as I never shut the door anymore. It helped me listen for noises throughout the house when I was doing my morning inventory.

He leaned against the doorframe and I sat up.

"I'm leaving in an hour. I need to find out how bad it's getting out there."

"How long are you going to be gone?" I asked. It was a perfectly normal question. I did live with the man.

"Few days, maybe a week, depending on what I find. I want you to come with me."

"I need to stay here." These people wouldn't know what to do if the disease came close. They'd need me.

"Rocky is coming with me. I don't want you going out a lot while I'm gone. Stay inside, don't breathe a word of this to anyone, and just stay out of sight. If someone gets sick, I don't want you to be the first thing they lay eyes on afterward. As long as you stay inside, you'll be fine. Tank will be here to back you up, but I don't think it'll go bad that quickly, and I'll be back soon even if it does."

"Nothing will happen quickly because they aren't going to get sick, and even if they do, they won't turn on me."

"Here," he said, walking over and laying a gun on the table beside my bed, as if I hadn't just told him I was fine. "Make sure you keep this with you. If someone threatens you, shoot them."

"What if I'm not sure they're threatening me?" I asked, imagining myself waving the gun through the community.

"Shoot them anyway."

"I was kidding."

"I'm not. I won't be gone long. Stay close to the house."

He paused, standing beside me for a moment.

"We should talk when I get back."

I knew what he wanted to talk about. I nodded, not looking at him now, as I didn't want him to see my skin ten different shades of red.

***

"Fudge? You up?" I whispered as I walked into her house just as the sun was starting to rise.

A yawning Fudge walked out of her bedroom. "Bookie ate the last of the roast before he went to go check on a pregnant foal, but I think I've got some cornbread you can snack on while I fry up some bacon and eggs," she said as she moseyed on over toward the kitchen.

"Did I wake you?"

She waved a hand at my comment. "No. There are plenty of other things waking my old bones, including Dax stopping by before he left." She went to open a cabinet and grabbed a plate for me.

"Fudge, I'm not here for food." It was understandable that she'd think that, though, since I was almost always looking for food.

But maybe… "I wouldn't mind a piece of the cornbread if you've got it while we chat."

"Tea?" she asked, pulling out the kettle and filling it with some water from the pitcher. The Rock had a pretty good setup, but not quite as good as the farm, and the running water wasn't always reliable.

"Honey?"

"Got a new jar yesterday." Honey was in high demand, but Fudge had already maneuvered her way in to the good graces of   several of the honey

80

collectors.

A few minutes later, I was settled on the couch next to her with a mug of hot tea warming my hands. A piece of buttered cornbread on a plate rested on my lap as I watched the sun rise with Fudge, while Bookie and Tiffy still slept in the other rooms.

"Dax thinks it might get bad. Are you scared?" Fudge asked as she sipped her tea beside me.

"No. Not for me, anyway. I'll be fine." Somehow I always was. It was always the people around me that didn't fare so well. "Are you?" I asked.

"I've had a good life. If I die, I'm okay with that. But I worry."

"Dax thinks I'm going to need to leave here."

"Dal—"

"No. They're going to be fine," I said. The way she'd spoken my name had said it all. But just like Dax, she hadn't spent as much time with these people.

She patted my shoulder and said, "It'll work out."

It was one of those things people said to you when they didn't know exactly *how* it would work out. Burned at the stake was a way of things working out too. Just not a good way.

I got to my feet, avoiding her gaze. "I gotta go."

"Wait, you don't want bacon?"

"No. I'm full," I lied. "I forgot about something I told Dax I'd do. I'll talk to you tomorrow." My feet couldn't take me back to   the house fast enough.

81

Chapter Eight

"They're looking at me funny, Bookie." I threw my stone across the lake's surface and watched as it did a perfect skip before disappearing. "Or maybe they aren't? Dax planted this seed in my head before he left a few days ago, and now I'm imagining it everywhere, with every look or greeting." I turned to see if I'd lost Bookie to boredom yet.

Not only was he paying attention, he seemed to be concentrating on my words. I'd been talking about it for a solid half an hour, and it was a subject that didn't even deserve a mention. Damn Dax for making me see shit that wasn't there.

"Even if they were, and I'm not saying that they are, it'll be okay. They've heard the rumors, is all. They know why Rocky left with Dax. They'll calm down after they realize they're safe." He threw a stone, and I watched it do one halfhearted bounce and then sink like the stone it was.

"So you think they are looking at me funny too?" Was Dax right?

"I just told you that I wasn't saying that."

"But you do?" He gave the shrug of the noncommittal, the one people do when they don't want to lie to you but don't exactly want to tell you the truth either. So maybe Dax was right. Just rumors of the sickness nearby and already this was what things were coming to.

"When I was walking over to meet you here this morning, Carmine and Angela were walking my way. They saw me and waved but then they turned around. I told myself it was just a coincidence, that they realized they were heading in the wrong direction, but now I don't know. Maybe it's not in my head. Maybe Dax was right." I grabbed a blade of grass by my hip and toyed with it between my fingers while I hoped Bookie would tell me I was crazy. But he was an optimist, not delusional, so my hopes weren't too high.

"Even if they did, it doesn't matter." He threw another rock, but harder this time. This one didn't even have a chance of skipping.

I was doing it again, dragging him into my messes. It was so hard not to, though. He was my Bookie, my best friend.

"Who gives a fuck

83

what they think anyway? That's what I'm saying. You're a tough woman who's been through a lot and is still kicking ass. Whatever happens, it'll be okay." He bumped my shoulder with his. "Even if they all start running away screaming, you'll always have me," he said, trying to drum up a little laughter.

I bumped my shoulder back into his. "I will, right?" I asked, even though I knew I didn't have to. Bookie would be there for me no matter what. He always was. He was the closest thing I'd ever had to family. And every time I thought of taking a step back from him, getting him out of harm's way, which was nowhere near me, where he might catch a stray bullet, I turned around and clung even tighter. It was selfish, but I just couldn't walk away from him yet.

With Bookie, I didn't have to pretend to be anything, because for some crazy reason he thought I was great as is. He didn't want to change me or make me into anything. Even though I had visions of grandeur, it was nice to be with someone who didn't think I had to become grand.

"Always. You're the Doxie to my Moobie," he said.

"I'm not having this fight with you again. I'm Moobie and you're the sidekick."

He nodded, but I realized I was laughing alone. "Bookie, you okay? You look a little green around the gills."

"I was in the stables

pretty late last night, is all. Damn foal didn't want to come out. Just tired."

As I watched, a single drop of blood trickled down from his nose. "Bookie…"

The world froze around me as his hand came up to wipe away the moisture he felt above his lip.

I couldn't breathe, couldn't think. "Bookie." In that single calling of his name, years of terror came out.

"Dal, I'm fine. Really," he said. "It was one drop. People get bloody noses all the time. It means nothing."

But it wasn't one drop—I watched a second drip down. It wasn't nothing.

His hand went back to his face, and I could see that even he wasn't so quick to dismiss it now. He didn't say anything as we both realized what might be happening. This was the very first sign of the Bloody Death.

He was sick. I knew it in my gut. The people around me always disappeared. Why was I so foolish to think Bookie would be different? Just like Bert at the trader hole had looked at me, I was death, and if you stayed near me, it was only a matter of time.

But please, not Bookie. No. I wouldn't let him go. I shot to my feet, scanning the Rock for a particular face. "Where's the doctor? Do you know where he is? We need to get you help."

He stood up beside me. "Dal, I'm…"

I thought he was going to say *fine*, but he didn't finish the sentence. His

85

face contorted as if he were trying to hold back a scream as the pain, the second sign of the Bloody Death, hit him. Everyone knew first came the bloody drip, then the pain.

He reached an arm out to me, looking for support as he stumbled on his feet.

"I need you to help me get back to your house," he said, his breathing ragged. "I don't want the others to get near me. If this is the Bloody Death, you're the only one with immunity." I knew Tiffy would be okay, but I didn't bother telling him. There was still Fudge and Tank to worry about.

I nodded, half listening as I looked around the place for help. "I need to get the doctor."

"Dal, help me get inside first."

"But we don't have much time."

Bookie grabbed my wrist, stronger than he looked capable of at the moment. "You have to get me inside. Don't go for the doctor. Don't tell anyone."

I hadn't seen the Bloody Death in action, but his brain was already going. In the Cement Giant we'd been sheltered from it, but everyone knew how it went down. "Why?"

"Because you'll be blamed for this and it's too late for me anyway."

"People survive. I did."

He was shaking his head. "I won't. Dal, I'm already dead. Do this last thing   for me."

I nodded and slung his arm over my shoulder, having no intention of doing any such thing, but he was having trouble walking from the pain. I had to get him to a bed and then I'd get the doctor. This was not going to happen. I wouldn't let Bookie die. Not him.

By time we were on our street, we'd been spotted by too many people to keep it a secret. There was a trail of blood running from Bookie's nose and down to cover the front of his white shirt. Not that I gave a shit anymore what anyone thought. The earlier discussion with him seemed like a pathetic waste of time now that his life was at stake.

I saw Tank as I neared the house.

His steps immediately faltered at the sight of Bookie. "Is he… Does he have…"

I watched the horror flicker over Tank's expression before he got his emotions in check.

Tank took a step forward and then one back, as if he couldn't figure out whether he should be helping or running the other way in fear for his own life. I didn't begrudge him his hesitancy. Most people would've just run from the first sight of us.

The only thing Tank would achieve by getting closer was to give me another body to care for anyway. I didn't want to waste one iota of attention on something other than Bookie, because he was going to need me if he was going to make it.

"Stay back," I said,

as much for him as for Bookie and myself. "Don't come back to the house. I'm going to bring Bookie there and stay with him. I need you to find the doc and send him over."

Tank nodded.

He lifted his hand toward Bookie where I was struggling to move forward toward the door again. "Do you need help getting him in?" he asked.

"No. I've got him. You're better off staying clear. Keep Fudge and Tiffy away from here as well."

Another nod and he took off, hopefully to go find the doctor.

I made our way inside, barely getting him to the bed before his legs gave out. I looked at the clock and thought about everything I'd ever heard or knew about the Bloody Death, including my own hazy memories. Seventy-two hours. That was all I needed. If he could make it past the next few days, he'd be like me, a Plaguer. It might not be the most enviable thing in the world, but he'd be alive, and that was all I cared about.

There was a rap at the bedroom window and I looked up to see Tiffy's face. I leapt off the bed where I'd been kneeling beside him as I saw her test the window, and was grateful I'd locked it.

"Don't let her in here," Bookie said.

"Tiffy, you have to go back to the house."

"But I want to help you. Let me in." Her small voice was muffled behind the glass that separated us, and I could see the beginning of tears as she looked in Bookie's direction.

"You can't."

"But I can help. I won't get sick."

The image of Bookie was already jarring, still bleeding and now tense with pain, and it was only going to get worse. But getting the kid to walk away was going to be tough, and there was only one thing I could think of that might work. "Tiffy, you need to stay with Fudge. You need to protect her, okay? Go back to the house and stay with her. She can get sick. If she tries to leave you, tell her you're scared. Don't let her come here. Tell her I said to stay away and that I'm taking care of him."

"But I can help."

"I can take care of him on my own. I promise you. But you need to take care of Fudge for me, okay?" She was hesitating, but I knew I had her, and her little head bobbed before she backed away from the window, wiping at the tears that were falling down her cheeks.

I turned all my attention back to Bookie and then to the clock. Seventy-one hours and fifty minutes to go. "We can do this, Bookie."

My normal ray of sunshine didn't look so optimistic.

"We'll get through this," I said, trying to force a conviction of steel into my voice when I felt more like rusted junk.

Chapter Nine

"After we leave here, I think we should start our own library somewhere. What do you think of that?" Bookie didn't speak, and I wasn't sure he heard me anymore. He hadn't responded in hours. I ran the damp cloth across his fevered brow for what might be the hundredth time. The water was lukewarm now, but I feared leaving him to get a new bucket.

I grabbed his hand, hoping he knew he wasn't fighting this alone, and looked at the clock on my nightstand. Only eight hours had passed, but he'd already lost consciousness. It wasn't a good sign. Everything I knew about the Bloody Death said the quicker a person lost consciousness, the quicker they died. Bookie hadn't lasted very long at all.

I wasn't a doctor and I didn't know how to save him.
The real doctor wasn't coming. I was sure Tank had
found him by now. He just hadn't been willing to
jeopardize himself for someone else. If Bookie could
just hang in there…

I grabbed his hand tighter. "We're going to see this
whole world, Bookie, you and me. We're going to see
every country there is, explore every ruin in the Wilds.
We won't stop until you have enough books to fill up a
library of your own."

A shiver ran through his fevered body, and I climbed
up on the bed with him and pulled his upper body onto
mine so I could wrap my arms around him and give him
my heat. I'd give him everything I had if I could.

"Bookie, I know you already know this, but you're
my best friend. So here's the thing: you can't die. You
just can't. Even if it seems easier right now, you can't. I
know, I'm being selfish, but I can't lose you." I dragged
an arm across my runny nose and forced my voice to
remain steady in case he was hearing me. "Do you hear
me, Bookie? You can't die. You can't. You said you
would always be there for me. You promised me that,
and I'm holding you to it."

I was bordering on hysteria and I knew it. Might
have even embraced it, because it was better than any of
the other emotions swirling in me, like absolute despair
and dread.

I clung to him,

wrapping my arms around him as tight as I could while I still had him here with me, because I feared it wouldn't be for much longer. I stroked at my magic like I had countless times by now, trying to infuse him with whatever I had inside me. I didn't know if it made a difference, but it didn't seem to.

I looked toward the ceiling like Fudge would and tried to talk to her god. "Take my magic and give it to him." If her god existed, he could gladly take everything I had. I'd thought that when the Wood Mist stole my magic, it had been the worst thing that could happen to me, but I was so wrong.

"Take whatever you want from me. Just give me Bookie."

I couldn't lose him, not Bookie. He'd been my crutch, the one who would back me up and be there with me no matter what I did or what crazy idea I had. He was the first person in my life that had loved me unconditionally. He hadn't cared that I was a Plaguer, even when he'd first met me. Even my friends at the Cement Giant hadn't accepted me the way he had. He'd risked his life to help save those friends because they'd meant something to me. He'd gotten me through when I'd lost two of them.

Now I would watch him die because no matter what I did, nothing seemed to make a difference. He hadn't opened his eyes in hours, and every time I touched his hands, they were colder than they had been—his heart struggling to pump enough blood to his extremities. I wished I could go back in time, and never told him to come here with me.

I rocked him in my arms as I spoke to him, refusing to give up on him. "Bookie, please. Don't give up. You can do this. I know because I did it, and you're a hundred-times-better person than me, so I know you can. Do you hear me?"

Tapping at the bedroom window drew my attention, and I saw Tank there.

"The doctor?" I asked without getting up, even though I knew the answer.

He shook his head, confirming the doctor wasn't coming. I didn't ask why. Didn't want to hear the excuses.

"I'm going to go and try and find Dax. If not, I'm going to see if I can round up some help," he said.

I nodded. So it was already getting ugly. How quickly they'd turned.

Tank disappeared and I pulled the blanket up around Bookie and me, bundling us up together the best I could as the fall night chill settled into the house. I had no wood left for the stove and I wasn't willing to leave Bookie for even a moment. If I could keep him warm, stay with him and talk to him, maybe he'd make it still.

"Don't worry, Bookie, I'm not leaving you." He never would've left me either.

***

Time didn't seem to exist after a while, and I found myself repeating my pleas to Fudge's god, and then to the Wood Mist, anyone who might listen.

I was pretty sure no one was.

The room was dark as we lay there. I wasn't sure when the shivering stopped, or when he'd made the last groan of pain, but I knew he was gone. The labored breaths had ceased some time ago, but I hadn't moved. Once I did move, once I got out of this bed, then there would be no going back. This would be real. As long as I stayed here, Bookie was still with me.

I gripped him to me. Another person, dead. Why did they all have to leave or die? Was it me? Was I cursed somehow to be alone?

I should've been better to him. I'd involved him in all my messes. I'd practically dragged him into them. Fudge had told me to leave him behind. Dax had, too. But I hadn't been able to let him go. I'd been too weak and now he was dead, paying a price that I should've borne.

I didn't know how long I'd lain there with him like that when I heard the noise, like something heavy hitting the front door.

I would've ignored it and still stayed there with him if I hadn't heard, "Go back where you came from, you dirty Plaguer, or we'll burn this house down to the ground."

Unclenching my fingers from where they were locked around Bookie, I took a deep breath and forced myself to face what lay ahead. I couldn't stay in this bed forever, even if I wanted to. I had to get to my feet and do what needed to be done. I'd hurt Bookie enough.

I wouldn't let them burn these walls down around him, even if I might deserve that end. Bookie deserved better, and he would get it. I might not have done right by him while he was living, but I'd do right by him now if it cost me everything I had, including my life. I owed him that. I owed him everything.

It was time to leave this place. Turned out Dax was right. He was right a lot. Maybe it was for the best I left here alone. Maybe I was one of those people who were meant to walk this world by themselves. It sure seemed like it right now. Maybe that was why I lost everyone, and I needed to accept it.

Chapter Ten

I left Bookie on the bed and made my way out through the living room and opened the front door, not fearing any of them. A rock wrapped in paper sat by the front stoop, a dent in the door's wood above it, with no sign of people. I reached down and grabbed it and shut the door again. I let the rock fall to the floor and looked at the sheet.

Leave or we'll burn you out.

I crumbled the paper and let it drop to the floor beside the rock before walking back to the bedroom.

"Bookie, they said they're going to burn us out.

Looks like we're in a real pinch this time, huh?" I asked.

I imagined him looking at me, stare lowered, just as he had when I'd talked to him in the stables before we came here. He'd say, *Is this going to be another lecture about how I could die?*

I wrapped my arms around myself. "No, I won't be giving you any more of those speeches."

There is a god.

"I hope so, Bookie. I really hope so."

Bookie was dead.

Dax was right. I should've left this place. I hadn't listened. Bookie would've come with me and then maybe he wouldn't be dead. This place was nothing but toxic, with its false mirages of safety and acceptance. I'd believed in a delusion.

Even now, the people I thought were my friends were watching the house. I hadn't seen them when I walked out on the stoop, but I could feel them. They'd be coming for us but I wouldn't let them get their hands on Bookie. It was time to go, and I wouldn't leave Bookie to rot in this house alone.

I grabbed my bag, the one Fudge had given me, and went through the stock in the kitchen. I wiped out Tank's stash of jerky, some cornbread Fudge had brought over yesterday, and a flask of whiskey I found in one of the cabinets. I moved about the place, packing what else I thought would be of need, leaving the stack of books untouched,   even though I'd yet to

97

read one.

I slung the bag over my shoulder. It was the dead of night. No one would follow me out of the gates if I left now. I couldn't wait for Dax to show up and bail me out—again. Maybe put a stop to what I had planned next.

I left the house and walked to the stables, feeling the eyes peering out their windows as I passed. I lifted my chin and continued on, hoping someone would get in my way, because I had enough anger to fill up this whole place right now and not a single outlet in sight.

The stables were empty when I got there and saddled Charlie, tying my bag to the back. He fidgeted the whole way back to the house, as if he was feeding off me.

I hadn't felt this alone in years, this sad or utterly defeated. But I wouldn't fall apart. There were things that had to be handled.

I walked Charlie up to the house and left him grazing on the front lawn as I went inside. Dax's bedroom door was open and I stepped inside it, breathing deeply. I ran my fingers over his jacket hanging on the doorknob and threw his on over my own, knowing I would need the additional warmth, and then shut his door.

I walked back to my room. Bookie was lying on my bed, his body lifeless. I sat beside him, and even though I'd thought there weren't any tears left, there still seemed to be more. "We're leaving here now, Bookie."

I wrapped my arms

around him, pulling him upward and close to me. "Why did you leave me?" I let myself devolve for only a few minutes into abject misery before I knew I had to pull it together. Once his body started to stiffen in death, I'd never be able to do what was needed.

I took the sheets from my bed and made a shroud, wrapping him snugly within, not wanting anyone to see him like this, so pale and unlike his true self.

"This will keep you warm while we travel. I know you're cold."

I dragged him from the bed and through the living room, wanting to preserve my strength in order to get him on the horse. I hated to bring him outside like this, for all the invisible onlookers to see, but there was no helping it.

I'd barely been able to lift him, but I got Bookie's body slung over Charlie's back and then walked Charlie and him over to Fudge's.

I slipped a letter through the slot on the door, making sure to not let the metal clank. She'd find it after I was way gone, and that was for the best. My path ahead was tough enough, and I wasn't sure I would be able to defend it at the moment.

I mounted Charlie and, with a hand resting on Bookie, clucked my tongue and urged the horse forward.

"They're watching us, Bookie, but you were right. I don't care what they think anymore."

I rode to the front of

the gate and it creaked open before I got close.

"I hope you get eaten by beasts for bringing your disease here," Tim, one of the night watchmen, yelled. It was the same guy I'd eaten a hamburger with last week and joked about the new plumbing system plans with.

I didn't reply, didn't even look over at him as I rode out of the Rock. It didn't matter what they thought. I was happy to leave. This place was nothing but a lie.

As the distance grew between me and the Rock, I thought of the words I'd written to Fudge as I kept my hand upon Bookie, selfishly looking for his support, even now when he had nothing left to give.

Dear Fudge,

I'll write this plainly, as there is no way to write it that will lessen the pain. Bookie died from the Bloody Death. I hope you know I would've done anything to save him. I would've given everything I had, including sacrificing my own life. He was the best person I'd ever known and I will mourn him until I die.

I'm hoping that my leaving will allow you to stay at the Rock with Tiffy and Tank. It's much safer for you to remain there than where I'll be going. I hope one day we will meet again in better times, that I'll be able to sit and share a meal with you again, but there's something I must do. I'm hoping it will bring us both some peace.

I'm also sorry that

100

I'm taking Bookie with me before you had a chance to say goodbye, but I needed to protect him, since he can't protect himself right now. If you want to visit Bookie, he'll be resting on the ridge to the west that has the most beautiful sunsets I've ever seen. If you don't know where it is, ask Dax. He'll know the spot. Bookie will be happy there. It's one of his favorite places.

Tell Tiffy to stay out of trouble and that I'll be seeing her again one day before this life is through with whatever it has left to offer.

As to Dax...tell him goodbye.

It only took Charlie a half an hour to get us to the ridge, and the sunrise was just starting to sparkle on the dew-laden grass. I dismounted and grabbed the shovel from where I'd tied it on the back of the saddle.

I walked around the place looking for the perfect spot until I stopped beside the rock we liked to use as a backrest. "What about here, Bookie?" I looked over at him, lifeless on the horse, and turned my head quickly before that became the last image burned into my brain.

"Yeah, this is perfect," I said, answering for him. I dug the shovel into the ground right where he used to sit, and started to dig. Each shovel of dirt seemed heavier than the last.

I dragged Bookie to the grave, having to stop a few times when the wrapping shifted off him. I settled him in then went back to the   saddlebags and dug out his books.

"I know you loved this one," I said as I laid a Moobie on his chest. "And don't worry, I didn't forget your other favorites." I tucked several more books around him. "And yes, I'm going to read that other book you wanted me to that I've been dragging my feet on. I told you I'd give it a try and I will, even if the lead guy seems like a total dick from page one."

My hands shook as I moved the books around a bit until they were perfectly arranged and he was surrounded by all his favorites. I climbed out of the grave from where I'd been kneeling next to him.

"I have to cover you now." I grabbed the shovel, eyeing the pile of dirt that I'd have to place on top of him. "It has to be done. If I don't, I'm afraid something will try and eat you or take your books. I'll be back. I'll come back a lot and bring you more books, but I have to leave you for a while. I have to find a way to fix this for you. You were the one that always said that the world would be as good as we made it. I'm going to make it good, Bookie, and I'm going to do it for you."

Chapter Eleven

I wasn't sure if I'd remember the way to Hell's Corner, one of the main hubs of the pirate stronghold. Part of me hoped I'd forgotten, because then I'd have a good excuse to not do what I was doing. I'd be forced to turn around.

But I did remember the way, and every mile farther away from the Rock, it felt like my heart was being buried back on the crest along with Bookie.

Dax would be angry, but there were more important things to worry about in this world than the revenge of one man. Or how leaving him made me feel like I was adrift in the ocean.

I hadn't realized how much I'd come to rely on him. It was better that I was leaving. I couldn't afford to rely on anyone like that. It was dangerous, made me soft, and I needed to be hard for what was to come.

My course was set. Jacob, King of the Pirates, needed me. I had some leverage with him and he had some leverage with the people I needed information from. There was only one path I was willing to go down, and it wasn't a U-turn. I needed Bookie's death to bring some good.

Fudge had told me once that she didn't believe people stayed in their bodies. She said that their souls went to a better place. I asked her where this place was, but she said she didn't know its actual location. Just said it could be all around us and yet out of sight. That was why she talked to her parents even when she couldn't see them. She said she thought they listened to her.

At the time, I'd thought it was ridiculous. I'd never seen her dead parents hanging around. That's how I knew how desperate I was when I looked around as I rode Charlie.

"Bookie? You out here?"

Nope. Nothing. I rode alone into Hell's Corner.

The place was just as creepy the second time around. Charlie neighed as he started to dance to the side, disliking this place as much as I had the first time I'd come here. I had a feeling that even the beasts avoided this place.

I looked to the weaving waterway, lined with trees but devoid of boats. Not that a pirate ship would fit here, but there were no dinghies or other smaller vessels to be found either. They'd come, though. I'd heard they policed this area regularly.

Patting Charlie's neck, I slid to the ground. "Don't worry, buddy, you're off the hook. I'm pretty sure horses aren't welcome where I'll be staying." My bag of insufficient supplies fell to my feet as I pulled the bridle off Charlie, afraid he might get it tangled on his way back home, and then gave his rump a slap. He hesitated.

"Go," I said, shooing him off. Like Fudge and Tiffy, he'd be better off behind the walls of the Rock.

"Go," I repeated. "Time for you to go home." His head ducked down for a moment as his big brown eyes seemed to hold remorse about the coming abandonment, but then he was galloping out of the place.

The small bank near the water that I'd come to before was a bleak campsite. I couldn't risk the attention a fire could draw, not out here on my own with no one to back me up while I was sleeping.

My back to a boulder, I pulled Dax's jacket snugly around me, breathing deeply. I could still smell him on it, and I wondered how long smells stayed like that on clothes. I'd needed something warm and it had been right there—that was the only reason I'd taken it.

I rested my head back on the boulder, and my knife stayed in my right hand as I pulled the flask I'd brought in my left and took a swig. I settled in to wait, having no idea when the pirates would come back here.

"What do you think, Bookie? Did I make the right choice?" I asked while I sat there alone, Dax's jacket doing a fairly good job of warding off the chill of the swamp.

You've got to do what you think is right. Bookie had said that to me on more than one occasion. I could almost hear him say the words now.

"And what if I don't know what that is? Or what if I can't accomplish it?"

Imaginary Bookie didn't have an answer for that, but he was as easy to talk to as the real Bookie had been. "You know, I don't say this a lot, but I'm scared, Bookie, really scared. I haven't felt this alone in a long time."

You'll always have me.

"I wish that had been true." I took one more swig of the whiskey before I cut myself off, waiting to see if I'd be doling out any death.

***

I hadn't meant to sleep. When I woke, it wasn't from a dream and the monsters weren't invisible, fading with the nightmares.

I felt warm air stirring my hair and touching my cheek. The heat from something massive was flowing over me. It was a beast and it wasn't Dax. I could sense the magic in it, so similar to Dax's yet distinctly not. That was when I realized that everyone's magic must have a certain fingerprint of a sort.

Eyelids still closed, I never let go of the knife. I wasn't sure whether it was better to feign sleep or let this thing know it was in for a fight if it attacked me. The idea of dying passively forced my eyes open.

We were nearly nose to nose, its fur brushing my bare arm where it squatted next to me, and its red eyes stared into mine, so close I could smell fresh blood on its breath from a recent kill. That was actually a plus. Hopefully the thing wasn't hungry.

He sniffed my hair before he moved downward to my shoulders. A slight rumble grew in its chest and my hand tightened on the knife as I looked for vulnerabilities around its neck. I was a second from attacking when it turned and took off into the trees.

***

The second night was almost over when I heard the boat moving through the water. I dug out the gun that I had close by, knowing I'd get longer range than with my knife, and had it aimed at the two-man crew before they got anywhere near me. It was a tough shot, but luckily, hitting my target was   my strong suit.

107

The small boat moved up the bank toward my camp and I watched as the two pirates got out in ankle-deep water. They pulled the dinghy up on shore, and I stayed still with the gun pointed in their direction in case this didn't go down the way I hoped.

Fifteen feet or so away, the two turned their full attention on me as we took each other's measure. I vaguely remembered seeing the shorter, stockier one the last time I'd been on Jacob's pirate ship, so that was a good sign. Not only were they pirates, they were the right crew as well. After all, I didn't want any old pirate ship, and I had no idea how many pirates there were.

The taller of the two pirates pointed at my gun. "I wouldn't be pointing that at us, being as you're on our territory and uninvited."

I lowered the gun—slightly. "I want to see Jacob."

"Girlie, why the fuck else do you think we'd be here? You coming with us or not?" he asked as I stood, gun still in my hand. The other pirate pulled out a lumpy cigarette and then lit a match using a nearby rock.

His buddy motioned for one for himself.

"Why can't you roll your own?"

"I do. I'm out."

"You say that, but you're always out."

I watched as the two bickered, and realized they really didn't care if I came.

"Where's the ship?" I asked.

"Around the bend,"

the taller one said, and then went back to arguing for a cigarette.

I took a couple steps to the left and past a row of trees, while keeping a healthy distance between us just in case they were faking non-interest.

Just as he said, there was a grand ship in the distance. I squinted and could make out Jacob's gold skull on the flag that was blowing in the breeze.

"You comin' or not? I'm not standing here until the sun rises."

I turned back to the duo and saw they were both smoking now.

I grabbed my stuff. As I got closer to the pirates, visions of their worst transgression played out in my mind: one bloody murder over a card game and the abandonment of some children. It wasn't great stuff, but these weren't the people in charge, either. And it wasn't the worst I'd ever seen. Plus, I had to weigh my options, and when one side of the scale was empty, the pirates were an easy win.

"Yeah. I'm coming."

I climbed into the dinghy with them, and they started to row us out toward the large pirate ship.

Chapter Twelve

The crew appeared to be just starting their day as I climbed aboard and the first rays of morning hit the deck. I caught a couple curious glances, but I didn't see any surprised looks as I followed the two pirates who'd brought me here, hoping we were heading toward Jacob. They led me to a cabin door below deck and left.

I walked through the open door and found the man I was looking for in a place that was nicer than I'd expected. It looked like Jacob had a thing for oil paintings and intricately carved wood. I walked across a rug that had to have come from the Glory Years, with its tight and perfect pattern, and approached the desk he was sitting at, getting within range.

The first time I'd met this man, my magic had been

on the fritz in a bad way. Everyone had been a blank slate. This time I was jacked up and ready to see what nightmares awaited me.

I was sure there was going to be something ugly in his head. Had to be. He was the Pirate King. You didn't get a position like that, leading this crew, if you were Snow White. Now I just had to hope it wasn't so bad I wouldn't be able to stomach working with him, because he was my only choice at the moment.

The second I got close enough, I was blasted by one of the strongest memories I'd gotten in a long while, which usually meant it cut the person deeply. A woman, dead by his hand. She'd been a small thing, maybe slighter than I, and she was lying at his feet, a knife protruding from her chest.

It wasn't a good sign, and I swallowed hard, wondering if I'd made a smart choice. But the problem was that I'd already made it. There wasn't any going back now, and I couldn't see a way forward without him. Jacob, his crew, and his ships were integral to my plan—if I could make it work, anyway.

"You're looking a little pale," he said as he watched me approach.

I shrugged, trying to push off the memory. "Rough night, is all."

"She was my wife, if you're curious."

Not surprising that he knew the full extent of what Plaguers could do. He'd known about the Dark Walkers and how I could ID them. Of course he'd heard about the memories.

He crossed his legs and readjusted his seat. "Strange how you didn't have this reaction the first time I met you."

"Not always reliable," I said, even as I knew this wasn't the type of person you admitted weaknesses to, unless you wanted your soft spots gutted later. But I'd rather have him think the memories weren't always a hundred percent than that I'd lost a large chunk of my magic for a while, which disclosed a much larger weakness.

His eyebrows rose. "Want to know why I killed her?"

"How do you know what I saw?" I countered.

"Easy. Because it's the only murder I remember. Do you want to know?"

"No. It makes no difference." And I'd rather believe it was something he'd had to do, or that she was about to kill him, because even now my fingers tingled, wanting the feel of my knife in them so I could right that wrong.

But I'd made a choice. Only problem was deciding if I could stomach him long enough to try and save the world. Was it worth it? Well, yeah. It was the fucking world I was talking about. I'd work with anyone to do that.

But he certainly wasn't my first choice. No, that person was probably just discovering I'd taken off from the Rock but I wouldn't think of him.

Then the image of a warm set of hazel eyes sprang to mind, and I could almost picture him standing beside me saying, *You've got this.*

Thanks, Bookie, I said in my head, because admitting to talking to imaginary dead people wasn't a great way to start a negotiation.

Jacob made an obvious show of looking behind me before saying, "You're alone."

Well *hear, hear* for Mr. Astute. Although I did have to admit that his three words clarified my situation, like a shovel scraping the raw metal on the bottom of a rusted wagon.

There was only me now. I was alone. My best friend, even though I still talked to him and imagined him beside me, was dead, buried by my own hand after I'd watched him die the most painful of deaths. Fudge and Tiffy, the only people left who felt like family, were miles away from me.

I wouldn't wake to breakfast tomorrow, or cross the way to the comforting smell of breakfast cooking, or the smell of sugar that always seemed to linger near Fudge as she laid a hand on my shoulder and tried to fatten me up. Tiffy's too-wise little face wouldn't be there giving me her sardonic looks, and Tank wouldn't be ribbing me. There would be no more exploring with Bookie, ever.

113

And Dax. I couldn't get my head around that yet. I'd run out on him, or that was how he would see it. I wasn't sure why thinking of him seemed the worst. Maybe because I knew how angry he'd be. There would be no happy reunion in a few years. The subject of him was better left buried, if I could bury it deep enough.

"Yes. I am alone."

"He agreed to let you go?"

He was obviously Dax. It was going to be really tough to bury him if people were going to dig him back up.

I weighed my answer. Would a pirate appreciate that I'd thwarted someone like Dax or be concerned about potential fallout from it? We were on a boat, surrounded by water. Jacob wouldn't be worried about fallout. "No, he didn't, but he doesn't own me."

"Does he know you're here?"

"No."

"For a girl, you don't lack for balls. That's for sure." Jacob leaned back, his white teeth shining against dark skin. Damn, the man had a good smile. He'd also killed his last wife, so that had a way of dimming the attractiveness. I didn't miss the insult, either. Just because I was a girl I wasn't supposed to have balls? Besides the obvious anatomical lack, I had more balls than him.

"No, I don't."

He used his foot to

push out the chair opposite him on the other side of his desk. "Why don't you have a seat and let me know what made you come here all alone?"

I took the offered chair, sitting at an angle that kept the gun inside Dax's jacket and the knife at my hip within easy reach, because that's the way this negotiation was going down.

He reached behind him to a shelf and grabbed a glass, placed it beside his own, and filled them both with what I presumed to be whiskey.

"You do drink?" he asked, after he'd already filled both glasses and placed the decanter down.

"Only on my good days." But not normally at the crack of dawn.

I took the glass and threw back the contents, knowing every action was being measured. I was going to have to negotiate quickly if he poured again, thinking my two-whiskey limit might need to apply to this situation.

The door to the cabin opened and my hand immediately went to the hilt of my knife, until I saw that it was just one of his pirates with two plates of food piled high with eggs, sausage, and potatoes. There wasn't any bacon, but the meeting was already going better than I'd expected if you factored the aromas into the equation, and of course I did.

Coffee was poured as I popped a fried potato into my mouth. It was starchy perfection after two days of jerky. I took a sip of the coffee, which was a little less perfect, before I ventured into the sensitive topic that had brought me here. "Have you heard of the recent outbreaks?" For a normal person, asking about the Bloody Death was an alarming subject. For a Plaguer, it was like waving a red flag in front of you. The Bloody Death was the last thing I wanted to remind anyone of, but I had no choice.

He raised both of his eyebrows, as if the question didn't warrant an answer. Great, another one that liked to make faces.

Damn, I had to stop thinking about Dax.

Jacob went back to spearing a forkful of eggs without the telltale glance at my hand I'd come to expect from people at the mention of that disease. That was what people did anytime the Bloody Death was mentioned. He simply had better self-control than most.

Wasn't sure what that said about killing his wife. Had he been in control at the time? An act of rage might have been better, if there was a better to that situation. Maybe control was a new character trait he'd been working on? Either way, I needed to make sure I never forgot who I was dealing with.

I reached forward to the whiskey that had also been refilled and threw it back in one motion. This day was going to need the two-whiskey maximum. "You have a relationship with the Skinners. When they wanted a meeting, they reached out to you. Do you still have contact with them?"

"I don't typically discuss my business with anyone."

"The Dark Walkers were giving the Skinners a cure."

Jacob didn't say anything, but I saw his muscles tense and his lips press together. "So the rumors were true."

I guessed he didn't know as much as he thought. I waited for that information to brew just a minute longer as I took another bite of eggs, fueling up in case I had to make a run for it at some point. "I want your help getting it. If we can get it, then maybe we can figure out what it is. Maybe even make more."

He didn't respond immediately, and I waited patiently, trying to get as much food in as I could while I waited. If this went south, I didn't know when I'd be eating again.

He didn't answer until I was nearly finished and halfway through my coffee.

"How would we do that?" he asked as he topped off my coffee with the pot left behind.

"Back in the Glory Years, there were people called chemists. There must be someone who still knows how to do what they did."

"It was different then. There were machines. Plus, why do I need it? I'm heading west, away from where the disease is spreading. Could be years before it gets there." His words might

117

have sounded cautious, but there was interest in his eyes.

"If the Dark Walkers have a cure, then there is a way for us to make it. I know your business is trade and transport. Can you imagine the power you would have if you had the cure? And you know it's only a matter of time before it hits everywhere. If it's not this outbreak, it'll be the next."

He placed the coffee urn down and weaved his fingers together in front of him. "You seem the type that would want to hand it out for free."

"I would, but I'm only one person. I don't have the resources you do. The way I see it, I'd rather have the cure getting to the most amount of people. Imagine the money and power you would reap from it? I ask only one thing: that you don't price it so high that only a few can afford it."

"I want to know what else I get," he said, and then took a bite of toast, as if he wasn't totally trying to screw me over. "So far, these are all things I could do on my own, perhaps had already considered."

"But you're going to get something for this. Why should I give you anything else?"

"Because as I see it, you don't have a choice." He leaned slightly forward as his elbows rested on his desk. "You didn't think I was a nice man, did you? That I keep this many people in line by giving things away?"

Oh no, I'd never thought that. "What do you want?"

"You, here at my

convenience, for one year." I was eyeing up the distance to the door when he added, "For work purposes only, unless you wanted to sweeten the deal."

"I'm not much into handing out candy," I said, trying to forget the images of his dead wife still fresh and floating around my mind. "What type of work?" I didn't cross my fingers that it was what I'd hoped, because he would see that, but my toes were.

"I want you to vet my crew. I think one year would be sufficient."

It worked, Bookie. It worked.

I'd known Jacob was nervous about the Dark Walkers, and I couldn't fault him there. It was all working out. If we were going to use his boats and crew to get the cure out to as many people as possible, the crews would have to be vetted anyway. It was the only way to be sure the cure wouldn't be tampered with. Still, I didn't want to jump at the offer. If I gave in too eagerly, who knew what else he'd try and squeeze me for?

I let out the weariest sigh, like I hadn't slept in a week, before I said, "I'd have to go from boat to boat? When would I have time to do anything else?"

"I would bring as many crews to you as I could."

I leaned an elbow on my chair arm, pretending to ponder the workload for a few minutes or so, and as if I didn't seek out those monsters on my own. "I guess it'll work. Do you need to take a vote or something?"

Jacob started choking on his coffee. "A vote?"

"Aren't pirate ships typically democracies? I thought I read that somewhere."

"Then you read too much. Don't be spreading that garbage around on my ships. There will be no votes here."

"Not a problem. Just asking." I lifted up my hands, surrendering the point easily. If he wanted to be King of the Dirtbags, he was free to keep the title as far as I was concerned, as long as they did what I needed.

I really wanted another shot of whiskey before I ironed out the last little itty-bitty detail, but I refrained. A year was a long time. There was no way that it wouldn't come up, so I had to handle it. "You know they're searching for me, right?"

"Which 'they' are we discussing? The Dark Walkers, the country of Newco, or Dax? Please tell me there isn't anyone else," he said dryly.

"You've got one wrong. Dax won't be searching." He didn't know where to look, and even if he did, he wouldn't. I'd walked out on our deal after he'd helped me countless times. He wouldn't care what happened to me; not even for his revenge would he come looking for me.

"Oh, I think he will," Jacob said. He sipped his coffee and watched me over the porcelain rim.

I didn't care what he

thought. I just wanted the subject of Dax dropped, because every time I thought of him or heard his name, this uncomfortable feeling gripped me deep inside.

"It's beside the point. Is it going to be a problem for you to handle?"

"I wouldn't have taken you on this boat if it was." Jacob nodded toward the bag at my feet. "Is that all you have?"

I looked down at the canvas sack Fudge had given me. It had started out as a loan that she'd never taken back. Besides the clothes on my body, that was the entirety of what I owned. "Yes," I said, reaching down and grabbing the strap a little too tightly.

"I'll show you to a cabin." He stood and I followed, my chair making an awkward scraping sound as I stood.

He didn't look at his wood to see if I'd done any damage, but I had a feeling he wanted to. I followed him out of the cabin, but not before I reached back and grabbed a couple of pieces of toast and tossed them in my bag.

He walked down the narrow passageway and pushed open a door to an empty cabin that looked lived in.

"We had a recent departure."

It was small, but no smaller than the cells at the Cement Giant, and the wooden bulkheads were much more appealing than the grey cement. Other than a bunk and some built-in shelves and cabinets, there wasn't much to it. I didn't need much. It was perfect for me.

"This is all mine?" I asked when I didn't see another bunk.

"Yes."

I threw my bag down, hoping the recent departure hadn't happened while he'd still been in the bunk.

"Thanks."

He nodded and went to leave the room.

"Jacob," I said, stopping him before the door shut. "Why is it that you believe in the Dark Walkers when so many others don't?"

He paused by the door. "I might not be able to see them the way you can, but that doesn't mean I'm blind. When I see enough smoke, I know there's a fire somewhere."

"One last thing. I get to interrogate every Dark Walker I find before you kill them."

Jacob's eyes wrinkled at the corners and a single dimple appeared. "I think you and me are going to get along just fine."

I smiled even as my skin crawled. What the hell did that say about me?

Chapter Thirteen

I nearly cracked my head on the wood above me when I woke. I'd fallen asleep shortly after I'd gotten in the cabin and it was still sunny? I peeked out the small porthole next to the bunk.

The sun was just rising, which meant I must have slept the entire day. There was a lot of ocean and only a small strip of land in the distance, the really far distance. If I was going to be a pirate, even if for a short while, I needed to learn how to swim, and quick.

As I got my bearings, I heard the muffled sounds of men moving about above deck, and reality was setting in like a bad case of the flu. I felt a little off right now but had a strong feeling I'd be in worse shape later.

I'd done the right thing. After making the deal with

Jacob, I was certain of it. I was trying to save the human race. How could it be anything but the right choice? The noble choice? Bookie would've agreed. If I asked him, he'd tell me I had to do the right thing.

I flopped back on the bunk. "It was the right thing, wasn't it, Bookie?"

Not even imaginary Bookie answered this time.

Bookie was dead. The thought wouldn't stop running through my mind like a dog chasing its tail. If we'd never gone to the Rock, would he be alive? What about Fudge and Tiffy and Tank? Were they okay? I'd just left them to fend for themselves. Doubts washed over me so strong I felt nausea chasing in behind it.

And Dax. But he'd forced my hand. I'd had to do this. He would've fought me on going for the cure. I'd had to leave, and it had nothing to do with how unsettled he made me.

Or maybe reality wasn't making me ill. Maybe I was actually getting sick. This boat rocked like a son of a bitch the farther from shore it got.

I got out of the bunk, tied my hair back with a piece of leather, and stumbled out of the cabin, trying to get my sea legs. The waves had definitely kicked up since yesterday.

Nose in the air, the smell of food led me to a small galley where a hairy little man, not even as tall as I was, tossed a bunch of eggs in a pan.

He looked over at

the new presence in his territory. "You the one I gotta be nice to?" he asked.

Only one person who would've given that order. "Probably? I'd appreciate the civility, but I won't hold you to it."

He went back to stirring the eggs about the greasy-looking pan. I looked around the place but couldn't find a single piece of bacon to be had. Fudge's kitchen this was not, but my growling stomach was giving me a thumbs-up on the eggs.

"Unless there's some other girlie on board, I'm figuring you're it. And there best not be. One girl on board is enough bad luck."

"I'll make you a deal…"

I waited for him to fill in his name. Took him a while, but he finally said, "Marty."

"Marty, you give me a plate of those eggs and you can go back to pretending I'm not here either." I smiled as wide as I could. All I cared about was getting a plate of those damn eggs.

My pleasant reaction seemed to annoy him further, and he was handing me a plate as soon as the eggs started taking a firmer shape. "I'd stay to your cabin as much as possible. The crew ain't gonna like this none."

I would've taken the plate and jumped into the ocean if that was what it took. My stomach was growling louder than Dax's beast on a bad day.

Leaving the galley, I

125

walked past the door to my cabin. The sun was shining. No way I was going to sit in there all day with the crazy cook.

There were some grumbles from the pirates on deck, but no one bothered me. I made my way to some crates by the bow, kicked my feet up on another crate in front of me, and settled in to eat my breakfast.

"Hey! Girlie!"

I turned from where I'd gotten comfortable, assuming I was the *girlie* in question. One of the pirates that had picked me up at Hell's Corner was standing a good ten feet from me smoking a cigarette that I could only assume was borrowed.

"Yes?"

"Jacob wants to see you." His message delivered, he turned and left. I guessed he figured I could find my own way, which I could.

Still eating as I walked, I took my plate of eggs down to his cabin to find his door wide open.

"You summoned me?" I settled into the seat I'd occupied the first day, swinging a leg over the side. If I was going to be here for a while, I didn't see much reason to stand on ceremony or act like I had some deeply hidden social graces. We'd struck our deal.

"Make yourself at home," he grumbled as I reached over onto his desk and grabbed his unused napkin to wipe off an especially messy mouthful of eggs.

"Thanks," I said,   ignoring the obvious

sarcasm.

He stood and walked over to shut the door before speaking. "One of my other boats is going to be here soon. You'll board it with me, but if you see a Dark Walker, I want you to alert me to it privately." He returned to his seat and started cutting up a piece of sausage.

"'Hey, there's a Dark Walker over there' not work for you?" I asked, wondering where the sausage had come from, but I didn't ask. It wasn't that important. It wasn't like it was bacon.

"No one else can see them. I'll be taking your word. That might not sit well with some of my crew."

"What happened to last night and this isn't a democracy?" I said, ribbing him a bit.

It took me all of a split second to realize Jacob didn't care for jokes at his expense. Dax would've laughed, maybe not out loud, but I could always tell when he thought I was funny. Now there was a guy who could take a joke.

Damn. I had to stop comparing everyone to Dax. And I also had to try and watch what I said. Keep the peace to get the cure. That was going to have to be my mantra.

"Of course you'd want to keep your guys happy, too, so I completely understand."

He nodded, not buying my cleanup attempt.

Holding on to my

plate, I got up and started making my way out, since I sensed the meeting was over. The less time I was around him, the less words I could speak. "What time's this shindig?"

"The ship should come into range sometime early afternoon."

"Got it. I'll be ready." I took a swallow of eggs and tacked "boss" onto the sentence at the last second.

The loud sigh told me he wasn't buying the act. I'd have to practice up on my bullshitting a little more. Looked like I'd gotten a little rusty since getting out of the Cement Giant.

***

By noon that day, I'd discovered the majority of the boat, even the parts I shouldn't have, like the main sleeping quarters where the rest of the pirates stayed. If this was going to be home then it was important to know every nook and cranny.

As I wandered the ship, most of the guys ignored me. A couple made lewd comments about parts of my anatomy. A few threw out some nasty remarks about being a Plaguer. All in all, I thought it was a fairly successful meet-and-greet.

I made my way up on deck just as another ship was coming in range. When no one else seemed to be concerned, I figured this was the one we'd been waiting for.

It didn't take long for the boat to make its way over and for Jacob to appear on deck. Ropes were thrown over, fastening the boats together temporarily, and several of the crew crossed onto the other boat. Trunks were carried from the new ship back to ours.

Jacob climbed onto the other ship and I followed, climbing from one deck to the other, while avoiding looking down.

I immediately spotted one. Wasn't what I'd hoped for. How could I trust a crew that had Dark Walkers, the very monsters I feared might be spreading the disease, to deliver a cure? I watched Jacob, waiting for his attention to land on me, which didn't take long, and I gave the subtlest nod.

His features tensed and his mouth flattened out a little, and I wasn't sure how the messenger was going to fare for a minute. Land was still miles away. I couldn't swim, but damn if I wouldn't do the meanest doggy paddle around if I had to.

He walked over to my side. "Who?"

"Red beard with the bald head."

"Go back to the other boat."

"That wasn't the deal."

"You'll get your crack at him, but I don't want it to be known you fingered him."

I nodded, not sure I liked it but not willing to take the chance of pissing him off yet, since my options were limited—as in I had none.

***

It had been seven hours since the other ship had left and I watched Jacob go to shore with several of his pirates, including the redhead I'd fingered.

I was rethinking every decision I'd made. Seven hours was plenty of time for the Dark Walker to convince them I was lying. That perhaps I was the traitor. It was too many hours to sit and wonder what was happening, and it was more than enough time for me to wonder if Jacob was reneging on his part in the deal.

By time I was called, I was making sure I had both knives on me and my magic stoked up to full blast. I'd overheard that the pirate I was following was called Stinky. As I walked behind him, I understood.

We walked to the edge of the ship and I climbed into a dinghy with Stinky and his slightly less smelly companion. As they started rowing us to shore, the other asked, "Why's he bringing you out here?"

"How would I know?" I said. Stinky and his friend clearly didn't think much of women, because their grunts of acceptance and glances at each other said they accepted that as perfectly plausible.

Stinky was out of

the boat first, and I followed him onto the beach. The other pirate dragged the dinghy up onto the abandoned shoreline of the small island, which didn't look like it had any inhabitants.

"Jacob is that way." Stinky pointed to a break in the tree line, and I was grateful for the full moon. My hand moved closer to my knife as I walked in the given direction, having no idea what the situation was going to be. I knew I could handle my own, but I had my limits, and I didn't know how many men would be waiting for me.

I stepped into a clearing about twenty feet wide. Worries over Jacob believing the Dark Walker over me vanished. The redhead was on his knees in the center of the clearing with his hands tied behind his back, looking half dead.

Jacob stood not five feet from him and didn't seem to have a problem getting his hands dirty, by the sight of his knuckles. Maybe preferred it that way? Another pirate I'd seen on the ship stood a bit farther back, his knuckles looking clean.

"He's all yours," Jacob said.

"I was supposed to be able to interrogate him."

"You can. He's still alive."

The Dark Walker's eyes were rolling around in its head and blood oozed from every opening he had. "What am I going to get out of this thing?"

"Probably the same   thing I got, which was

131

nothing."

"Really? Nothing?"

"Nothing. But at least I know you weren't lying," he said, lifting a hand in his direction.

"How's that?"

"There's never been a human I couldn't crack. They usually talk by time I'm breaking the fifth finger. By time I get to pulling teeth…"

Jacob kept rattling off all his interrogation methods, but I had to tune him out so that I could keep my dinner down.

"Did you hear me?" he asked, and I realized he was done with the torture itinerary. "I'll leave my guys here to clean up the mess after you're done."

"You aren't going to stay?"

"If I couldn't get anything from him, nobody can."

I believed him as I watched him leave the clearing. I wondered myself if there was a point to this, but I had to try. I walked over to the monster. "You're in a lot of pain, aren't you?"

He didn't answer. I was relieved he didn't beg. I hated seeing anything in pain, and somehow that included Dark Walkers, to my great annoyance.

"I can help you." I used my best Pollyanna voice, but if he believed that, he'd believe that I could fly around this clearing, too. Wasn't a slew of other options. I couldn't *re-beat* him to near death. Jacob hadn't left much gas in the tank for me to work with. "I don't want to hurt you. I just want answers."

His one good eye—and by good I mean the one that was able to partially open—met mine. A garbled mess of sounds came out.

Even if he was willing to tell me what I wanted, how was I supposed to decipher it? Well, didn't this just make things a little more awkward?

"I'm sorry, but could you repeat that?"

He did, but I still couldn't understand it. Then he hacked up a mouthful of blood at the end of the sentence.

"One more time?" I asked once he seemed to get it all out.

I would've sworn the good eye got a little squintier.

"I think he's saying 'I'm not telling you anything,'" Stinky said from somewhere behind me and to the left. Hmmm. I let it roll around in my head for a second, and the sounds did seem to match up to Stinky's suggestion.

I turned, giving the Dark Walker my back. I knew you were never supposed to turn your back on your enemy, but between the pirates and the Dark Walker, it was a tossup these days which side should be forward. At least the Dark Walker couldn't stand. Hell, if he could take me out in his current condition, I probably deserved to die.

"How did you know what he was saying? What? You some kind of mind   reader?"

Stinky made the best derisive sigh I might've ever heard in my entire life. Like, totally nailed it. It was the perfect mixture of *I ain't got time for this* and *you're so very stupid*. I was going to have to practice that sucker later on myself.

"No. He's been saying it the whole time." If he'd added *dumbass* to the end of that sentence it would've been mockery brilliance. Between the torture and mocking, I was starting to think there was a lot to be learned from these pirates.

I turned back to the Dark Walker, or maybe he should be more accurately named the Dead Walker right now. I grabbed my knife and ran a clean cut across its neck, this time in mercy. I could handle death, but I was finding torture to be a little hard to stomach.

The thing's head wobbled and then dropped forward. Jacob had been right. So had Stinky. This was useless. But eventually I'd find one that would crack. "Okay, boys, do whatever it is you do with your dead."

I walked out of the clearing thinking how nice it was to not be the one having to bury them for a change.

Chapter Fourteen

I was sitting on the sand by the two boats left, admiring the ocean and the nice breeze it was giving off, when Stinky and his cohorts walked out of the clearing. Something had changed in the last ten minutes it had taken them to bury the body. The way they were looking at me, I didn't think I was going to be asked out for a tea date.

I wouldn't exactly say I saw sex in their eyes, like I'd recently come to recognize, but there was a hint of that and something else I was very familiar with. Violence. I didn't need them to give me the specifics to get the general sense of bad shit heading my way.

I stood and wiped the sand off my butt, my hands stopping close to my knives and staying there.

"Jacob is expecting a report from me when I get back, so let's hurry it up," I said as I took a step toward the boat I'd arrived in.

"She thinks she can order us about," one of them said, and the other three laughed. It wasn't even a good joke. Yep, this was about to get ugly.

They edged in closer, two of them moving around me to block in my sides as one approached head-on with a man at his back.

I felt myself tense and wondered if they noticed it. It wasn't because of what they would do to me. They wouldn't hurt me. I'd killed groups of Dark Walkers, so four men posed no threat. But I might kill them—and I couldn't, no matter how much they provoked me, because I needed Jacob, and killing his pirates after a couple of days on the job might look bad.

"Guys, this is a very bad idea."

What a shock. They continued anyway. A strange hand was groping my butt, as one of the men on the side got impatient.

"I know I might not look like much, but you don't know what you're dealing with, so I'd remove that hand."

I'd been concerned things might come to this, and not because I was that in tune. They'd basically said as much every time Jacob wasn't around. I just thought it had been a bluff, them fluffing up their pirate colors and acting the part.

"If you don't take your hand off me I might have to turn you into a walking cliché, hook and all."

There was a grunt, or maybe that was a laugh. "What's a little thing like you going to do?"

I could see from the smiles that no one thought I could back up my words. Still, I gave them one more chance.

"You've got about three seconds before I remove the hand." And hopefully he'd take me up on that extended timeframe, because I had a silly feeling that Jacob wouldn't appreciate me carving his pirates into pieces.

Instead of removing it, he actually squeezed. I'd let this go way too far. I should've put them in their place after the first insinuation. Now I might have to chop off pieces. Maybe not the whole hand, though. That seemed like a strong warning. Perhaps just the pinky? How angry could Jacob be over a pinky? After all, it was a nearly worthless little digit. Then again, maybe taking a pinky might be more upsetting than I thought.

My fingers grazed the knife at my hip and I set my mental aim then spun into action. The offending hand was quickly removed, although still attached to the offender, who was now at my feet. I had my right foot on his chest. I held one hand out and dug my knife partially into the flesh above his wrist.

I made sure it was the perfect spot, a place that wouldn't do irreparable damage. I wasn't looking to be trapped on a boat with someone wielding a hook. The grudge might happen anyway just from the embarrassment of being bested by a small female, but I'd limit the damage.

I watched as everyone else took a step backward. And then another one.

"Next time your hand touches me, you lose it. Is that clear enough?"

I waited until he nodded before I took my foot off his chest and released his arm.

"Great. Now my knife is all dirty." I found the nearest tree and scraped the blood off the best I could.

"How'd you do that to Murrell?" Stinky asked.

I tucked my knife back into the hook I used to hold it at my hip while they all looked on. "I never miss my mark." I took a step toward the boat. "I'm ready to leave now."

There were looks shooting this way and that between them before Murrell, who was still bleeding, finally said, "You ain't gonna say nothing to Jacob about this, are yuh?"

"Not if you get me back quickly. If I don't get a good sleep, I get real cranky, so I'd double-time it with the rowing."

Finally I saw a little urgency in their steps.

I was a few feet from the boat when I heard a familiar chiming. A quick glance around told me I was the only one hearing it.

I shook my head and

continued over to the boat that would take us back to the ship, but the chimes got louder.

"I'm not talking to you. You tried to kill me. Go talk to someone else," I said, not caring what my companions thought. They'd probably been ready to tell Jacob I'd fallen overboard and been eaten by a shark. Did I really care if they thought I was nuts?

The pirates looked at me like I was the craziest bitch around but didn't ask who I was speaking to. Good. I leaned back on the seat I occupied alone.

It wasn't very surprising how the night had gone down. Humans had pecking orders, same as a pack of wolves did. I'd just shown them where I fit in.

I was an alpha and they better not forget it. There was only one person alive who I considered my equal, and he wasn't here at the moment. *Good luck, boys. There's a new bitch in town.*

Chapter Fifteen

Three weeks later

Jacob's door looked solid, but I knew a good kick would bust it right open. Instead I rapped my knuckles against the surface, ignoring the more violent inclinations. I'd been on this boat for three weeks. I hadn't made contact with the Skinners but I'd vetted six of Jacob's ships already, with word the schedule was going to pick up. Which also had me wondering how many ships there were.

This was a much larger organization than I'd realized. It was another thing that kept me in line, and not because I personally cared about my own welfare. The larger the network, the more use I could put it to.

Considering the ships I'd already vetted and the time I'd agreed to stay on, this bastard had a fleet of at least a hundred. Once I got my hands on that cure, that would be a hundred ships distributing it. So no matter what kind of sicko this guy was, we were going to be best friends for the foreseeable future.

"Come in," Jacob said without asking who it was. I guessed it was nice when you were surrounded by people who all licked your boots, and his crew did—and they didn't even see the sick shit in his head like I had. Would love to know what other little good deeds he did on a daily basis to encourage the ass-kissing I saw from a crew like this.

I walked in, doing a mental wipe of all the concerns I had so that I could plaster a mask of calm tranquility on. I took the seat on the other side of his desk without waiting for an invitation and leaned forward, eyeing up his breakfast plate that made the eggs I'd just eaten look like they'd come from an anorexic chicken. My sea of tranquility might have caught a couple of waves if I'd seen bacon, too. Either way, I settled the score by leaning forward and plucking a biscuit from where it rested on the corner of his dish.

He didn't say anything about it. That was the beauty of leverage at work. I had to play nice, but so did he.

"Are you helping me or not?" I asked.

"You really aren't very good at diplomacy. I can see how you and Dax got   along."

141

"Is that a yes or a no?" I snapped. I didn't need his opinion on my compatibility with someone I was trying to not think about every damn minute of the day.

"I told you I would, and I am. I honor my word."

"I think you're jerking my chain," I said, having recently learned that new saying from one of the books I'd lifted from Jacob's booty. This man got everything: clothing, booze, you name it.

His chin tilted up. "What does *jerking my chain* mean?"

I thought back to the passage in the book I'd read it from. There hadn't actually been a chain anywhere in the scene, but the meaning had been fairly clear. "Screwing with me."

He pursed his lips and tapped a single finger to them. "But what's that got to do with a chain?"

"It's too long to explain." I hoped he left it at that before I had to get creative. I'd had no idea either when I read it.

"I could say the same for you, pulling the chain link. You've only found one Dark Walker in my crew so far."

"First off, it's 'jerking my chain.' If you're going to steal my sayings, please get them right."

Jacob shrugged in a hesitant agreement. I thought back to when I'd first shown up and hoped I wasn't going to end up thrown overboard with my neck slit. Even two weeks ago, I would've gotten a squinty look. Now he nodded, no   pretense, no show.

142

Were we best buds? Not in this lifetime. Someone who could kill a person they were mated with would never make it to my inner circle. But we weren't two armadillos going at it either. And when we were alone like this, we'd come to a sort of truce. I didn't shit all over him in front of his crew, and he cut me more slack than anyone else, knowing I hadn't signed up to be one of his pirates and he needed me almost as much as I needed him.

There had even been that night a week ago when he'd tried to take our relationship a little further. He'd hit the whiskey pretty hard from the smell of it. I'd declined as politely as you could with someone like him. Luckily, he hadn't seemed to care much. I thought I'd been more of a convenience than a desire, since there was nothing but men on board, and that didn't seem to be where his inclinations lay.

"Second, your crew has been clean. If I were the dishonest type, I would've thrown you a name just for your sake. There's a couple names I'd love to give you right now. Is that what you'd prefer?" I'd been sorely tempted after a few of the encounters but hadn't pulled the trigger. No matter what happened from here on out, no matter how desperate I might become, I had a code. Most people don't plan on doing bad things. They just do. There's always a rationalization, if you look hard enough, why it was for the best or it wasn't their fault.

Sometimes, my code

was the only thing that kept me going when the ache I felt turned to an almost palpable pain. But I was trying to do the right thing, and I'd had to leave the Rock, or more specifically, I'd cut ties with people by doing so. People who I tried not to name or think about, no matter how often that damn man showed up in my head.

That's what's good about a code. You can't rationalize black and white. If I let go of my code, it might be a slippery slope until I found myself standing over someone I had loved, bloody knife in hand. I looked at Jacob and wondered if he'd had a code at some point. What had gone so wrong, and did I even want to know?

"We getting this done or not?" I propped my chin on my hand, trying for a cross between bored and losing my patience. It was a tricky combo. Too much bored and they thought you didn't care. Too much impatience and you looked like you cared too much.

He put down his utensils and picked up a sheet of paper that was folded and sealed with wax. The seal crumbled and he glanced over the sheet before putting it aside. "They agreed to meet you at a trader hole in two days a bit west of here," he said before he took another bite of eggs.

"When did you get this?" I picked up the dismissed paper and read over the short message that only stated a time and place. There wasn't any need to work on feigned annoyance   anymore.

144

He finished chewing his eggs before he spoke. It was sort of amazing how refined Jacob could seem on the outside when I knew what dwelled beneath. That's the thing about monsters. You don't always know who they are. I did, but there were a lot of suckers out there with no idea. Until I'd had that lapse when I couldn't glimpse into a person's memories, I'd never known how scary it could be, and I never wanted to be in the dark again.

"I just got the message this morning. Sorry if I wanted to eat my breakfast before running to do your bidding."

I grabbed a link of sausage off his plate, just for making me wait like that, and relaxed back in the chair. They'd agreed to meet. Would they bring some of the cure? What if they didn't?

"Do you ever stop eating?"

"I've got a lot of meals to make up for," I said, and stood. I needed to think in silence. I grabbed his last biscuit before heading toward the door. "It took a little long, but good work, by the way."

"Of course, I'm only here to serve you," he said as I shut the door, laughing to myself.

Chapter Sixteen

I swallowed the last bite of biscuit but knew this was going to be a two-meal morning. There was no way to think clearly on one plateful, so I detoured to the galley, wondering what was cooking for lunch already. I'd never missed Fudge's food as much as I did now after three weeks of this crap.

I poked my head over Marty's shoulder as he stirred the contents of the large pot, and saw carrots and potatoes breaking the surface. He started edging his body slowly in between me and the stew like a mother protecting her baby from a predator as I tried to lean in closer to get a better whiff. Marty's stew was hit or miss, and more often the latter.

"Smells good." Had to hedge my bets because bad

stew was still better than no stew.

He nodded, knowing my game by now. "They'll be no stew until noon."

"Are you still pissed off I took that hand off you last night?" I'd wiped Marty out of a week's pay at poker night, which was technically five nights a week, and I didn't feel a lick bad about it. I knew the only reason the guys had invited me to the games in the first place was they thought I'd be easy pickings. Turned out I was a natural card player.

"That was a lucky draw," he said.

"You are so right," I agreed. Let them all keep thinking it, too, as I kept building up my emergency stash.

Deciding on another tactic to get Marty to hand over some stew, I grabbed a seat on the bench in the corner.

"What do you think you're doing?"

I never sat in the galley, even when I was eating. It was way too cramped for my tastes, and the swinging pots hanging from the ceiling freaked me out even though I was a good two feet shy of hitting them. "What? A girl can't sit and relax?"

"You're not getting any until lunch bell."

"Sure, Marty, whatever you say." I kicked my feet up on the bench across from me and let it rip.

"The girl from Malarky saw a little sharky and giggled all the way home," I belted out. It didn't matter that my singing voice

would make mirrors crack. Marty hated that song no matter who sang it.

"Don't you keep—"

"She came back the next day, after a roll in the hay—"

"Stop! You win." I watched as he grabbed a bowl and filled it generously.

I stood, wondering why I'd ever thought pirates were so tough. "Thank you," I said, smiling as I took my bowl and grabbed a spoon.

A thump emanating from outside the boat rattled the stuff on the shelves above the stew pot, and I shot a glance over to see Marty's reaction.

"Who the hell you got coming on board this ship today?" I asked.

He shrugged. I knew a couple more crew members were showing up. Jacob had given me a schedule, but whoever had just boarded sounded like a giant.

I choked back the stew in three bites and headed above board. It was a lot easier to check out the newcomers before they scurried off about their day and I had to track them down, especially in the pit of the boat, where you never knew what you'd see.

***

The bright sunlight hit me and the sky was the brightest blue I'd seen in weeks, above water that was startlingly clear. The pirates called this place Panther Bay. No, wait—Panama Bay. Yesterday we'd sailed through the tiniest little river that they'd said had been dug out in the Glory Years, but now we were back on open water.

The breeze was fresh on my skin and I'd come to appreciate the smell of salt air. It was one of those days that had to turn out well or it would be wasting its perfection.

I leaned my head back, letting the sun beat down on my face as the wind lifted my hair off my shoulders. Being free like this would never get old, ever. Even living on the ship wasn't as horrible as I'd feared. I could get used to this life. Wide-open space as far as a body could swim, if a body *could* swim.

Not that it was all perfect. There were gaps, or maybe, more accurately, gaping wound holes. I tried to ignore the aches, like the one when I thought of Bookie and another that I tried not to think of at all.

It would go away. I was sure of it. Time was all. Everything faded with time; even the most stubborn of things faded out given enough distance and time. I'd just expected some more fading to happen by now.

"Bookie, I did the right thing. Didn't I?"

Imaginary Bookie didn't respond. He was fickle that way, but I still talked to him. Couldn't seem to stop myself even though I knew he wasn't there. No one was. Even though I was surrounded by pirates, I was on my own.

I'd been on my own in a sense my whole life. When I walked away from the Rock, I'd essentially cut ties with Dax. I'd known exactly what I was doing, even in the emotional wreckage of Bookie.

It was times like these I couldn't stop myself from thinking that maybe I should've at least left Dax a note. Left him something. But everything I tried to write seemed inadequate, and I'd balled it up and tossed it.

Logic told me it had been the right move. I couldn't do what I needed to do with him around. I had to be free to make the moves I deemed necessary, and he'd said himself he didn't think that looking for the cure was the right thing to do. I had to leave.

When I left the Rock, I'd thought the gaping hole inside of me was mostly Bookie. I hadn't realized what a large chunk had been Dax.

It was strange that even now, as I thought of him, I could feel that strange, familiar buzz I used to get being close to him, like my body was trying to mimic him being there or something.

"Glad to see you've been safe all this time."

Shit. Now I even thought I could hear him. What was my problem? I was alone on a pirate ship in the middle of Panther—Panama Bay. I needed to stay tough. I needed to obliterate all memories of him.

A hand gripped my arm, spinning me around until I was face to face with the man himself. Oh no, this was definitely not my imagination. Not the dark hair I wanted to touch or the eyes that felt like they were scorching me. His face looked like he wasn't shaving regularly, and a dark lock of hair fell almost in his eyes. It did nothing to detract from his presence, even added to it somehow.

"Dax." He looked just as perfect as I remembered. I went to reach for him and wrapped my arms around myself before I grabbed him like I was drowning in the ocean and he was the only thing that could keep me afloat.

I should've been nervous. Maybe even scared. I'd walked out on our deal. But I wasn't because standing there with him, the sky looked even bluer than it had, the air fresher, the breeze on my skin crisper. It was as if part of me had just woken up from a three-week coma.

Even the anger I could feel spreading out from him didn't dampen the rush he gave me. I'd told myself over and over I wasn't sad he was gone, but how did I convince myself I wasn't ecstatic to see him when the feeling of elation was near bursting from me and it didn't matter how angry he was?

Angry might've been an understatement. He wasn't screaming or doing anything really, but even the guys on the deck were giving us a wide berth.

This was bad, but I'd made the right choice. I was trying to save humanity, for fuck's sake. If his revenge had to be put on the back burner so the world could live, he'd have to get over it.

His eyes ran my length, and I suddenly wanted to fuss with my hair that had seemed to grow even wilder since I'd lived on the boat, the ocean breeze blowing it dry every day.

"Strange finding you alive like this when I've been searching for your dead body."

"Why would you think I was dead?" I asked while I took a step back. This might be a little worse than I'd expected.

He grabbed my arm, stopping my retreat just as common sense started to kick in and I realized this was actually *way worse* than I'd thought.

Still, this crazy part of me didn't care why he was grabbing me, and was thrilled that he was touching me, because that was all I wanted to do to him. I was so happy to see him it was hard to hide it, and I was wondering if I'd lost my mind at sea. Dax being here was a bad thing, and I needed to stop this stupid happiness that was all rainbows and unicorns.

"Because Charlie, your horse, came back to the Rock with a bloody saddle?"

Oh shit. Bookie's body must have bled on him a bit. Hadn't thought that one through. Or maybe it had been my blood. Burying him was a blur, but I remembered noticing cuts on my hands afterward from digging rocks out of the soil.

"What a crazy mistake," I said, grasping for some reason. "So, you thought I…" Maybe I was better off not beating this particular dead horse.

"Along with reneging on our deal, yeah, I thought you were dead," he said, and I was starting to have a hard time reading him. As if he were pulling back all his emotions now.

Mine, on the other hand, wouldn't stop bubbling up. I'd walked away, hadn't even left him a note, and he'd looked for me anyway because he'd thought I was in trouble?

"And you still tried to find me?" I took a step forward of my own volition, emotions boiling up on overload and so fast that I couldn't even fathom most of them anymore. I knew logically who this man was, that most would've been leaping into the ocean at this point. But not me. I didn't put up the smallest fight to leave his side, because the hole I'd been living with was all of a sudden full to bursting.

"You walked out on our deal. No one screws me over." His glacier wall was firmly in place now. But instead of being protected by it, I was getting chilled to the bones this time, and all the heat I'd felt was wiped out.

I nodded. It was no less than what I'd expected of him. I'd left out my destination in Fudge's note for a reason. But for a few minutes there, I thought he'd crossed half the world because he'd been worried about me.

I bit my lip, looking out across the sea while I fought down a strange sadness over being wrong.

As the weeks had passed being away from him, in my weaker moments, I'd had daydreams of what it might like to see him again. It was always after I'd found the cure to the Bloody Death and everyone knew my name and no one cared that I was a Plaguer.

He'd see me, see what I'd become, and he'd be proud. He'd understand why I left. I'd meet him standing tall, not this ball of nerves that I was right now that didn't know which direction to turn.

"We're leaving." He pushed me in the direction of the bow, where he probably had a dinghy waiting, but I didn't budge any farther than he'd moved me. If he was this mad now, the rest of this reunion was not going to go well.

"I won't. I came here for a reason. And even if I wanted to, I made a deal with Jacob," I said just as the man himself appeared on deck.

Dax stepped closer, trying to use his height and size advantage against me. "You made a deal with me and you're honoring it," Dax said.

I must have seemed like the ballsiest girl ever to the guys on deck because I didn't even step back, relishing in the proximity, the smell of him, which was this unique blend of forest and clean air and made me think of being surrounded by   nature.

"Dax," Jacob said, pulling me from my Dax stupor. It was a good thing, too. I needed to get a grip. Nothing had changed. The world still needed saving.

"Jacob," Dax replied.

It was like shards of ice pinging back and forth between the two men. This was nothing like the last time I'd seen them together. I didn't know whether to step back so they had room to kill each other and I wouldn't catch any blood splatter—because bloodstains were the worst—or step closer, maybe even in between the two, and possibly avert the coming fight.

I needed this particular Pirate King alive and kicking, especially now that I had an impending meeting with the Skinners. I didn't know where this particular trader hole was or how I was going to get to it without a massive boat to sail me there.

"I think we should talk in private," Jacob said.

"Lead the way," Dax replied. My gaze instantly shot back to Jacob, and I wondered if he knew that talking in private just gave Dax cover if he had to turn into a beast and rip him apart.

When Jacob nodded and headed below, I had a strong suspicion he didn't. There wasn't a single chance to warn him off or let him know that Dax could sprout a nasty set of claws, and his fangs weren't too small either. Who was I kidding? I wouldn't have told him anyway.

The three of us made

our way below deck and stepped inside the privacy of Jacob's cabin like three fighters about to do battle. As long as one of the opponents, who might be me, didn't get close enough to smell another opponent, who might be Dax, didn't lose her train of thought, I might be able to hold my own.

It was best if I started. I was the one who'd left him high and dry. I'd just explain the situation and he'd come to see I was right. "Dax, as much—"

I was immediately cut off by Jacob, who said, "She stays. She agreed to give me one year. She gave me her word." He slammed a hand down on his desk.

I nodded. "I did—"

"You mean this agreement or last time you met her and tried to strike a deal? Come on now, Jacob. Did you really think I'd let that fly? You knew she was mine."

"She gave me her word," Jacob said, both hands now on his desk.

"You made an agreement with someone who wasn't in a place to agree to anything. It's null and void. Obviously her word isn't worth much, and you should vet your partners better. Either way, not my problem. She goes with me." Dax shot me one of the nastier stares in his arsenal, one that had usually been reserved for other people.

Well, that stung. Now I was being cut off and insulted. Yes, he might have a point. But that look? The one he gave to the dirtbag who'd gotten too close to his bike outside a hole one day? That was the look he thought I deserved?

Jacob edged forward toward Dax and me, like he might be crazy enough to step in between us. "I won't let you take her. I wouldn't have let you on this boat if I'd known you were going to be unreasonable."

Jacob let him on? As in knew he was coming? What the hell was he smoking?

Dax stepped closer to me, making it impossible for Jacob to get in between us unless he wanted to bowl him over. Jacob might not have known, but there was no way he was bowling over Dax.

"Try and stop me. We both know why you haven't come to port in so long and why you 'let me board,' as you put it."

Hmmm, I had noticed we didn't go to shore much, but I'd thought it was just their routine to stay out of port. I guess it wasn't. Did I have more leverage than I'd realized in this situation? How badly did Jacob want to keep me?

"And that was a nasty trick, by the way. I needed that oil," Jacob said.

"I wouldn't have burned it all if you hadn't knowingly taken what's mine."

Wait a second. I'd let all the other territory stuff go, but this was getting out of hand. "Excuse me, I'm not—"

"Dax, we've known each other for a long time. It would be a shame for

157

our relationship to go badly now," Jacob said, puffing up a bit, like he was trying to stretch another inch out of his already large frame.

Dax still remained calm. Like, scary calm, though. "I don't give a fuck."

Yeah, I could've told Jacob how that extra inch would serve him before he'd gone through the effort.

As interesting as it was to see how this was going to play out as merely a spectator, I did have a stake in this, being the one they were fighting over. I cleared my throat this time before trying to speak, just to give them warning. "I—"

"I need her. She's already found a Dark Walker on one of my ships," Jacob said.

What? Was I invisible and mute to them? I took a step to leave the cabin. Maybe I should just leave the two of them and make my own way. Let them figure out I was gone after they were done fighting over me like I wasn't even there. Would serve them right.

I stepped around Dax's back and he moved with me, stepping in front of the door as I moved in that direction.

"Oh, so you do realize I'm in the room while you talk about me."

"I'm fully aware of where you are and when you run out on me."

There was that look again, the one that punctured something within me even if the wound wasn't visible. Between the words and the look, I was starting to feel like I was shriveling up inside.

He had no right to look at me like that. I'd temporarily stolen his revenge. That was it. And knowing him, he'd find another way to get it anyway. I hadn't betrayed him, not really.

He turned his attention back to Jacob, and I was relieved. Still, I didn't try and leave while he was in front of the door. Figured maybe I'd just hang back out of the way while they fought this out.

"Make it worth my while and we'll stay on—for a bit, anyway," Dax told Jacob.

Wait, now he was willing to stay on? Dax didn't compromise. Why was he willing to give in at all?

"I'm helping her find the cure. What else do you want?"

"That's for her. What's in it for me?"

"Then what do you want?"

"Information, and with your ships and network, I'll get it that much quicker."

"Deal."

"And I also want free crossings from now on. You pay for your oil and gas like everyone else."

"Fine, but she finishes vetting all my crew before you leave."

"As long as it's in a timely fashion." Dax grabbed the bag he'd dropped on the floor by the door and waited there. "Come on. Show   me where you sleep."

159

My world just spun on its axis, righted itself, and then went off orbit altogether. I was still getting the cure I wanted, but Dax was staying...and in my room? He was looking at me like I was lower than the mud on the bottom of his boots, and I still couldn't get over the urge to wrap my arms around him. No, this cabin sharing was not a good idea.

"You're going to stay in my cabin?" I said, like I was hard of hearing and couldn't possibly have heard correctly.

"Yes. That's what I said." Bag in hand, he walked out the door, expecting me to follow him.

I didn't follow. I turned to Jacob instead. "Don't you have a cabin for him?" My hands flailed in the general vicinity of where Dax had just exited. I couldn't stay with him, not in the same room. Hell no. I was having enough trouble standing next to him. And not for a second did I think he was going to go along with my plans. I wanted to save the world. He wanted revenge, possibly against me now too. They were incompatible goals at the moment.

Jacob squinted. "How big do you think this ship is?" He looked over toward the door and then back to me before leaning down and whispering, "I didn't want him here. He's here because of you. Your problem, not mine. If he hadn't started causing me issues because of *you*, he wouldn't be here at all."

He walked back to

160

his desk and sat down, looking over maps, dismissing me as clearly as if he'd screamed *get the fuck out.*

I watched him for a few seconds while he ignored me before I gave up.

Chapter Seventeen

Dax was waiting in the hall when I walked out of Jacob's cabin, looking both satisfied and pissed at the same time. It was the most perfect silent expression of *you started this fight but did you really think you'd win against me?* I'd ever seen.

It was a mouthful of a look, but I recognized it. I'd used it myself in the past, back when I'd been someone who believed in happily ever afters and was a connoisseur of a great expression. But even then, I'd never been able to nail that one as good as he did.

Most of the emotions I felt these days I preferred not to display. Like the mixed one I was having now, something close to elation that he was back and utter terror of his closeness at the same time. I'd moved on. It had been painful, was still painful, or had been until he'd shown up, but I would've gotten over it if I had enough time. I was sure of it. That feeling of having a gaping hole had been an adjustment period. Now he was back and I didn't know whether I should hug him or try and push him overboard.

He was pissed. I'd left him without so much as a note, and that was going to buy me some time. He'd keep me at arm's length even if I couldn't stay away from him. Because if he started kissing me the way he had back at the Rock, I might not be me soon. I'd be following him around like a puppy, weak and vulnerable, and I didn't have time for that. I had a world to save. No, he'd keep his distance, because he didn't like me very much right now, and that was a good thing even if it didn't feel like it.

"Are you going to walk me to *our* cabin or are we going to stand outside of Jacob's for a while longer?"

Yeah. There was no denying it. The situation between us was going to be ugly for the foreseeable future.

I started walking toward my cabin and paused outside the door. "Stay right where you are," I told him as I opened the door to my small space.

"What—"

"Do what I do," I said, stepping in front of him. "Step over this." I pointed to a spot on the floor where I had a trip wire that

163

would release a knife. It was set up so it would swing down in an average man's groin area. "Now duck here." I pointed to another fine filament that was nearly invisible in the daytime but impossible to see at night. "This one is lethal. I figured if they didn't take the hint with the first warning, they deserved what they got."

I waved my hand about the five-square-feet space left in front of the bunk. "This area's safe."

He tossed his bag down, not looking any happier than he had a few minutes ago, maybe worse.

His eyes were as hardened as I'd ever seen them. "Nice setup you've got here."

"It's a means to an end."

"How's that working out for you?"

"It's working."

He leaned a hip against the edge of the bunk as his eyes grazed over my form and stopped at my face. "Really? It's been three weeks. What have you accomplished so far?"

"You don't need to know what I've done. It's not something you deemed worthy enough to bother with," I said, getting my own jabs in as I got a little tired of being on the receiving end of all the blows. It wasn't like I didn't have cause.

He voice was dowsed in ice as he said, "I misjudged you as the loyal type. I usually read people better."

His words stabbed at me, deeper than I thought possible. "I am loyal."

I'd known he'd be mad at me for leaving. "I had to go and I had to do this. You're mad I left, but I had to or…" All I read from his expression was betrayal. "It doesn't matter. Think what you want."

"You're fulfilling your obligations to me."

He moved about the room, which consisted of a step and a turn in the limited space available, checking out the place, and I thought we were done speaking, but I was wrong.

"I saw Bookie's grave," he said, knowing me too well in spite of what his words claimed.

I faced the bunk, as my fingers twisted in the fabric of the rough cover, worn thin from too much use. My mind went back to happier days of soft coverlets and afternoons spent exploring the Wilds with Bookie.

I nodded. It was as much as I was capable of. If I spoke, or turned to look at him right now, saw my feelings of loss reflected, I might lose it altogether. I couldn't afford to do that.

Some of Dax's own words from when I first got to the Wilds repeated in my head. *Dal, you're in the Wilds now. If you're soft, you're dead.* He'd been right then and the words were even truer now. I had too much in front of me to fail. There wasn't any room for messy emotions.

"It was a good spot. He would've liked it," he said from somewhere slightly closer. But Dax didn't try and crowd me or hug me. He wasn't that type, even when he did like me, which definitely wasn't the case at the moment. He was the type that gave you your space until you didn't want it. And I'd told him by leaving that I wanted it and more.

Dax walked over to one of my trip wires, the subject of Bookie dropped, and looked it over for a moment. I thought he was admiring my work until he reached over and grabbed the knife off my hip and snapped one of my traps, setting the knife swinging into empty space.

"What are you doing?" I asked, placing myself in between him and my next trap. He ignored me and stepped around and followed the line to the gun.

"Stop!"

"You don't need this crap anymore and I need somewhere to sleep where I don't have to worry about rolling over and getting shot or stabbed."

"You can leave your stuff here but you can't sleep in here. They'll think I'm having sex with you."

"So what?" he said as he finished undoing my handiwork.

"So? The pirates don't get girls that often. They'll think I'm available."

He was already taking things out of his bag and placing them on the shelves. "They won't touch you."

"They wouldn't touch me before this either, but now I'll have to kill them to make sure."

"They aren't going to try." He let out a long sigh as he leaned on the bunk and looked out the porthole, sending me to the opposite side of the cabin.

"And why is that if they think I've gone all loosey-goosey?"

His eyes squinted halfway shut. "Loosey-goosey? What are you reading these days?"

"It means sleeping with a lot of people."

He had the nerve to scoff.

"What was that for?"

"No man that's been out of the womb for more than a day would believe you were loose."

"What's that supposed to mean?"

"That you're as green as spring grass and there's no missing it. And if you think that would stop them anyway, you're delusional too. Do you really think that these men care how much experience you've had?"

He stunned me into a pause as I thought of some of the comments the pirates had made about being my first. Then shrugged off the memories because it didn't matter anyway. "That might be true, but—"

"They won't touch you because you're not theirs, and I'll make sure every man on this boat knows it."

"They already know I'm not theirs. I told them." Damn, this man was stubborn. He didn't get it. I didn't want to have to start chopping off hands.

"Were there certain ones in particular you're talking about?" he asked, some of his heat seeming to sneak through the glacier.

"No. I was speaking in generalities." I crossed my arms over my chest and looked about my small cabin, which had been a perfectly good size before he arrived. "Fine. Let's say that's not a problem. I don't want you in here." My palms were already sweating and my heart was going all pitter-patter. I wouldn't be able to even get any sleep if he stayed in here.

"I don't care. You broke our deal." He took a step toward me.

This time, I took a step back. It had nothing to do with fear, or not fear of violence, anyway. He was back less than an hour and he was already making me out of sorts with myself. "I didn't break our deal. We never had anything clear-cut. I ID'd Dark Walkers and you helped me figure out my magic. How long was that supposed to go on? There was no time laid out. No fine print, no contract."

"That's bull. I had your word and you left before you were done doing what I needed."

"You didn't do that much for me. It's not like it took a long time to help me with the magic."

"And what about the fact that I broke you out of that hellhole, not once but twice? That wasn't that much?"

He was staring at me as if I was the lowest of the low, as if I weren't loyal. He turned his back on me, and I was relieved to not have to see that look in his eyes anymore. I watched as he rested an arm on the bulkhead as he stared out the

168

porthole to sea. And I couldn't drag my eyes from him.

"You got spooked and you ran for the hills," he said, not bothering to look at me while he spoke.

"That's not what happened."

"Not only did you break the deal, now you're a liar too." He let out a soft sigh that was heaped with regret. "I knew I shouldn't have gotten involved with a kid."

I had a feeling that last sentence wasn't meant for me, but I couldn't let it go.

"I'm not a kid."

"You ran like one."

"I wasn't running."

"Sure looked like it to me."

I forced myself to hold my position in the face of the disapproval he was dumping on to me. He was wrong. I'd done what I had to.

He didn't say anything else. Simply shook his head.

Here he was, standing less than ten feet away from me. How many times had I imagined having him here when I'd lie in the bunk at night? But this wasn't turning out like anything I'd imagined.

Now he was here and I didn't know what to do. So I did the only thing that might make me feel better. I went to the galley for food.

***

"You can't sleep

here," Marty said as I slumped in the galley's booth hours later after dinner had long passed.

"Why not?" I asked him as he stood looking down at where I sat.

"Couple reasons. One, I'm afraid to leave you so close to all the food."

"I couldn't possibly eat another thing." I was afraid if I did that I wouldn't be able to breathe, because there wasn't much room left for my lungs after I'd tried to eat away my worries. "What's the other reason?"

"That's my bed," he said, pointing to where I sat.

Shit. I got to my feet and headed back to my cabin, the place that was my sanctuary until he'd shown up and stolen it.

I opened the door to my cabin and found him spread out on the floor, a blanket draped across his hips and lots of skin showing above it. "You're really sleeping here?"

"We're not revisiting that subject again, are we?" he asked, as if I were the most redundant creature to walk the Earth.

We were about to, until I realized just now how futile it would be. Normally, I would've walked over to the shelves I was using for my few belongings and dug through it for the shift I used for sleeping, but I had nowhere to even change.

I looked about the cabin, trying to determine the easiest path around him and to my bunk, glad his jacket that I slept with was

170

tucked out of sight. He'd think it had something to do with him, and the only reason I slept with it was that it was warm and smelled like home. That was because Fudge had probably laundered it for him. Not because *he* smelled like home. But he might get some stupid idea that it was him. So now I wouldn't even be able to take it out, and how was I supposed to fall asleep?

I realized the only way to the bunk was stepping over his legs. He was ruining my sleep and my cabin.

"You're taking up too much room."

He ignored me. I climbed onto the bunk and got settled under the cover and realized I could smell the jacket from where it was tucked, or maybe it was that he'd brought more stuff from home. Instead of having trouble sleeping, I drifted off as soon as my eyes closed, not even answering his question first.

I shot up in the bunk and there was no hiding the night terrors now, even if I didn't scream, not with him in the same room. At least he had the decency not to say anything. I looked over, wondering if maybe by some long shot he was actually sleeping.

He was awake, but it didn't matter anyway. He'd say nothing and neither would I and we'd pretend it never happened.

"What are they about?"

Huh? I shook my

head. It was bad enough I had them. I didn't want to talk about them, too.

"Just random stuff. Nothing important." Nothing I could change, anyway, if that was a requirement of "important."

There were a couple of minutes of silence before he spoke. "You hold too much in."

My adrenaline was still pumping, so he'd picked the wrong time to start preaching about what I did wrong. "You want to talk about holding stuff back? Why aren't you trying to drag me back to ID your Dark Walkers and find your vengeance? I want to know why you are staying here when it's obvious you don't even want to be around me."

"You're right. I don't want to be around you. I don't like people who go back on their word. I've decided it's the easiest way forward without having to chain you to my side."

I stared at the ceiling above me while I bit the inside of my cheek to stop from defending myself. I was doing what I had to. He could see it however he chose. Didn't matter.

"Try and hold it in a little better if you aren't going to talk about it. I'd like to get some sleep," he said before I heard him moving around. My eyes shot to where he was lying on the floor. He'd turned on his side, giving me his back again.

I stared at his dark

head and the line of his shoulders for a moment before I rolled over and did the same.

Chapter Eighteen

The meeting with the Skinners was today. I didn't know what strings Jacob had pulled to get this meeting and hopefully the cure, and I wasn't asking. There was already one too many things I already knew about in Jacob's mind. I didn't want to know any more, not one iota of detail for the rest of my life.

I leaned up slightly and looked down at Dax lying on the floor. He looked like he was sleeping soundly for once, lying on his back, his face peaceful like I'd never seen it.

I eased out of the bunk, trying to avoid the part that always creaked as I slid down onto the floor silently. I tried to ease around him, which was next to impossible with how much space he was taking up. He cleared his throat and I knew he was awake before I took two steps.

"Why do you pretend to sleep?"

"I don't pretend anything. I was resting."

"You've never rested this much since I've known you."

"I've never been stuck with you on a boat." He opened his eyes only slightly, which made him look sexier than normal. That was a very bad thing in my book. "The meeting isn't for a few more hours. Why are you up so early?"

He knew about the meeting? I might as well climb back into bed and try and get another hour of sleep in, since I wasn't going to be able to dodge him now.

"Of course I know about the meeting."

"Did I just say that out loud?"

"Your face nearly screamed it. And before you ask, yes, of course I'm coming with you."

He'd read that question wrong. I'd already known he was going to come. This sucked. Only one thing to do now. Eat.

***

An hour later and the boat that was taking Dax and me to the meeting with the Skinners neared the shore. We were in a little-known area that was just shy of the border of the country called Cali. I hopped out, hoping by some miracle Dax

175

would stay behind but knowing better.

There, not far from the beach, was the trader hole Jacob had described, with its green metal roof and whitewashed walls, a few horses hitched outside it.

"Hang on a second," Dax said as I moved to go inside.

"Why?" I asked without slowing my pace.

"What is your problem? You walk out on me and you're the one with the attitude?"

"You wanted nothing to do with this. This is my mission. Why are you insisting on coming? You know I'm going back to the boat afterward."

He didn't get it. I was meant to live this life alone and I needed to go about my life like I had been for the past few weeks. I'd gone from the Cement Giant, and having my whole life dictated to me, to living with Dax. Who tried to dictate my whole life to me. Who'd also made me feel safe. And I shouldn't have gotten so comfortable, because look what happened. Bookie had died.

Now, here he was again, broad and strong and perfect in almost every way you would want a man to be. It would be so easy to hand over the reins and let him take control. And then one day, he'd disappear like my parents did or die like Bookie, and I'd be there, trying to stitch up the gaping hole he'd left, but maybe this time it would be too large to fix.

He took a step in

front of me. "Because you are going to hold up your end of the bargain. If that means I need to dog your every step to make sure you stay alive in order to do it, I'm going to. There's no damn way I'm letting you step in that place alone and die, screwing me over in the process."

"Jacob needs me just as much as you do, and he set the meeting up this way."

"Hate to break this to you, *darling*, but the only reason no one else is with you is because he knew I'd be here to make sure it didn't go south."

My hands found my hips as I took a step away from him and said, "That's bullshit."

"Ask him yourself when we get back," he said, pointing to the ship in the distance.

"You know I can handle myself."

"But against how many? You don't know what you're walking into." He straightened, his hands relaxed at his sides now, and his voice softened as he asked, "Do you really want this cure or was it an excuse to run?"

I tried to not flinch at the accusation...or to think too hard on it either. Nothing mattered right now but this meeting anyway. "You know I do."

For a minute, all I heard were the birds chirping away as we stared off. I was indeed stuck with him. There was no magic I was aware of that would get him back on that boat. "I'm taking the lead. Don't step on my toes."

He cleared his throat and then rolled his eyes, adding a slight shake to his head at the same time, just for that extra flavor. "Your memory is still intact, correct?"

I was narrowing my eyes at him. "What's your point?"

"My point is, we don't know who's meeting us here, and some of these people are going to take less than kindly to you after last time."

I didn't get a chance to speak before he was talking again, but in a quieter tone now. "The last meeting is not going to help you get any cooperation. Don't let your ego make your decisions."

The memory of standing outside the Skinners' fortress, countless beasts ready to fight beside me, or at least looking like that, had me forcing down a smile. I wished there were more cameras in the world, because I would've loved a shot of that. It had been scary as hell at the time, but damn, it was a cool-ass memory.

But it did give me a pause. Did he have a point? I'd trampled all over their egos like a herd of buffalos over eggshells. Their leader had been practically crying uncle by time I was done.

"Maybe it will help?" I said, hearing bullshit in my words.

"Or maybe because you don't have a herd behind you now it's going to hurt. The way that went down is going to leave a lasting impression."

Every sentence was

like another stroke of the paintbrush, making the picture uglier and uglier. "You were there, too."

"In beast form, so it doesn't matter."

I knew that, but it still grated on my nerves like sore skin rubbing against tree bark. "Fine. Let's go."

We walked into the small hole where Jacob had made arrangements. We got settled at a table and ordered some drinks so we blended. It wasn't worse than any of the other ones I'd been in, and the whiskey might have been a hair better. There weren't too many people in it either, which was good, since Skinners didn't have a large fan club, and for once I wanted my target alive. Although I wasn't sure if people in these parts would even know what a Skinner was.

Two men I didn't recognize strolled in fifteen minutes late. They didn't have the markings on their face, and from the leather pants and shirts, it looked like they were trying to blend. But the way they scanned the room, it was definitely them.

They stopped in front of our table and I didn't doubt my looks had tipped them off to who I was. My hand went to my knife. Dax didn't budge.

The scruffier of the two dropped a bag on the table. "All yours. Tell Jacob this was everything we had left."

"You're just going to hand it over?" As far as smooth comments went, it wasn't my best showing. I stared at the small bag on the table as if they would snatch it away at any   second.

179

"The shit isn't working anymore. Rather have free passage than hold on to this crap. All it's doing is making people sick."

"This was the cure, though?"

"Up until a month ago."

"Why didn't your leader come?"

He leaned toward me, hands on the table and his face uncomfortably close as he said, "Because he's dead, you idiot."

There was a blur of motion and a thump, and then the guy was bent over the table, his face pressed against the surface so firmly, his cheek looked a bit malformed. Dax's hand was on the back of his neck and our glasses were lying broken on the floor.

His companion didn't move so much as an inch to help him out, either. Chicken. I didn't like the Skinners to begin with, but I liked one that wouldn't lift a finger to help his friend even less.

"Watch yourself," Dax said, his hand still firmly gripping the guy's neck.

I clucked my tongue before I said, "I didn't need you to do that. I could've done it myself. I chose not to." I'd showed constraint and he'd beaten me to it. And why had he done that? Dax didn't even like me. Why would he care if some guy got in my face?

I heard some shuffling and saw the few other patrons were leaving now that they smelled trouble. "Great. And you caused a scene."

"Not the first time," Dax told me as he let go of the Skinner's neck but kept his attention focused on him. "If you want to walk out of this place, as opposed to crawling on two broken legs, you'll make me believe you're telling the truth. If this is a swap and bait, I will find you and I will kill you."

The guy straightened but didn't stand quite so tall anymore. "It's not fake," he said as the other nodded. "Jacob made a deal with us to get us somewhere new. He got us here on one of his ships and we got him what was left of the cure. People are dying all over the damn place back home."

"Go," Dax said.

They hesitated, as if trying to sense if it was a trap, before scrambling toward the door.

People are dying all over the place.

"Don't think about it. You can't. Not now," Dax said, confirming he was thinking about the exact same thing I was: everyone back at the Rock and the farm. If only it were that easy to push it from my mind. But that was why I was here and I couldn't stop now.

The bag sat on the table. I grabbed it and opened the small string that held it closed and peered in. It looked like a shriveled-up black clump. "What do you think?" I asked as Dax peeked in.

"They smelled like they were telling the truth."

I glanced over at him but didn't ask what a lie would've smelled like.

181

It wasn't important. I held a link to the cure in my hand, and even knowing the Skinner had said it didn't work, it was as close as I'd ever come to a cure.

"Since you're *in charge*, what's the plan now?"

I answered the question as if it weren't asked with a cutting edge. "I'm going to find a chemist."

"There are none in the Wilds." He held up two fingers to the barkeep.

"There must be."

"Not that I know of."

"That doesn't mean they don't exist."

"Did Jacob know of any?" he asked as the barkeep placed two whiskeys in front of us, not making any mention of the broken glass. "Bet he didn't."

The eyebrow arch and that certain tilt to his head was infuriating. "Why do people ask questions when they already know the answers?"

He shrugged. "Can't answer for everyone, but I'd say it's my preferred method of gloating."

"Seeing that you know everything, do you have a useful suggestion on where to get a chemist, since you said there aren't any in the Wilds?"

"Actually, I do."

"Are you going to share it?"

"I'm going to show you. I might know a guy. Come on," he said, threw back his whiskey, and got to his feet.

"Come where?"

"Back to the boat.   We're going to need a

182

lift."

***

Dax swung the door open to Jacob's cabin without bothering to knock. At least I gave the pretense I wouldn't barge in.

Jacob, seated behind his desk, rolled his eyes before placing his sandwich on his plate. "A man can't even eat a damn meal in peace anymore."

"We need you to swing the boat around and take us to Sling City," Dax ordered, as if he were the one commanding the ship.

"Where do you want to go?" Jacob asked.

"Where?" I asked.

"Sling City," Dax repeated.

Jacob was shaking his head. "It's completely out of my way. Even I don't like to go there."

"That's where this person is? The chemist-type person?" I asked.

"Yes," Dax said. "It's an island off the coast of Cali. It used to be a part of the country of Cali. Sling City soon started to become a problem. The country of Cali let them break off on their own because the manpower needed to police them outpaced the amount of money they were able to get out of the place. The entire island is nothing but holes dedicated to the trade of everything. You've got something to sell, that's where you'll find a buyer. Gold, oil, people—whatever you need or want."

Jacob looked at Dax. "What do you need there? I'm guessing it has something to do with what you picked up from the Skinners."

"Yes, and this can't wait until next week. The stuff we have is already past its prime. The longer we wait, the more it'll decompose and the tougher it's going to be."

Jacob shoved his plate away from him. "Last time I was in that port, I lost ten crates of whiskey."

Dax leaned forward on Jacob's desk. "Don't forget how well you stand to do from this. Ten crates of whiskey will be nothing compared to that windfall."

The mention of the wealth to come practically danced across Jacob's face. "I guess we're changing course. Still going to be a couple of days. I'm a sailor, not a magician."

Chapter Nineteen

"They're worse than they used to be," Dax said from his makeshift bed not far from my bunk.

It was pitch dark out and I hadn't even screamed. Dax said he slept, but I wasn't seeing much evidence of it.

"I don't know what you're talking about. I—"

"If you're going to wake me every night, I think I deserve to know why."

The bunk creaked as I tried to find a comfortable position that didn't exist. "Like you even sleep. You're always awake."

"I do sleep. I just don't need as much as you do. You telling me or not?"

"It's nothing new. I've always woken up at night. A

lot of people do."

"Not everybody thrashes around like they're fighting for their lives. You going to tell me or not?"

"Have I told you yet?" No wonder I was so tired lately. It was worse than even I'd known.

I turned on my side as if I were going to try and get back to sleep, even though my sleep was done for the night. I was still tired and there were hours before morning, but once I woke to one of those, I could never fall back to sleep.

"I'll make you a bet. You lose, you tell me what you dreamt of. I lose, I'll sleep somewhere else."

This had to be a trick. "Why do you want to know?"

"Curious, is all. Why are you so scared to tell me?"

"I'm not. What's the challenge?" I asked, realizing I'd just let him goad me into something else. Why was it that he was the one person in my life that could push and prod me so easily?

"We both ask the other a question they should know the answer to. Whoever gets it right wins. In case of a draw, we ask another question." There was a pause before he sweetened the pot: "I'll even ask first."

"Shoot."

"What is the color of the gas tank on my bike?"

I'd only ridden on that thing for countless hours. Was he trying to get out of here? Maybe he'd decided he didn't like sleeping in my cabin. "Grey."

"Wrong. It's blue."

How could I have gotten that wrong? Was I color-blind? Okay, well, he still had to answer one of mine. "What's the only way I won't eat eggs, unless of course I'm starving or something, because then I'd eat tree bark if I had to."

"Sunnyside up," he answered almost immediately.

"How could you possibly know that?" I asked, sitting up in the bunk, feeling like I'd gotten conned but not sure how.

"The only time I've seen them on your plate, you pushed them around and made a mess of them instead of eating with your natural vigor."

"And you noticed and remembered that?" It seemed unbelievable that he'd know that, but it wasn't like Fudge was sitting in the cabin beside him feeding him answers.

"Yes."

"I can't help it. I don't like how they run all over the place." Damn me for hating runny eggs. If I could've just learned to love them I wouldn't be screwed right now.

"Spill."

"It used to be the Dark Walkers. Now Bookie is there as well," I said, giving him the barebones of it without all the nitty-gritty details gumming up the works.

"You lost the bet," he reminded me.

A sigh escaped my

lips before I was aware I was doing it. The cabin was still dark but I wasn't sure what his eyes could see. I knew his hearing was always better than human, so I forced my muscles to remain relaxed as a last-ditch effort to downplay the whole affair. "They're attacking me, but unlike when it happens in real life, they're winning," I told him, not mentioning the fear that always clung to me afterward or the sound of chimes I'd hear. The suffocating fear that everything up until then had been for nothing because the Dark Walkers would drag me back to that life that was as far from living as a person could get without being dead and buried.

"And Bookie?" he asked.

And even with all the fear and pain, I could handle it if it weren't for the newest part. That was the worst. The new addition. "Right before they kill me, they make me watch Bookie die."

Every night since Bookie's death, I relived the loss in my dreams. Then I wondered why I couldn't get past it. How could I? It was fresh pain every day. As far as Bookie, time stood still.

He didn't ask anything else. I closed my eyes and wondered if I should get up or pretend I had fallen back to sleep.

"You aren't the reason he's dead."

"I know that," I snapped. I did, on some deep logical level; I knew the Bloody Death had killed him. Then the thoughts of bringing him with me to the Rock invaded. What if I'd left him at the farm? He might never have been exposed. That was pretty logical as well.

"He chose to come."

Dax didn't understand. Bookie would've never let me go alone after I asked. Even then, I'd known that and I told him anyway. He was the one person who would've always been there for me. He was the kind of loyal that didn't exist in this world. Now because he'd been loyal to me, he was dead.

"You told me to leave him alone. You wanted him to stay, so don't lie to me now. I already know what you believe."

"And I relented because I knew he was going to follow anyway."

I shook my head as I lay in the dark. "He wouldn't have known where I was."

"Bookie knew the Wilds as well as anyone around. He would've known right where to look."

"I could've told him I didn't want him around."

"And he would've come anyway because that's the person he was. You didn't create the Bloody Death. You aren't responsible for who it kills."

Dax was quick with answers, and I wanted to believe him but I didn't. I couldn't argue my guilt anymore either. If I did, I might lose the glue that was holding me together, and I'd been holding on for weeks now. If I did lose it, it would be of   epic proportions.

189

"Why are you even talking to me about this?" I asked. "It's not your problem. I'm lethal. For someone who says they know so much, why don't you know that?"

When he didn't speak for a while, I thought that was finally going to be the end of it.

"Is that what you think?" His voice was soft but clear across the dark cabin.

I tried to steady my breathing so I could answer without a tremble. "It's what I know."

I wrapped the blanket around my shoulders and jumped down off the bunk and over him as I headed out of the cabin, away from Dax and away from the questions.

***

The bustling port was in the distance as the crew dropped anchor. A few miles was as close as Jacob was willing to bring the ship. A pirate would have to row us the rest of the way in. We climbed the rope ladder down to the dinghy below, with the two pirates who were going to drop us off at shore and return tonight.

The closer we got to Sling City, the more amazing I realized the place was. I didn't think I'd seen so many people like this outside of Newco, with the hustle and bustle of stalls and people selling their wares and produce.

But it was different too. Maybe it was a child's memory, but there had been an oppressiveness in the Newco cities. People always looking over their shoulder, a subtle sense of a repression that lingered, as if words were never spoken before they were thought over. Come to think of it, even if I hadn't gotten the Bloody Death and never been branded a Plaguer, I still probably would've ended up in trouble.

There were buildings here too, just like in Newco, but again different. Everything in Newco had been state owned and painted in greys. Not so here. The stores and houses were painted in vibrant colors, plants hanging from rails, creating a kaleidoscope for the eyes.

I climbed from the boat before it stopped moving, thirsting to get into the crowd and feel the hustle of life around me.

Dax grabbed my arm. "Don't go too far."

I wrenched my arm away from him without saying a word. He knew I only had one destination in mind, and there was no purpose to his threat other than he was pissed off I'd left him once.

I turned back to him, loaded with a nasty comeback on my tongue. This wasn't like the other times. He seemed…different. Like some of the anger I'd seen in him had seeped out a bit. I mentally snapped the safety back in to place, the words left unspent.

"I'm not kidding around. This place is rougher than it looks," he said. "Are you hearing me?" he asked when I just stared at him.

"Yeah, I hear you." I was afraid to think it, but he seemed more like the Dax I used to know. The one who was there for me, no matter how much I pissed him off. As we stepped forward together, it almost felt like old times, walking into this town with him beside me. Knowing if the shit hit the fan, he'd be at my back.

"Yahoo!"

I turned to see where the shout came from, and a young man around my age, dodging in and out of the crowds of people with a burlap bag tucked under his arm, was racing toward us—or, more likely, away from whomever he'd just robbed. A middle-aged woman, who was seriously outpaced, was trying her best to catch up to him, but it was a lost cause.

Dax stepped to the left just as the kid was about to pass us. The would-be robber went flying through the air before making an awkward spill, face first in the mud, his stolen goods falling on the ground. Dax leaned down and grabbed the bag.

The kid pushed up and out of the muck and turned to find his attacker. Dax stood there, bag in hand, more than willing to supply a fight if that was what the kid wanted. It didn't take too long, approximately three seconds, before the kid nodded and said, "Guess you can't win 'em all, matey." He took off in the opposite direction, a smile still on his face.

"Here," Dax said to   the woman slowing

down.

"Thank you so much, mister." She started digging through her bag that had just been returned and offered him several lemons. Dax shook his head.

"But I'm looking for a man named Bitters," he said, and all of a sudden I realized where the good-guy act was going.

The woman's hand started fluttering in the sign of the cross, which I recognized from Fudge. She held her bag tight to her but then nodded and gave us vague directions.

"Would you have helped her if you didn't need directions?" I asked as we headed toward where she'd said.

"I helped her. Do the reasons matter?"

"Sometimes, I think the reasons matter more than the act itself."

"Tell that to the woman who went home empty-handed and see what she thinks about it."

Chapter Twenty

After wandering around the forest on the outskirts of Sling City and taking a couple of wrong turns, we finally found something that matched the description of the building the woman had given us. It was a small hut that looked no better than some of the holes I'd been in. In the Glory Years, chemists had machines, but this place had no signs of modern technology.

I remembered what some of the technology looked like from pictures of the Glory Years Bookie had shown me, and fuzzy recollections of seeing some in Newco. They often looked like strange trees that had no branches or leaves, but weird lines of power. The lines of power would have nowhere to run from. There weren't any great places of mechanical wonder that pumped out that energy here.

It wasn't a make or break, but I would've felt better if I saw something other than a roof made of grass and sod, and dried leaves hanging in the windows.

"We sure this is the place?" I whispered to Dax, as if someone or something else might hear me as I looked at the tiny shack that couldn't contain more than one room.

"We followed the directions. This is it."

"The guy that lives here is going to be a scientist with cutting-edge technology?" I asked, my words dripping in sarcasm. This couldn't be accurate. We had to have the wrong place.

When I didn't get a verbal response I looked at Dax, who was more fluent in face talk than words sometimes. His face-to-English translation said, *This is about what I expected.*

He took a few steps forward while I remained behind. I was going to trust the only cure I'd ever had to whoever lived here?

He stopped walking and turned back to me. "Do you have someone better lined up?"

He did have a point. I stepped forward and caught up to him.

The door swung open before we got within five feet, and we heard him before we saw him. "I know we've got guests! Don't you see me opening the door?"

The man that stepped over the threshold looked like he wasn't just pushing a hundred, but like he'd already rolled it right off the cliff and took the tumble down with it, wearing the same clothes he was in now.

"Are you Bitters?" Dax asked.

The man leaned forward, squinting and with an expression that could only rival Dax's face. "If you don't know that then why are you here?" he asked, and then shook his head, the few white hairs still left on his head swaying as he walked back inside.

He left the door wide open. I didn't look at Dax before I followed Bitters in. If I could handle a gang of Dark Walkers on my own, I didn't think this man, with one foot and a couple of toes in the grave, was going to be much of a threat.

From the look of his home and his clothing, I would've imagined him living in poverty, but when I walked inside the dimly lit room, there weren't many surfaces that didn't have either animal pelts or dried meats, or any of the other things that were considered so valuable in the Wilds.

The abundance of wealth stored here, alone with only this old man, made me nervous for him. How was he living in the worst place known and still alive with all this wealth?

"You live out here by yourself?"

"The people around here wouldn't touch me. Even if they did, girly, I'm nearly two hundred years old. This life doesn't owe me one more minute—no, one more second. If we're going to get right down to it, I'd return a couple if I had my wits about me." He laughed heartily at his own joke, and it was a robust sound that didn't appear to come from a man of his vintage age.

A large black crow that was perched on the back of a chair cawed, as if laughing with him. I noticed that was the only other living creature in the place, and the one he must have been speaking to when he opened the door.

I'd never seen anyone quite like him. He looked like he could have lived the two hundred years he was claiming, but how was that possible? No one lived to two hundred. A lot of people in the Wilds didn't live to fifty, unless you were like Dax.

Bitters was stoking a fire under his kettle and I looked at Dax, eyes squinted with a *this guy isn't all here* look.

He shook his head, disagreeing with my assumption.

Really? Two hundred? I mouthed. How was anyone supposed to believe that?

Yes.

"So, Bitters, you lived during the Glory Years, then?" I asked, still not buying his story.

"Yes, I did. You don't believe me? I don't blame you." He walked over to one of several chests lining the wall and started digging through it until he pulled out a framed picture.

He handed it to me,

and then tapped the glass where a young man in his twenties stood in front of a car. It was taken during the Glory Years, the heyday of civilization. The man's arm was wrapped around a pretty young woman. It was a nice picture and all, but didn't prove anything. Bitters could've found it in a ruin. I'd found plenty of pictures.

"I don't look much like that anymore, but still got the mole and the scar."

I looked down at the picture again and then at Bitters, with the same scar on his right cheek that ended at a dark mole shaped like a crescent moon.

Was this guy really from the Glory Years? Two hundred? What was he? I would've asked, but I had a feeling it might be a rude question, and we needed something from him right now.

"Glory Years, those were the days. Not that it was much different out here, mind you, but my wife insisted we live here. She was a witch. Said the cities and people drained the magic."

"What do you mean, drained the magic?" I asked.

"She used to carry on how there was only so much magic in the world. I didn't believe her until after the first wave of the Bloody Death started wiping people out. Then things got interesting." I waited until Bitters turned his back, going to retrieve the kettle from where it hung over the fire.

"Tea?" Bitters asked as he turned back around.

"No thanks," Dax said as I shook my head.

"She died some time ago, but I was too settled to bother moving at that point," Bitters said as he swirled his tea.

"So she passed? I'm sorry," I said, laying down the picture I still held in my hand and wondering if that was her.

"Don't be. She was a witch, and I don't just mean magic, either. Bossed me about like crazy. Marrying her was the worst mistake I ever made." He stopped his tirade to have a sip of tea before looking at the two of us as if we were suddenly unwanted guests. "What did you people want?"

"Are you a chemist?" I asked.

His robust laugh made a return. "Is that what they're calling me?" he asked, and I nodded slightly, unsure of the desired answer this fickle man wanted. I shot a glance over at Dax, who shrugged like he hadn't misled me.

"I'm a wizard! You think living this long happens to just anybody?" His crow cawed and flew over, landing on his shoulder. "What are you needing? You came here to get something. You all do. Everyone wants something."

"We want to know what this is," I said, holding out the bag we got from the Skinners. It wasn't much, and I hesitated to hand it over to some guy that said he was a wizard and whose emotions seemed to rock back and forth worse than the ship   in a storm.

He walked over and took the bag from me before I came to my senses.

Dax and I both waited and watched as he opened it up and gave it a sniff. "Doesn't lack for aroma."

I smiled and nodded.

"What is it?" Dax asked.

"That's what we want you to tell us," I added.

"I've got my ideas," he said, but seemed more interested in looking at my gloved hand than saying anything. "You're a Plaguer."

"What's it to you?" I asked, taking a step back.

He started reaching for me. "Let me see it."

"Why?" I asked, knowing he meant the brand. I wrapped my arms around my midsection, tucking the hand close to my body.

"What's your interest?" Dax asked, sounding more annoyed with the guy than I did as he stepped slightly in front of me. "She's not your concern. Tell us what we came to find out and what you want in exchange, and that's the extent of our business."

"All I want in exchange is to see her hand," Bitters said, almost as obstinate as Tiffy on her worst day.

I wasn't a fan of being a freak show, but if all he wanted was to look at it in exchange for telling us that cure? Didn't seem there were many options. I stepped forward, except I couldn't get around Dax, who was still blocking me.

"Why?" Dax asked,   firmly in place.

200

"Because I've seen those brands before and I want to see if it's a fluke."

I forced Dax out of the way by making my will known, partially by bumping into him. "What's a fluke?"

"I'll explain after I see," Bitter said, holding out his hand for mine.

I tugged the glove off and felt a tiny buzz when Bitters took my hand, and wondered if that was his magic. He turned my hand this way and that, holding it up to the light streaming through the window and then moving us closer to the fire to judge it there. I held my tongue, not wanting to seem overly sensitive about something that was part of my past, whether I wanted it to be or not.

"This isn't how it used to look, but I still see some remnants," he said.

"I cut off the original scar."

"Do you remember how they gave this to you?"

"No." All I remembered was the pain. I hadn't looked at what they'd done, keeping my eyes firmly closed. It bothered me that I didn't have more information, but I had been only four.

He looked closely at it one more time before releasing it. I tugged the glove back on.

"I don't think that is a normal burn. I think it was caused by something else. I found it odd the first time I saw one and I find it odd now. You don't bother doing something fancy to mark someone when they could've easily used an iron."

I had no answer for this, and neither did Dax.

"What do you think they did?"

His shoulders popped up. "How would I know?"

He walked to where he'd placed the bag holding the cure, dropped its withered contents on his table, and chopped it in half.

"This should do. You can come back in a couple days."

"You don't know what it is now?"

"I'm a wizard. Quality wizarding takes time. Not even I can figure this out in five minutes, even though I am the most brilliant wizard of my decade."

When neither of us moved quickly enough, he said, "We're done now."

"I'll be out in one minute," Dax said, urging me toward the door.

Not sure what he needed privacy for, but I didn't ask either. Maybe it was some sort of beastly affliction he didn't want to fess up to with me around.

I left him in the hut, and as soon as I stepped out of Bitters' place, I heard them. It wasn't a shock. I'd been half expecting them as soon as we got deeper into the forest and away from the main community, because the Wood Mist loved to lurk deep in the trees.

There was no sight of shimmering, but they were close. "Shut up," I said.

They got progressively louder as I waited.

"I don't care what you want."

"Who were you talking to?" Dax asked as he stepped outside of Bitters' a few minutes later.

"Myself." I tilted my head toward the hut. "Why did you want to talk to Bitters alone?"

"I'll tell you later." I looked back at Bitters' place one last time before we started making our way to the pickup point, where a pirate should be waiting with a dinghy soon.

"You think this Bitters guy, wizard, whatever he is, can figure it out?"

"He seemed to already suspect."

I ran my fingers over the leather covering my right hand. That hadn't been the only thing he seemed to have a hunch about.

"What are you thinking about his opinion on my scar?" It wasn't a question I would've asked him yesterday. But today seemed strangely different in the way it felt almost like old times.

"I'm wondering if the brand wasn't so much about marking your skin as testing you."

I hated when we thought alike. "But for what?"

"I don't know. That's the problem," he said, and then we both fell silent as we started getting closer to the edge of the town and possible eavesdroppers.

"Maybe we should stay local," I said, looking about the place and wondering

203

if it might be better to keep tabs on Bitters, and half of the last known cure.

"We go back to the boat. I don't want to heat this place up too much with too many people seeing you."

He was right; even this far out it wasn't worth the risk. He'd been right back at the Rock too, but things were different now. I had a plan, and each set of eyes that landed on me and figured out who I was would bring the Dark Walkers that much closer.

I hadn't seen any yet, but they were probably still back east, focused on the Rock and the vicinity around it. I'd known all along being on the boat was the safest place, but it didn't make it any easier to leave Bitters behind, and half of the only possible cure we had vulnerable.

"It's only a couple of days more," he said.

"I know that."

"The disease has been around a long time."

"I'm aware of that, too," I said as I saw our escort nearing the dock, conveniently early.

"Then what's wrong?" he asked.

And then I was startled by the warmth of his hand wrapping around mine, so similar to what Bookie would've done, and I answered before I thought about it. "Even if we had it today, it would still be too late."

He didn't try and argue with me, and let go of my hand as I climbed into the boat.

Chapter Twenty-One

My eyes popped open and I couldn't get enough air in. I tried to calm my breathing, knowing Dax woke at the slightest noise. I didn't want any more questions.

The bunk squeaked as I shifted, and I ended up having to freeze in the most uncomfortable position to not make any further sounds. It was a miracle he hadn't woken already. Then I heard him moving and realized I'd called the miracle a little early. I shifted into a comfortable position, the bunk creaking away.

Dax walked over and stood beside me. "Move over."

"Why?" I asked, remaining right where I was. He started climbing into the bunk anyway, and it was move or get squashed.

"What are you doing?" I asked while he took up

more and more of my bed as he got settled, his shoulder pushing into mine.

"Sleeping in the bunk with you." He shifted about until I was left with barely any space between him and the bulkhead.

"Why?"

"Helping you get some sleep tonight so that *I* can get some sleep tonight," he said, and then tugged half of my blanket over himself.

"How does you sleeping here, and hogging my space, make me get some sleep?" I asked, as I had less than half of the room I'd had. "What makes you think that this is a good idea?"

He repositioned the pillow under his head. "I'd tell you but I don't think you're going to like the answer."

Oh no, he wasn't pulling that crap on me with his top-secret reasons when the real reason was probably that the floor was too hard. "Tell me anyway." I was propped on my elbow, staring at him and daring him to withhold.

He was completely calm as he stared straight at me. "Because you've been sleeping with your hand curled around my jacket, the one you have stuffed beside the bunk. If my jacket is helping you sleep then I figured I might work better."

I froze, my stare-down turning into something that had a bit less spine involved. "I was using it as a pillow, was all." I turned quickly and settled in, looking at the wall.

"Except you weren't using it as a pillow."

"Yes, I was," I said.

"I would almost believe that if you hadn't taken another one of my shirts since I've been here."

I'd lifted it from the laundry, paid Stinky to tell Dax that it had been ruined, and hidden it under the blankets of my bunk. How did he know? I'd never been so glad for a dark cabin as my skin lit on fire.

I wasn't saying anything. I was mortified beyond speech, and there was no lie or excuse that was going to climb this mountain of evidence. How did you tell someone you were trying to kick out of your bunk that you fell asleep better when you could smell their scent next to you? Even the thought of uttering those words made the heat in my face spread down to my neck.

"I make you feel safe. It's not a big deal. To be honest, it's actually kind of cute."

I pulled the blanket over my head. If any more blood left my heart to swarm to my face, I was afraid I'd have a heart attack.

***

I woke up in the crook of his arm, my fingers gripping the front of his shirt while my leg laid claim to the top of his thighs like I had the right. After all my carrying on about him sleeping beside me, I was stretched out on him like he was my life raft in the ocean.

How to extricate myself was the problem now. He wasn't moving. By some miracle of the Wilds, could he actually be sleeping? Please, please! Let it be so. I needed one miracle to finally stick.

I also needed to work quickly and in order of priority. The leg was the worst offender. If he woke to the rest of me gripping him, it would be bad, but the leg was oh so much worse.

I tried to brace my body and lift my leg a fraction of an inch at a time, waiting with my breath held to see if he was going to wake up.

He turned on his side, slipping from my grasp as his breathing remained deep and even. Was he ill? I'd never seen him sleep like this before. I'd worry about it later.

All body parts detached and accounted for, I strategically sought a way off the bunk without touching him again. It was tough, but being able to utilize a spot between his calves and the wooden rim, I was free in under two minutes and out of the cabin in under three. No one would be the wiser about my apparent need to cling in my sleep.

***

"Hey, Marty," I said as I stepped into the galley and found him in his usual spot in front of a pan. "Eggs?" It was always eggs, but for some reason I kept thinking he was going to surprise me one of these times. Or maybe I was just hoping? Either way, it never happened.

"It's always eggs," he said, and then scooped a portion onto a plate that was nearly twice what I normally got.

"Thanks."

"Share them with your man. This way you don't dirty two plates. My hands get wrinkled." He looked down at his fingers and then to me. "I don't like that."

My brain was stuck on only one part of what he'd said. "I don't have a man."

"You're saying Dax ain't your man?" His eyebrows met almost in the middle. "Sure seems like he is."

I didn't want to know how it seemed. Was actually too afraid to ask. "It doesn't matter what it might seem like. He isn't."

His eyebrows seemed nearly stuck together and his mouth twisted. "I think he is."

"I just said he wasn't, and I don't want his eggs." I grabbed the spoon from him and dumped half the contents of my plate back into the pan. Well, almost half. At minimum, a good quarter.

"But it seems like—"

"Are you not hearing me?"

"Yeah, but I got eyes and ears too, and they see real clear." He took his spoon back and used it to point out said features.

I took my plate, forcing myself to keep my mouth shut and stop arguing. It was getting me nowhere and I could be eating. Plate in hand, I went up on deck and grabbed a seat by the bow, in line with where a few of us sat every morning.

The second I settled down, Buck, a guy I'd played poker with more than a few nights, scooted away from me.

"What are you doing?"

"Nothing," he said, keeping his eyes on his plate.

"Move back over here this instant."

"I like where I am," Buck said, which was ridiculous considering he was now elbow to elbow with Stinky on his other side.

"Fine." I scooted across until there was only the tiniest sliver of room between us.

Buck jumped up, looking like I'd just put a gun to his head. He moved to the other side of the ship and remained standing. Stinky, who'd been sitting next to him, looked at the now open space, decided to be preemptive, and stood before he was the one right next to me.

I stood myself and waved my hand at the empty crates that we used for seating. "You can all sit again, you big bunch of chickens."

I went and leaned against the rail, like I wasn't afraid of falling in. The eggs

210

tasted worse than normal, even though Marty made them the same every day. I took a couple more bites before I gave up and went to find the source of my problems.

Dax was getting his own eggs by time I found him.

"I thought you were going to share," Marty said, shooting a dirty look at Dax's plate when I stepped into the galley.

"And I told you I wasn't," I replied before I proceeded to ignore him and focus on Dax. "I need a word with you in private."

"It's a little chilly out. Should I grab a jacket?" He delivered his question with the innocence of a babe.

It wasn't chilly out at all. The misplaced humor didn't find a home with me, but a blush found its way to my cheeks. "In our cabin," I snapped.

"Our cabin," Marty mimicked, and then rolled his eyes as if his point was made.

"You!" I pointed at Marty. "Shut up or I start singing."

His mouth snapped shut.

I took off down the passageway and heard Dax following not too far behind as I walked into what used to be *my* cabin.

"What are you telling everyone?" I asked as soon as the door shut behind him.

"I don't know what you're talking about. You'll have to be more precise." He leaned a hip against some shelving and continued to eat his eggs.

211

"Are you telling them we're together or something?"

"No." He continued to eat, unbothered by the notion.

"Then what are you doing?"

"Dal, I don't know what you're talking about."

"Why are they all scared of me?" And why was I near screaming while he was relaxed and eating?

"I don't know, but that's a good thing."

"No, it's not because you're the reason. I want them to be scared of me because of me. Because I'm scary." I stabbed my chest with my finger.

"There's nothing I can do if you didn't scare them enough on your own." He continued to eat, but I would've sworn he was laughing on the inside.

"I *was* scaring them."

"Then what's the problem?"

"You," I said, turning my pointing on him. "You came along and you're taking over again and handling everything, and I need to do this on my own."

"I haven't taken over. I've helped out where needed. Some people, ones of maybe a saner variety, might even be grateful for it." He was still calm, while I felt as if I were wrapped inside a tornado.

I let out an awkward groan as I dragged both hands through my hair. "I don't want you to help me. I need to do stuff all on my own. Don't you understand that?"

I stormed up on the deck and away from the stubborn bastard. Unfortunately, he followed right behind me, and I thought perhaps my storm might have finally touched his calm.

I was halfway across the deck when I heard him calling, "Honey, why are you doing this?" It was the sweetest voice I'd ever heard escape his lips. "I just wanted a little morning romance. Don't be mad."

"What are you talking about?" I said, watching how every single pirate there was listening, and not being polite enough to even pretend they weren't.

"Oh baby, don't be like that," Dax said, making it look like we'd had a lover's quarrel.

I put my hands up, warding him off as he approached, and heard muffled laughter as he pursued me across the deck. He wrapped his arm around me and kissed my neck in front of the whole crew.

My hands on his shoulders, he leaned in by my ear. "Now this would be considered me trying to take over."

He gave me an extra squeeze before letting me go and walking away.

Chapter Twenty-Two

It was after midnight, if I read the moon's position correctly. I found a nice little place to perch, in between the latest crates to arrive with Jacob's booty. The breeze washed over me and I took in the stars. Feet up on the rail, I could almost pretend I was completely alone in the universe, and right now, alone felt perfect.

I could get used to this life. First time I'd ever seen one of these ships I'd been terrified to get on it, but the place really grew on you. And space. I'd never seen so much wide-open space as the ocean.

Maybe not so alone. I leaned my head back and tried to pretend I didn't hear the faint sound of chimes. Or maybe, even though we were miles from shore, someone had hung up a wind chime somewhere? I searched the horizon for the golden mist that helped give the Wood Mist their name. It wasn't visible, but that didn't mean shit when it came to them.

"I know you bastards are watching me. If you're not going to go away, you might as well show yourselves and spit it out already."

I sat forward, glad I had a knife on me while I waited for some shimmer. Nothing showed, and the chimes were still muted, but joined by a scratching noise coming from the crate I was sitting on.

Beside my leg, letters started to form, as if the wood was carved by some invisible tool. The shape of a B appeared with agonizing slowness. I looked around, knowing it was them, but where were they? Why didn't they just talk like normal? They had a voice.

Then again, I'd only ever seen them in the forest. Before coming to the Wilds, I'd never heard of such a thing as the Wood Mist, but maybe they didn't like the cities.

If they were connected to the forest somehow, what did most vegetation hate? Salt. There was a reason the saying "salting the earth" had come to be.

"Ahhh, we're too far out to sea for you guys, huh? Maybe not a fan of all this salt water? Reduced to carving?" I leaned back and relaxed again. "Sucks to not have all the power, doesn't it?" I shouldn't have giggled. I'd be on land again soon, and it was nearly impossible to avoid forests. Then I laughed anyway, because that was the kind of *piss on your shoes* mood I was in.

The carving stopped. I guessed the Wood Mist got a little sensitive when you pointed out their shortcomings.

"We both know you deserve a little ribbing, so don't get all touchy now. Might as well spit it out, since you're so intent on talking."

I closed my eyes, listening to the waves hitting the boat when I heard the carving start back up. Whatever they wanted to say, they weren't giving up that easy. I looked down and had three letters now.

B U R

"What's this? If you're trying to tell me something, I need a little more."

A couple minutes later, an I was carved, then an E and a D.

"Buried? That seems like a lot of work to write something that doesn't make sense." What did that mean? I'd done a lot of burying in the past month, but I couldn't see how any of those deaths had anything to do with them. "You trying to say I shouldn't hold a grudge because it's done and buried?"

I looked around, searching for a hint of shimmer in the night sky. "Am I supposed to let it go that you tried to kill me? If I remember correctly, you weren't overly concerned about burying

216

the hatchet with me. If I'm alive, it's by my own doing, and I do hold a grudge. I'm one of those people." I'd never understood the concept of forgive and forget. Someone screws you over, there's no forgetting that.

There was no reply, and I didn't particularly care. I wanted to be alone, and that included company from creatures of the wood. It wasn't as if I could go to my cabin alone anymore, because the person who was messing with my head the worst was currently occupying the space.

Damn him. I'd been so miserable when he was gone, and now that he was with me again, I wasn't sure I felt any better. I didn't know how to fix what was wrong with me where he was concerned, or how to get rid of the anxious feelings. The whole thing was bizarre. The nightmares weren't the only thing messing with my sleep.

And every time I saw him getting dressed, which was nearly daily because he had absolutely no modesty whatsoever, I kept thinking of the sexy books I'd read with the half-naked guys on the cover. It was probably only because he was half-naked too, but still. The man needed to get some modesty. Meanwhile, I was changing buried under the flimsy blanket, which was a near disaster most times.

Stupid sexy books. I didn't know why I'd ever read them. Or why I kept rereading the one I had. They were stupid books. The women in them always fell madly in love with some guy who made them crazy. Then the worst part was that all they wanted to do was have sex. It was all they thought about.

No wonder I was having problems. Those books had burned sex into my brain. I wasn't in love like they were, though. It was that book. And reading that book over and over again when I'd been sitting in that cabin alone had only made it worse.

I looked around, making sure I was still alone before I talked to Bookie. "You were right. The dragon books were much more worthy of their spot on the bike that day."

I could see Bookie in my mind, nodding as he agreed with me.

"Well, you should've stopped me."

Who could ever stop you? By the way, weren't you the one that tried to sleep with Dax?

Imaginary Bookie was getting to be a wise-ass.

Yeah, I'd thought of sleeping with Dax, but it was purely a business arrangement that would've satisfied my curiosity at the same time. It was a good thing I hadn't. Dax already made me crazy because he was bossy and controlling and always thought he was right. Who knows how bad it might've gotten if I'd slept with him.

My senses were already heightened around him because of that crazy

218

magic he had. And it was potent stuff. Lately, it was making me think all sorts of crazy thoughts. Even back at the Rock, it had started to get to me and made me funny in the head.

Come to think of it, maybe I was better off taking my chances with a spare hammock and the potential rapists. Or maybe I should sleep on deck.

I was still mulling over where I should sleep when I heard Dax come aboveboard. He didn't come over to me but walked to the railing. Didn't matter. I knew he was checking up on me.

I'd never had anyone do that before. It was awkward and smothering. But when he was gone, I'd missed it in spite of myself.

I watched him, and for once, he looked almost as conflicted as I was.

His body turned to me as he rested his hips on the railing as only someone who could swim would. It was hard to make out his features now with the moonlight at his back.

"When you were at the Cement Giant, did you have any friends before Margo, Cindy, and Patty?"

My body immediately jerked back at the question that came out of nowhere. "How is that any of your business?" I asked. Just when I started softening, he seemed to poke me right in my sore spots.

"Just answer."

"No."

"Because you had none?"

He'd backed me into a corner. If I said nothing, he'd think I didn't, and for some reason the idea of him thinking everyone had always hated me was worse than facing what had happened. "Yes. I did."

He nodded as if he'd already assumed as much.

"What happened to them?"

"I'm not in the mood for an interrogation." Not about that, not right now. I didn't want to talk about other Plaguers and the horrible rumors of how they'd ended. It was hard enough dealing with the bad endings I knew of for certain.

"And I wasn't in the mood to chase you down for weeks. Now answer my questions."

I didn't need to see his face. The set of his shoulders silhouetted by the moon alone told me he was digging in. If I said nothing, this would escalate into another fight. As mad as I got at him, as much as he was getting under my skin lately, I didn't want to fight with him. We'd just gotten to a place that wasn't ugly. I didn't want to take a step back to where we had just been.

The bickering we used to do before I'd left had been more of a sport, putting my wits up against his and seeing who could poke the hardest. What happened between us since he'd shown up was rubbing me raw. I didn't have any more room for pain. I was all stocked up.

"What happened to

them?" He crossed his arms and relaxed his frame against the side of the boat. "I know they were already gone. They weren't on your list when you went back to the Cement Giant."

"I can't tell you what happened to them. They disappeared. One day they were there and then they were gone. All I've got for explanation is rumors."

"That happened a lot to you. People disappearing."

I shot to my feet, hating that he'd driven me to running, but I couldn't take this. Not so soon after Bookie.

He stepped forward, blocking my way.

"Sit."

"Fuck you. I'm not going to sit so I can listen to you tell me how everyone around me disappears. I already know it. I live it."

"Just sit."

When I didn't listen but moved to get around him, he said, "I only want to talk for a couple minutes."

With him blocking my way, I didn't have much choice but to do as he said, or drown. The water didn't look so bad, but I was pretty sure I'd change my mind after a couple mouthfuls of it. I wasn't miserable enough to kill myself. I'd never be that miserable.

I went back to my perch, wondering if he was going to drive me to throw myself into the ocean soon anyway, to hell with a lungful of salt water.

Dax sat beside me,

his arm grazing mine as I tried to ignore him and watch the moon's reflection flickering in the waves. For all the times I'd thought of him when I'd been here alone, I stared straight ahead, hoping he'd just say what it was and leave me alone.

I watched him out of the corner of my eye, waiting for the next strike to come and knowing that this was why it was better to be on my own. Togetherness was an illusion for the weak. From the second we're born, we're alone, and maybe that's how it should be. All people did was hurt you, even when they didn't mean to.

A low sigh escaped his lips, which was so un-Dax-like it caught me off guard a bit.

"You're scared," he said.

"I'm not scared of anything." What was there for me to be scared about? I didn't need anyone and I'd slay a roomful of Dark Walkers without batting an eye. "As far as I know, mind reading isn't on the list of your abilities, so don't tell me I'm scared."

"Yeah, you are. The funniest part about it is, most people are scared to be alone. You seem to have the opposite affliction."

"Like I said, I'm not scared of anything." I wasn't, and I didn't bother explaining the benefits of being unencumbered, not when he was obviously looking to argue. He thought he knew everything. I wanted to be alone because it was the best thing to be.

He leaned back and

222

propped his foot up on a nearby crate as he reclined next to me. "I look exactly the same as I did on my thirtieth birthday."

My head jerked toward him as a little shock went through me, and it had nothing to do with the fact that he wasn't aging anymore. I'd figured that out a while ago. But why was he was telling me? Dax didn't tell anyone anything. From what I'd gathered, I didn't think even Becca—a woman he had been sleeping with—had known his secrets. First he attacked me and now we were sharing? Was he one of those schizophrenics Bookie had talked about?

I didn't know whether to talk or say nothing. If I talked, maybe he wouldn't continue, and I really wanted to hear this. If I didn't speak, maybe he'd think I was uninterested, which I was anything but. I gave him a minute, hoping that his words would kick back in and I wouldn't be forced to risk it either way.

"I've never been sick. I can walk through a crowd of people, all in the throes of dying from the Bloody Death, and not so much as sneeze the next day."

I stayed unusually still, afraid the slightest movement would jar him into realizing he was telling me way too many of his guarded secrets. I did try to smell the air for whiskey, wondering if he'd gone on a drinking binge. But his voice was clear and I didn't notice any scent of booze lingering.

"I'm exceptionally

223

hard to kill because I heal quicker than a human can, and my skin and muscles are tougher than tree bark."

Hmmm, had he actually tested his skin against the strength of tree bark? I knew he was densely built. I guessed that could make sense.

When he remained quiet for a while, I figured I wasn't risking much in asking my questions now. Of all the things I'd thought I wanted to know, there was one burning the strongest. "Why are you telling me all of this?"

"Because I want you to understand." His eyes met mine, a determination in them that was just shy of overwhelming.

There was no guard, no glacier. Right now, maybe for the first time in all the time I'd known him, he seemed completely open to me. Even his energy seemed different, still throwing off that same buzz, possibly stronger, but this time not setting my magic off, almost calling to it, and I could feel an answering warmth in my chest that was completely out of my control.

"Understand what?"

"I'm not going anywhere."

I was the first to break eye contact. "You act like you can't die," I said, scoffing even while a part of me hoped he'd tell me I was wrong. But I wasn't. His brother had died. Dax was hard to kill, but he wasn't invincible.

"I can. Everything can. It's part of life. But I'm about as close as you   can get to immortal."

I couldn't stop myself from looking back to him. It was as if I could see the many long years of hard living in his gaze, a bittersweet expression born from knowing too much and having mixed feelings about the wisdom he'd earned.

With a nod, as if he had said all that he needed to, he stood. I watched as he went below deck, giving me space but leaving a chill where there once was the comforting heat of his body beside mine.

Chapter Twenty-Three

When Dax and I got to Bitters the next morning, we found him hunched over a single cleared spot on a workbench. But not before we had to bust in a barred door because he'd ignored our banging. If he hadn't popped up his head, I would've thought he was dead.

"You couldn't have knocked before deciding to break my door?" Bitters asked, oblivious to the panic he'd caused.

"Bitters, did you figure out what the stuff we gave you was?" I asked, ignoring his question. My heart was still pounding over the possible setback while he was wiping the sleep from his eyes.

"Of course I did. I'm the greatest wizard of the last decade." He stood and started looking over another bench that was overflowing with papers and bottles.

"I've never met another wizard," I said.

"Exactly my point." He seemed to find what he was looking for as he picked up a corked bottle. "Your stuff came from a living thing, something your people call a Dark Walker."

"But what is it?"

"I think, I don't know for sure, but I think it's their flesh."

"I thought you knew?" Dax asked.

"I do. Mostly. You'll just have to double-check, is all, and as it happens, I know one personally. Poor thing came to me for help. I couldn't do much. What's wrong with him was way beyond what I could fix, but that's where you'll get your answers."

"None of them talk." I leaned a hand against the wall of his shack as I tried to remain patient. I thought I was so close, and now I had to go and track down another Dark Walker for answers? Standing there, I had to remind myself that I wasn't a quitter.

"This one will," Bitters insisted.

"Why would this one after so many others haven't?" I looked over at Dax and shook my head, already doubting a reason I hadn't gotten yet.

Dax remained quiet, waiting to hear Bitters out.

"Because of this," Bitters said, holding up his bottle.

"What is that?" Dax asked.

"Now that's between

me and my client. He's going to be mad enough you're delivering it, but my old bones don't feel like hiking out to anyone. I don't care what I'm paid." He walked over to the table, and with a swipe of his hand, papers and spices all fell to the ground. He fetched one paper from the scattered ones on the ground and started drawing on the sheet. "Here. This will get you in the general area, and then you'll have to dig around a bit."

Dax took the sheet and we both looked over the crude map.

"Why doesn't this person come to you?" I asked.

"He did initially, until it became nearly impossible. The rest you'll have to discover on your own because it's not an easy picture to paint.

"Don't forget this," he said, handing me the bottle. "And I wouldn't sample that if I were you."

***

It took us about three hours to get there on foot after a fight over stealing a horse. He cursed my code. I told him he needed to have a code. He responded to get back to him in fifty years and we'd see how shiny my code was then. All in all, we were almost back to normal.

Neither of us talked about last night's discussion. He didn't take any verbal jabs at me, and I returned the favor. By time we got to our destination, it made me wonder how many reset buttons we had in this relationship.

"This?" I asked as we stood in front of a seaside cave. I took the directions from Dax's hand and glanced down at the crude drawing.

"This is it."

I walked up to the opening and stopped. "Go ahead."

"Go ahead?" he repeated, as if he doubted the words he'd heard. "You aren't going to argue to go first? Tell me how you have this covered and you can handle anything and everything?"

The opening looked dark and small, and gave me the general sense of a black hole. "Nope. Not after the last couple of months and not today. You see the hole we're about to walk into? I'm claustrophobic. And if I'm going to lay all my cards out on the table, I'm not particularly fond of the dark, either. I think I'd rather risk death by starvation than walk into this thing first. I'm taking the day off from being my normal kick-ass self, so if you have some overwhelming urge to take charge, like you usually do, today is your free pass." I waved a hand toward the cave. "Have at it."

Dax walked into the dark, small cave laughing. In my mind, this was simply building the case that he was insane. Only a crazy man would walk into a place like this laughing.

The cave opening wasn't so small that I had to bend over to enter, but Dax did. I couldn't see a thing in front of me, and I reached

229

forward to feel for where I was going and felt Dax's hand wrap around mine instead, leading me forward. It was a sure grip, like he wouldn't let go no matter what happened, but not so tight I felt like I couldn't pull away.

"I hear someone back there," he said as we progressed down what seemed more like a tunnel than a cave.

"Who is that?" The gravelly voice came from deep in the cave. I couldn't see anything, as my eyes were still adjusting to the darkness.

Another few feet and the tunnel opened up into a larger cavern. There was a single chair beside a flat rock, which looked like it was being used as a table of sorts. A single candle lit the place and revealed some clothes folded and piled on a natural ledge, along with some unlit candles. I heard a dragging noise coming from another opening at the back of the cave, and I wondered if that served as a bedroom, since I didn't see any kind of bedding.

"We're friends of Bitters. We've brought your bottle." Dax squeezed my hand before he whispered, "Prepare yourself. This is a rough one."

I waited to see what was coming toward us that Dax had already seen.

"He shouldn't have sent you here."

My eyes slowly focused on where the voice was coming from, and I felt the bile start to rise in my throat. Bitters had said this was a Dark Walker, but it didn't look like any of the ones I'd ever seen.

In my entire experience, the only discernable difference between a Dark Walker and human was the dark haze that surrounded them and the sickly sweet smell. The thing standing at the back of the cave, fifteen feet in the distance, had no resemblance to a human beyond having similar proportions.

Every inch of flesh not concealed by the loose pants and tunic it wore was wrinkled, red, and raw looking, with occasional patches of black spots that looked more like tar than skin. Its eyes were yellow and reminded me of a reptile. Was this what they really looked like? Or was there something wrong with this one?

"Here is your potion from Bitters," Dax said. He placed the bottle on the rock table and then stepped in front of it. The message couldn't have been clearer if he'd carved it into the stone wall.

In my head, I tried to remind myself of all the horrible things these creatures had done to me, and yet when it started moving forward, each step causing a contortion of pain, I felt bad for it.

"What do you want?" it asked, eyeing up the bottle.

"Answers," I said.

It nodded. I wasn't sure I believed it would be willing. Dax must have seen some truth there I hadn't, because he stepped out of the way.

"So you know what

231

I am?" it asked, slowly making its way to the table and grasping for the bottle Dax had left there, then uncorking it and taking a deep swallow. I could see some of the tension leave its form as it did. A painkiller, then?

It slumped into its seat, hand still wrapped around the bottle.

I inched forward, close enough to catch the sweet scent of him. "Why don't you look like the others?"

"This is a bad day, even for one of my kind. My skin is almost completely worn out."

"Your skin?"

"The hide I wore. I had a good set." His eyes landed on the bare skin of my arms. "A Plaguer hide. They last longer than regular humans, but nothing lasts forever."

I clenched my hand, imagining a knife in my grip as I sank it into his chest. I couldn't believe I'd felt bad for this thing, even for a minute. Ever since I'd heard the Skinners had collected hides for the Dark Walkers, I knew what it meant on some level that I hadn't wanted to acknowledge. But to stand here in front of one that might have slain someone I knew in order to steal their skin?

"Is that why they hunt me? For my skin?"

"No. They hunt you because they're fools and think you aren't a regular Plaguer." Its eyelids sagged as it answered, and I was afraid that if it took too many more swigs from that bottle, it would fall over.

"What do you mean,   not a regular Plaguer?"

"Those tests they ran on you when you first got to the compound, do you remember them?" His yellow eyes stared at me as he waited for a response.

I should've taken a step back, but I moved closer. "How do you know about that?" I asked.

"Because I was there. You wouldn't recognize me now, of course. At the time, I appeared to be a grey-haired man in my fifties. Wasn't my favorite set of skin, but it worked for what I needed at the moment. My name's Croq, but I went by Mr. Edward when you knew me."

He said it all so calmly, as if he wasn't the monster I remembered. If I didn't want the cure so badly, I would kill him right now in the most agonizing way I could come up with.

Dax's eyes were on me. I could feel him but didn't turn to look. It was something I didn't speak of, ever. There was nothing about that first year at the Cement Giant I ever wanted to talk about. I didn't want questions from him, either.

Dax moved closer, standing only a foot from my side. I hoped his attention would shift back to the Dark Walker soon. If he didn't stop looking at me like I was a china doll that was sitting too close the shelf ledge, I was going to have to punch him in the face to remind him of exactly who I was.

"Should I kill him, long and slow?" Dax asked, and I saw the anger burning there, as if this monster had wronged him.

"No. Even if I want you to... No. Not unless he can't help us, and then I'll do it myself." If anyone would be killing him, it was going to be me.

Croq tilted the bottle to his lips again and Dax kicked his chair. "Tell her why they hunt her."

"They think you can get them our cure." Croq's eyes started to glaze, and his speech wasn't as clear as it had been.

"Why would they think that?"

"I don't know, but I never believed it anyway. There's only one thing that can fix me, and you aren't it." He waved his hand toward me and then leaned on his table, his head falling to the side as if it suddenly weighed too much for his neck. "I'd tell you everything if you could get the Wood Mist to fix me."

"They can fix this?" I asked, not doubting for a minute that there was something wrong. I had trouble even looking at him.

"Thousands of years ago, we walked the Earth like gods. Until the things you call the Wood Mist cursed us," he said, nearly babbling in a stupor now.

"Why did they curse you?" I asked, my voice getting louder as his lids drooped lower and lower.

"To get rid of us." He looked at me, then took another swig of Bitters' concoction.

As much as I wanted my own answers, I knew our time just got cut down to a few minutes. Unless I took the bottle, but then he might stop speaking completely. "Where does the cure for the Bloody Death come from? Is it your flesh?"

There was the slightest shifting of his head. "Healthy flesh, not like mine."

"If you were healthy, could you cure people?" I asked.

"But I'm not." Croq's eyes widened slightly, as if I'd said something that made him want to stay alert. "Can you get the Wood Mist to fix me?"

Dax's eyes narrowed but I kept my attention on Croq. "I don't know. What's it worth to you?"

"If you help me, you won't need a cure."

He took another swig of his potion and I didn't try to stop him. "We'll be back."

Chapter Twenty-Four

We walked out of the cave and down the beach a ways, as the little bits and pieces of information started to glue themselves together. There weren't as many Dark Walkers in the Wilds because maybe they feared the Wood Mist. The Wood Mist feared the oceans, or more accurately, the salt in them that was deadly to most plant life.

I sank to the ground and planted myself on the beach as I sorted through all the possibilities. Dax remained standing, but he stood nearby.

"You want to talk about it?" he asked.

I let out a sound that could've been a laugh if it had held even a drop of humor. "I thought you knew me better than that."

"I do. It was a test. I wanted to make sure you were of sane mind the way you were talking in there. It sounded like you wanted to make a deal to heal him and get tangled back up with the Wood Mist in the process." His face softened in the setting sunlight, but I wasn't fooled about what he thought of that idea.

"I'd make a deal with the devil for a cure." It wasn't a bluff.

"And that's exactly what you might be doing."

"I know."

"At least some of the Wood Mist tried to destroy you."

"I am aware." I leaned back on my arms and stared at the waves breaking, trying to keep my own nervousness under control, since I didn't see any other options to move forward. It wasn't like you woke one day and decided you wanted to dance with the devil. Sometimes he was the only dance partner available.

Dax shrugged, looking out at the sea too. "They might not be willing to speak to you. Why would they undo a curse in order to help?"

"I don't know about the curse, but they'll definitely speak to me," I said.

His gaze snapped back to me. "Will they?"

"Pretty sure."

He looked as happy as I felt.

"And how do you know that?" The question was wading knee deep in accusation. I wasn't sure when I'd signed an agreement to share all with him, but he certainly seemed to think he had the contract in his back pocket.

This next little tidbit wasn't going to be appreciated either. "Because they've been trying to talk to me for a while."

"The chimes?"

"Annoying as hell, too, when you're trying to pretend they don't exist." From his expression, my bad joke didn't lighten the mood.

"And do you know what they want, as well?"

If he actually had a signed contract, this was when he would've waved it in my face and yelled about breaches and such.

"No. They got one message through to me, the word 'buried,' and that was it."

"Buried?"

"No idea, but they want something from me and now I want something from them. There's a chance this could work, and we've got to take it."

"They still might not be able to do anything for him. This is all based on one creature who was foxed out of his mind."

This time it was me with the expressions, and mine said clearly, *I have to try*.

He crossed his arms. "Why? You owe no one—except me, that is."

My eyes broke with

his and I let a handful of sand sift through my fingers. "If the Wood Mist can do this to the Dark Walkers, they have the knowledge to destroy them."

"If he's telling the truth. We don't know how good his information is."

"If there is a chance to get rid of this disease, it's worth anything, including my life."

"No, it's not."

I stood and brushed the sand off my pants. "I have to do this, so if you aren't going to help, then stay out of my way."

His eyes narrowed. "I don't understand why you would care about a world full of people that turned their back on you, hunted you for what you are."

"Maybe it's not just for them, or the ones who died. Maybe it's for every Plaguer that will survive only to be hunted for their parts, hiding in corners. I can't live with that."

"Like you've ever hid." He shook his head.

He disapproved, but it wasn't the first time, and I'd still do what I felt I had to. I walked closer to the ocean, longing for the safety of the salt water before I threw myself into the tangled vines of the Wood Mist.

Dax approach me and stopped close enough that I could feel his magic. "Give it another hundred years and then talk to me about what you can live with. What happens if we return this creature to its former glory? You don't think that'll have ramifications? You didn't cause this disease, and it's not your problem to fix."

I looked at him. "I've made up my mind and it's not changing." I could see my words shift something in him, the set of his eyes, the tenseness of his muscles. He was thinking about taking it out of my hands completely, or trying to. I knew him well enough to know what was coming. "Try what you're thinking and I'll never forgive you."

His face was stone. "You'll be alive and have time to get over it."

"But I won't get over it."

"Maybe that's a choice I can live with."

I didn't want to go to this place with him. Didn't think I could forgive him if he managed to take this chance from me. I didn't want to find out if we'd used our last reset button.

"Dax, this won't be another fight. This will be war between us."

He stood there looking as unmovable as me, and then all of a sudden, I saw a softening. "How much would you sacrifice to do this?"

"Let's put it this way: I'd like to be buried next to Bookie if it comes to that."

"Don't say something you don't mean."

"I'm not. You'd really stop me just for your revenge? I understand the desire, but—"

Something flickered

behind the glacier. "You still don't get it."

He walked away from the coast a bit and started gathering up driftwood.

"What are you doing?"

"Making camp. We won't make it back to Bitters tonight. We'll have to leave in the morning."

"Why are we going to Bitters?" I asked as I followed him now, wanting to know what he was up to.

"Because there might be a solution to this we both will be able to live with, but we're going to need him for it."

"You want to stay here?" I asked, and pointed to the cave.

"He's the least of our problems."

Chapter Twenty-Five

My eyes fluttered open and I felt Dax's heat underneath my hand and along my side.

Not again! At least in the bunk, it was almost unavoidable to touch him. Here, I'd had the entire beach to roll around on.

I could tell from the location that he hadn't come to me—I'd moved closer to him. He was the same distance from the fire as before I'd drifted off. Why was it I couldn't go to sleep anywhere near him and not end up cuddled into him?

Shit, shit, shit.

Calm breath. I could detangle and he wouldn't be any the wiser. Follow detangle protocol and all would be good. Leg first. Get the leg off him from the place it had decided it should drape over his and then tuck itself in between his calves.   Damn, my leg was a total hussy.

I'd just managed to detach my torso from where it was partially resting on him when he seemed to stir, and I leapt to my feet, as if I hadn't been anywhere near him.

He sat up and stretched, looking about until he saw me. Whew, looked like he had no idea I'd draped myself all over him.

"Couple hours until dawn still, but you want to get going?"

Good. He'd assumed I was getting up to break down camp. "Let's get going. Definitely."

***

"Bitters?" Dax shouted as he busted into the one-room hut without knocking. I was starting to realize Dax had a real problem with putting knuckles to wood.

I should've been more nervous as we walked into Bitters' hut. When Dax had tried to explain that Bitters could use his magic to help protect me, I hadn't cared about the details. I'd been immediately all in. Anything that would lend me some protection against the Wood Mist was all right in my book.

But now that we were here, and I watched as Bitters was getting up from where he'd been lying on his bed, a cigarette of some sort in between his fingers and the air especially pungent, I wasn't so sure I should be adding this chapter to my book.

Maybe I should've left this sucker closed.

Bitters coughed and some smoke escaped his lips. "What are you doing? I could've been in the middle of something very dangerous or maybe top secret!"

"But you're not," Dax said.

Bitters just shrugged, as if to say, *Okay, so I wasn't.*

"Are you capable of doing a Grounding Spell?" Dax asked.

Bitters walked over to his table, heaped so high now that it looked like there would be an avalanche at the slightest tap, and sat on the chair beside it. He leaned back and found the last three inches of space left on the surface to prop up his heels. After getting himself quite comfortable again, he took another drag from the cigarette in his hand and answered, "I'm the best wizard I know. Of course I can do a Grounding Spell."

"So that spell does exist?" Dax asked.

"Sure," Bitters said, his hand waving the cigarette and leaving streams of smoke ribbon in the air. "It's been about a century since I've done one, but shouldn't be a problem."

"I need you to do one on us," Dax said, pulling me beside him.

"Who's the anchor?" Bitters asked, eyeing us up and then pointing at me. "She doesn't look too sturdy."

"She's sturdier than she appears," Dax said.

"You know it can't be undone, right?"

All the nerves that

had started to wake up before suddenly felt like they got a bucket of ice water dumped on them. "Wait a second. What is this exactly?" I asked.

"I told you. It's something that'll keep you alive."

"Am I doing it or not" Bitters asked as he started rifling through dusty bottles sitting on the table with his free hand.

"Yes," Dax said to Bitters, and then turned his attention back to me. "You said you'd do whatever it took. This is part of the price."

No denying I'd said that, but doing "whatever" was an easier thing when you were doing it in the far-off distance. "What exactly is a Grounding Spell?"

"It ties our life spans together."

"What does that mean?"

"When you talk to the Wood Mist, they can't kill you unless they kill me as well. The downside is, when I die, so do you. As I've mentioned before, I don't die easily."

"That's all it does?"

"Yes."

"So I could talk to the Wood Mist and they couldn't get inside of me and kill me?"

"They might be able to get inside you, but they can't kill you unless they kill me too."

This didn't sound so bad. This was definitely something I could get behind. "Sign me up."

Bitters walked over

to a roughly drawn calendar hanging on his wall. "What am I getting paid?"

"What do you want?" Dax asked.

"Hmmm. I'm not sure. I don't really need anything. We'll work it out later." He started tapping his finger on the blocks. "Come back on Friday."

"That's almost a week from now," I said. Croq looked like he might not have two days left, let alone a week, especially if he kept hitting up his cure.

"I know. I can count. It's also the new moon." Bitters stabbed the calendar with his finger, and I saw the little circle inside the box he was pointing at.

"Wouldn't you want the full moon?" I asked. In every book I'd ever read, the good stuff always happened on a full moon. If we needed a moon cycle, that seemed like the one we'd want.

"Noooo," he said. "Or I would've said come back in three weeks. Who's the wizard here?"

Looking at it that way, one week was better than three.

***

Dax and I got back to the ship late. I stopped to grab a snack from the galley, and by time I got to the cabin, he was already settled in my bunk.

"You're really going to sleep there every night?" I asked as I climbed up onto the bunk next to him, liking how he threw off so much heat. The place had been a lot chillier before he'd shown up, that was for sure. And if I was going to start admitting things, at least to myself, it was nice knowing I didn't have to bar the door or step over trip wires. Everything about the sleeping arrangement was an improvement. Only problem I had was I became a stage-one clinger in my sleep.

I'd settled into my corner like I usually did when he surprised me by saying, "If you really want me to leave, I'll go."

Shit. He would? "No, you wouldn't," I said, and then closed my eyes, hoping to end the conversation.

"Really, go ahead. Tell me you want me to go."

"I don't know why you even say that. You wouldn't leave." I pulled the covers up over my shoulders and hoped he'd shut up about it. "You never do what I tell you to."

"Are you asking me to leave?" he asked.

"Didn't I just do that?" I asked, knowing I hadn't actually asked him to.

"No, you didn't. Are you?"

This was getting tricky. Why was he trying to get me to ask him? Couldn't he just shut up and go to sleep? "Would you if I did?"

"Immediately," he said. "If you didn't feel like cuddling anymore, I wouldn't want to crowd you."

"What are you

talking about? We don't cuddle," I said, so glad I was facing away from him and he couldn't see the panic that was surely written all over me.

"I'm not sure what else you'd call what we do every morning, but okay," he said.

I turned, forced to defend myself against how bad it looked. "I get cold at night. That's all it is."

He remained lying on his back as he stared at me. I watched as his hand reached up, and then it cradled the back of my head as he pulled me down to him. His lips grazed mine feather soft as I leaned on his torso.

His hand dropped and then he was shifting out from underneath me and rolling on his side, giving me his back.

"Goodnight, Dal."

"You're going to sleep?" I asked before I thought about how that sounded and what I'd implied.

"Yes. Why?"

He was really going to sleep. I wanted to plant my foot on his ass and shove him out of the bunk. What did he think he was about? He gets me all jazzed up and then rolls over? What? Did he think I was going to beg him to roll back on over? Because I wasn't.

I turned over, giving him *my* back and trying to be noisy enough about it that he'd know.

I shouldn't say a word, but I couldn't resist. "Just for the record, you aren't always very nice."

"Neither is leaving   without so much as a

note."

Chapter Twenty-Six

The door swung open to my cabin just as I was pulling my shirt over my head. If I hadn't sensed Dax, I would've known anyway, because no one but him would have the balls to barge in like that. They could talk all the trash they wanted when Dax wasn't around about how they could take him, but no one ever tried.

He walked over and placed a small packet wrapped in fabric on the bunk. "This is yours," he said.

He turned to leave but paused by the door. "Also, looks like Jacob's about to take over a ship. I don't think there's going to be much of a fight from the looks of it, but you may want to stay down here," he said, and then went to shut the door.

"Wait! You can't say that and just leave," I said as I threw on my boots and grabbed my knives. "The pirates are taking a ship?"

"You know, I knew this wasn't going to go smoothly," he said, shaking his head and talking to himself. "Try not to get involved. We need this ship and people to sail it."

Well damn it all to hell and triple shit, I hadn't even had breakfast yet. He had a point, though, about stepping on toes. It was bad enough we were stuck waiting, and Jacob hadn't taken too kindly to his schedule getting interrupted because we couldn't leave the area yet. But still. I had to do something. "What about negotiating on their behalf? How do you think that would fly?" I asked as I thought of the best approach.

"My guess? It would probably depend on if Jacob enjoyed his eggs today."

I hated being a guest. The shit was almost worse than being a prisoner some days. You had to go along with whatever they wanted and you couldn't even act pissed off about it.

I let out a stream of curses, unlike any tirade I'd ever let loose before. That was one of the good things about pirates. I had a whole arsenal of new curses to add to my vocabulary to spruce things up when needed.

I headed toward the door and he put out an arm to stop me. "Just keep in mind, if it gets ugly and I have to kill everyone, they'll be

251

no one left to sail the ship for us. Who's going to sit with it in port when we go ashore?"

"I get it. I'll try and keep the peace," I said, and stared down at his arm until he dropped it.

Dax followed me as I made my way on deck. I figured he was going to go do his own thing once we reached topside, but he dogged my steps all the way over to the rail as I spotted the new ship in the distance.

We hadn't even gotten to the other boat yet. "What are you doing?" I asked. "I told you I'd try and do this peacefully. Don't you believe me?"

"I'm here to watch the show."

"The show?"

"Yes, the one where you try and tell Jacob how to run his crew while not insulting him. I need something to amuse me on this damn boat."

I nodded. I could see a certain amount of entertainment value in that. It also wouldn't hurt to have someone like Dax there beside me when I was arguing my point. "So you're going to back me up?"

He tilted his head back and crossed his arms before he said, "Would never think of stepping on your toes like that. You don't need anyone, remember?"

Eyes narrowed, I tried to think of a fitting response, and couldn't come up with anything reasonable that wouldn't make me have to eat my own words.

Lacking a good comeback, I rolled my eyes and huffed. It was lame, but

I had bigger issues, like saving however many people were on the ship we were about to take over.

"Jacob," I called as I approached where he was standing on the upper deck, looking through the coolest set of binoculars I'd ever seen.

"What is it? I'm busy right now."

This didn't appear to be going down the way my interrupting his breakfast normally went. I turned, looking for Dax and wondering if I could use the appearance of him to my benefit, even if he didn't actually support me. He managed to plant himself ten feet down and was looking as uninterested as possible, with a smug *Oh, you need me?* expression pasted on.

No, I don't. I watched as the ship got closer in range and hung back. I'd take this minute by minute. Or more likely, blow by blow?

The closer the ship got, the more splintered and worn the wood appeared. The boat was half the size of our ship, and yet there were more than twice the amount of bodies we had, just topside.

No one offered a fight when the pirates strung the boats together, or even as they boarded. Jacob was one of the first on deck of the taken ship, and I was close behind.

"Jacob, these people have nothing to take," I said to him.

There was a slight nod as he examined the group. Their clothes were filthy and their hair greasy. The boat itself carried an odor from having too many passengers on board. Even the ship was near broken, with holes in the decking.

Jacob moved forward, making his command known. "I control these waters. What are you doing here?"

An older man stepped forward. "We didn't mean to trespass. We're simply trying to get as far from the Bloody Death as possible."

There were murmurs of agreement that ran through the crowd.

"How bad?" I asked.

"It's taken over the entire southern East Coast."

Jacob took a step backward, fearing anyone who'd been in a plague-stricken area.

I could see him give the nod to his men. He was going to let the ship go, and quickly.

Things had been going so smoothly and then I saw her, tucked behind a group of people. I'd almost missed her. The grey mist that hovered around Dark Walkers was barely noticeable until the sun had come out from the clouds and hit her just right. She was my age, tops, or so she looked. Between Dax and the Dark Walkers, I'd learned you could never truly know how old someone or something was.

I could let her go. Pretend I'd never seen her. But it wasn't a *her* and that skin she was wearing was probably from a person she killed.

"Don't let the ship go yet," I said to Jacob.

A quick nod and he was reversing the silent orders. He hadn't become the Pirate King by being stupid.

I walked closer to the group, not having the fear of catching a disease like the others, and used my knife to point at her. "You, front and center, now."

I saw it in her gaze. She knew she was caught. Had probably been waiting for this from the moment I'd stepped on board with my flaming red hair and gloves. I didn't know how, but they all seemed to recognize me.

There was only a second's hesitation before she stepped forward. I saw the change as she emotionally prepared herself to die.

I'd been through this too many times and didn't bother with the bullshit anymore. "You going to talk, or should I just skip forward and kill you?"

She tilted her head back, offering me her neck. Of all the things I didn't know about the Dark Walkers, I did know this: most were loyal to a fault. Was it by choice? Who knew, but it didn't change my situation.

I gripped my knife as I focused on what I had to do while everyone waited and watched. Only two others, Dax and Jacob, knowing what was about to happen.

The mist was so slight around her that I had to keep telling myself there would be no logical reason for it to be there other than she was a Dark Walker.

I had to keep reminding myself she wasn't really a young girl, either. The signs were there, and only a Dark

Walker would offer themselves up like this. A human would be pleading for her life.

Maybe I should try and question her anyway, but I already knew I wouldn't get answers from this one. If I waited much longer, I'd talk myself out of doing what needed to be done.

With a quick slash, I ran my knife across her throat and she fell to the deck a minute later, motionless.

I heard the gasps of surprise and then outrage from the captured boat's passengers. I turned back to Jacob. The pirates might have remained quiet, but I could see the surprised looks on their faces. They didn't understand what had just happened or why.

"Have your guys throw her overboard," I said, knowing the telltale rotting would take place if the passengers on board tried to save her body for a land burial.

Jacob nodded and gave the order, understanding the problem.

I walked back across the plank onto our ship and headed toward my cabin, feeling like the coldblooded killer everyone appeared to think I was.

Chapter Twenty-Seven

Settled on the quarterdeck, I took a sip of whiskey and watched the pirates celebrate their recent coup. It seemed like a silly celebration to me, as they hadn't won anything. The people on the ship had had nothing to win. In the end, it hadn't even been worth taking the ship itself, it had been in such disrepair, but I guessed the pirates didn't like missing an opportunity to party.

And there was Dax, drinking right beside them like he was part of the crew. They were welcoming him in as if he were one of their own, like a long-lost brother or some shit.

I leaned back against the bulkhead and tilted the bottle to my lips, the image of killing that girl—that Dark Walker—playing over and over in my head. She'd seemed so young, so human. I kept wondering if I'd made a mistake, but all the signs had pointed to the fact that she was a monster.

So I'd killed her, like I'd killed so many of them before her. I'd stopped counting the kills after I hit double digits, especially as I just kept finding another one to kill and the number kept growing.

Living so close to death for months was starting to do strange things to me. Staring it in the face, over and over again, so close that it felt like I could almost see into the abyss of nothingness, it made me want to cling to life even more firmly.

I saw Dax break from the group. He headed below deck, hesitating slightly as our eyes met. Now there was someone who knew something about death. He nodded slightly before he continued on his way. He knew I was off just as he knew there was no perfect string of words that could fix the mood I was in.

I looked over at the group he'd left behind, all deep into their cups, and wondered if a good fight might make me feel better. Even drunk, I doubted they'd take me up on it. No one so much as breathed in my direction anymore.

I took another swig from the bottle I'd claimed and kicked a foot up onto the rail as I toyed with the faceted red stone that hung from a golden chain. After I'd killed the Dark Walker, I went back to the cabin alone, looked at what Dax had left for me earlier, and discovered it was a necklace.

Today was the first day of November, and also my birthday. Dax must have seen that in my file from the Cement Giant. He'd gotten me a birthday present.

I ran my finger over the stone, wondering when he'd gotten it, or how he'd managed to find one so close to the shade of my hair.

A couple more swigs and another option of how to spend my evening—one much better than a fight—came to me.

***

I walked into the cabin as he was taking off his shirt and took another long swig of whiskey, needing to make sure that my liquid courage didn't dry up before I saw the job done. I placed the bottle on the small ledge by the door and walked over to him. His eyes narrowed as I tugged the shirt he was about to change into out of his grasp and tossed it to the floor.

I reached my hands out and laid them flat on his warm flesh, surprised at the contrast of smooth skin over ridged muscles. As my fingers drifted over the corded muscles of his abdomen, a low rumble began building from his depths that I could feel through his flesh. The sound was so primal and raw in its intensity it reminded me of his beast. It called to me and my hands drifted lower, to where his   pants hung low on his hips.

As if I'd reached some unknown boundary, he grabbed my wrists, stopping my hands and removing them from him before he took a couple of steps away. "You aren't ready for this."

I'd sought him out almost uncertain of what exactly I'd do, as I'd been fueled by liquor and the fear of death, my own and that of everyone around me. Now I knew for certain exactly what I was seeking.

I closed the gap between us and laid a single hand on his arm. Then I asked a question that never would've crossed my lips if it weren't this moment and today hadn't happened, and I didn't feel so absolutely desperate to feel something other than death weighing down upon me. "Don't you want me?" I stared at my hand on his arm, afraid to look into his eyes and see rejection.

"Dal, it's *never* been about wanting you," he said, his voice rougher than usual.

I shifted my gaze up, and the way he was looking at me made my skin burn. "Then what?"

"I think you need—"

"No. Stop trying to tell me what I need or what I'm ready for. What I need is to forget about death for a while and feel like I'm alive."

I saw his gaze linger over me and stop to pause on my lips. I could feel his energy cranking out, and I was starting to realize there was a pattern there that might have more to do with him wanting me than anything else.

Then he contradicted everything I saw and felt with one word. "No."

"What? Do you have to call all the shots always? Maybe you don't always know best. Ever think of that?"

He picked up his shirt from where it had landed near the bunk and pulled it over his head before crossing the room toward the door. "You're trying to mute out the killing. I get it. But it's not a good idea."

I watched him as he placed his hand on the door and a desperation gripped me. I needed him. I felt like I was breaking off into little pieces and he would be the one that could make me whole.

His hand was on the door when I said, "Either you do it or I'll find someone else. This is a big ship with a lot of men. Hell, even Jacob offered to do the honors. I wonder how he feels about the timing?"

I knew I had him when he stopped moving, and instead of walking out the door, he now seemed to be blocking it. "He did, did he?"

"Uh huh. I bet I could walk down the hall right now and he'd happily oblige me." I was playing with fire. I could see the last of the glacier Dax hid his feelings behind melting in front of me. I could feel the heat he was throwing off.

"That will never happen." The magic was near boiling in the room, and even with my whiskey haze, I could sense I was treading into dangerous territory.

Maybe Dax was merely afraid if I got involved with Jacob, he might lose me for good. At the moment, I didn't care what worked, only that he did what I needed. And this was beyond want. I needed this or I was afraid I'd be lost in the emotional abyss soon.

I'd turned nineteen years old today and had spent my birthday killing a girl who looked just as old as me. I knew she wasn't what she seemed, but neither was I, and I too could die at any moment. And then as I'd sat and held the first birthday gift I'd gotten in over a decade, I knew what I needed, and I wasn't letting him walk away.

"You think you can stop me? You're not the only man on this ship."

He reached back and pulled the shirt off again. The muscles of his abdomen and arms rippled with the movement as he stripped away the rest of his clothes and stood there in front of me, more perfect than I'd ever imagined.

"But I am the only man for you. Take off your clothes," he said as he stood across the room looking as raw as the beast that lay beneath the surface.

It was do or die. I knew if I hesitated, he might be just as likely to sleep in front of my door as in the bunk with me. He still hadn't committed fully, and I knew if he saw any question he might leave. I didn't hesitate, pulling my shirt up.

It hadn't cleared my head yet when he was standing in front of me yanking it off the rest of the way.

"Nobody touches you but me," he said before his mouth covered mine and he gave me exactly what I was hoping for.

He yanked my pants down roughly and I knew I had him. He'd chosen a new course and committed to it. There would be no going back from here. I could feel his determination in the grip of his hands on my waist, as they circled around and grasped a handful of my ass before he lifted me.

My back hit the bulkhead and my legs raised to wrap around muscled hips that now claimed the space between the juncture of my thighs. I had never been so exposed, or cared so little, in my life.

He pulled me tightly against him, and I could feel the hardness of his dick pressed against me. The intensity only increased as he shifted my body into a slow rocking motion, causing me to ride the steel ridge of his dick. My hands twined in his hair, trying to find a solid place to grab as the rest of me reeled.

My thighs tightened around his waist. I hooked my ankles behind his back as I wondered how much better he would feel inside me if he felt this good now.

This wasn't the same man who'd taken his sweet time with the teasing kisses of the past. This was a heat I'd yet to experience, and it was torching me from the inside out. All the fighting and near-death experiences didn't come close to the intensity of life I felt exploding within me in at this moment. This was what I'd been looking for, the thing that would blast the taste of death from my mind until all I could do was feel.

His eyes scorched into mine. It was as if he was gauging each movement made and the effect it had on my body.

One arm held my hips to his as I felt his finger from his other hand entering me, testing me. I gasped in amazement and my back bowed in reflex, pushing my breasts hard into his chest.

I had just gotten used to the strangeness of having a part of him in the most private part of me when another finger joined the first. This time when I gasped, his lips were on mine to capture the sound, and his tongue delved into my mouth to tangle with mine, and then to pump in a slow rhythm that mimicked the motion of his fingers.

His groan vibrated through me as if he liked what he'd discovered. I threw my head back on a gasp and his mouth moved to my neck. He hoisted me higher and I felt his lips close over a nipple, biting and then sucking away the sting before moving to the other.

His mouth left my breast as he slowly lowered me, and I could feel something much larger than his fingers pressing against me.

With agonizing slowness, he lowered me down onto him, stretching and lighting every nerve ending on fire as he did. His eyes locked on mine, watching as my lips parted on a gasp, his mouth nipping at my lower lip as I did.

I arched into him, wanting more. Then he was pulling out almost all the way, just to sink even deeper within me.

An intensity was building within me that had me digging my fingers into him and urging him forward until my head dropped back and I was shuddering on an explosion of exquisite sensations surging through me in waves.

"What was that?" I asked, breathless and weak, leaning on him.

"That was the beginning," he said as he walked us over to the bunk, his hands already strumming my body to life again.

Chapter Twenty-Eight

The cabin was empty when I woke the next morning, only a blanket to cover my skin. Vivid memories of what I'd done with Dax the night before made my skin burn again, even as my head pounded from the hangover.

The girls at the compound had said that your first time having sex was usually horrible, painful even, but maybe they'd not had someone like Dax. Actually, of course they hadn't. There was no one like Dax. Still, they said when it first went in, there was always pain. I wished Fudge was here so I could question her.

It was better than I'd ever imagined. And more intense, like I hadn't even been myself. And the things I'd done. Was that normal? How could I even look at him after some of that? And I was stuck on a boat with him, so I'd have to. Even worse, now that I'd done it, I wasn't sure if I'd ever   be able to stop.

I pulled the blanket up over my head, already mortified, and there was no one even in the room with me.

No, it couldn't be that different with Dax. I wasn't going to get all stupid about it. I forced myself out of bed and yanked on a shirt and some pants as I realized I smelled like him. He was on my skin somehow, and I liked it even though I shouldn't.

"Bookie, why did you let me do that? You're supposed to be looking out for me wherever you are, like Fudge's parents look out for her."

I told you not to get those sexy books.

"No, actually, you didn't. You just looked at me funny and turned red," I said, arguing with my *imaginary* Bookie while I got my boots on and wondered how I was going to look at the *real* Dax after all the things we'd done. I wasn't sure if you were supposed to get that close and intimate with someone else's body—were you? There were parts of me he'd seen last night that I couldn't have described if asked.

Nope. Wasn't going to think about that. I was going to get dressed and go about my day like nothing had happened last night. Head up high, I went to the galley and grabbed a plate of eggs. I was heading across the deck when I spotted Dax.

He nodded, or I thought he did, as I looked about the ship finding deep interest in everything that wasn't Dax's face.

"Where you going?" he asked as I walked past the place I normally sat.

"Huh? I don't know." And I didn't. I'd been staring at the wooden crate across the deck and not paying attention to where I was walking.

He let out a deep sigh and ran a hand through his thick hair. I remembered how wonderful it felt last night. He had great hair. It was silky and thick, and my fingers clenched at the idea of touching it again.

"You're acting weird."

"No, I'm not." I jutted out a leg and scoffed, trying to sell my act.

I'd never understood back at the Cement Giant when the girls pretended they didn't care about someone they'd slept with. I got it now. Once sex got involved, things got really strange. I just wished I knew why.

"You're like a scared bunny about to take off in a sprint. Your heart is pitter-pattering a mile a minute."

"You're so wrong." I wouldn't have called it pitter-pattering. It was more like a stampede of buffalo.

He leaned forward, getting close enough to almost kiss. "No, I'm not. I. Can. Hear. It."

"You can hear my heart?" I asked, not one ounce of me believing that bullshit. Beast ears or not, it had to be a bluff.

The hint of a smile appeared on his face. "Of course I can. I'm a predator."

I was so pissed I

didn't even deny it anymore. "This is total bullshit. I want a list of all this weird shit you can do. Otherwise it's an unfair advantage," I said, keeping my voice down, as I knew every pirate in our vicinity was trying to listen.

"I've got lots of unfair advantages."

Oh yes he did. Even the thought of how many naturally given advantages he had made me start blushing. I tilted my head down, trying to gain some cover in my hair as that weird magic thing that happened between us was lighting my chest nearly on fire, along with some other parts a bit lower. It had me torn between ripping his shirt off and jumping in the water, even if I couldn't swim.

"I knew this was going to happen."

"Knew what?"

"You can't even look at me straight."

"Yes I can," I said, forcing myself to look at him and hold it for a full second before I looked back at my eggs.

Dax stiffened.

"What? Something wrong with eating now?" I asked. My eggs didn't look that good, but they never really did here.

He didn't say anything, but I heard a low growl.

I looked up, wondering what had set him off that wasn't me. I turned to see that the noise I'd heard on the other side of the ship was just the pirates coming back, but they had company.

"Rocky?" I almost couldn't believe it when I saw that auburn head of hair and smile heading toward me. I put my plate down on a crate before I dropped it on the deck.

"Yes. Rocky." Unlike myself, Dax didn't seem so happy to see him.

"Dal!" Rocky strode right over to me and was hugging me in the next second.

"What are you doing here?" I asked.

"What do you think? I came to help you."

"You came all this way?" We were halfway across the globe and miles away from the Rock. "How did you know?"

"I heard there was a new petite, redheaded pirate. Wasn't hard to figure it out after that." His glance shifted to Dax and then back to me.

"Why didn't you wait for me to get back? You didn't have to go to Jacob for protection."

I shook my head, realizing what it must have looked like to him. "No. It wasn't like that." I looked around at all the eager ears. "Are you hungry? Marty, he's the cook, just made eggs. Get something to eat and then we can talk."

Chapter Twenty-Nine

The three of us sat on deck, Rocky a foot from my left and Dax a foot from my right.

I'd put Rocky's bag in my cabin, although I wasn't sure where he'd be sleeping. I was on the brink of sleeping with the other pirates, rather than sleeping in a cabin with both Dax and Rocky.

I'd caught Rocky up on everything that had happened while he ate a plate of Marty's eggs. Found out that Tiffy, Fudge, and Tank were okay, at least when he'd left the Rock. Now that he was done with the food, he was digesting the extent of everything else.

"It's nice out here," Rocky said, although his interest seemed to lie more with Dax and me.

"Yep, it is," I replied.

Dax didn't say anything, but looked like he wanted to toss Rocky over the side of the boat.

Rocky stood and moved about the deck, like he couldn't find a good spot to stand still. Was it Dax or me? Or both.

Did he know something was different between me and Dax? Nah. No way. Although if my face started heating up, he might guess something was up.

"You're doing pretty well with your sea legs," I said as I watched how easily he rocked with the ship. It had taken me a couple of days to adjust myself, and it was the prefect distraction to not talk about all the things that needed to be said.

"I've been on quite a few boats," Rocky replied, paying more attention to Dax than me now.

Dax sat there and said nothing. He didn't need to, though. When I looked at him, all I could see on his face was *what the fuck is he doing here and I should really toss him overboard.*

I did my best to ignore Dax as Rocky and I focused on small talk, the bizarreness of the situation not lost on me.

"I thought you were staying at the Rock?" Dax said, and I knew a can of worms being opened when I heard it. The curtain was officially being closed on the fake niceties.

"I thought you weren't going to look for her?" Rocky shot back.

"I changed my mind."

"So did I."

"Rocky, I know you want to help her, but this isn't a situation you're cut out for."

As I watched Dax standing there, I suddenly realized this wasn't just about me. Dax liked Rocky, always had, even when he was annoyed with him. Part of this was about trying to protect him.

"Why? Because you're here?" Rocky asked.

"Rocky, this isn't your…"

I heard Dax's words drift off just as I was trying to figure out how to help the situation along. It was something so unlike Dax that it drew my attention to him and to a Dax expression I'd never seen before. I stood and then froze, knowing something was very wrong.

"This isn't what? Finish your sentence," Rocky said, and I turned to see what he was making of this unexpected behavior.

The plate I'd held in my hand crashed, as my fingers suddenly turned numb. The sound drew the attention of several other pirates who were on deck.

"He's got the plague!" I heard someone scream, and there was a burst of energy around us as everyone even remotely nearby evacuated our area. But it all seemed to happen in the distance, somewhere in a haze, while Rocky stood crystal clear in front of me.

As I watched, Rocky

brushed his hand beneath his nose, and it almost seemed like everything had slowed down. He raised his hand and saw the blood on his fingers, while I remembered a scene just like this not long ago. His face drained of blood and I could see the effort it took him to stay on his feet as the truth of the situation hit like a punch to the gut.

His gaze rose to mine and there wasn't any need for words. I saw it all there in his eyes. He was a dead man walking and he knew it.

My legs felt like wooden appendages but I forced myself go to him, even as I relived my own nightmare.

"Rocky, it's going to be okay," I said, thinking back to how I'd said the same thing to Bookie and how that had ended. "We've got a lead on a cure."

He wasn't listening, and I didn't have the strength to make him. I wasn't delusional enough this time around to fill his head with promises that seemed beyond reach.

Dax appeared beside me. "I'm going to put him in our cabin," he said, immediately picking up the slack as I stood frozen, and Rocky looked like he'd already seen his grave.

Dax's action finally spurred me and I sensed the threat all around. The pirates on deck looked like if they weren't afraid of touching Rocky, he would've been thrown overboard already.

Dax grabbed Rocky's arm and threw it over his shoulder.

"I'm going to go talk to Jacob," I told him.

Dax nodded, completely in sync. If Rocky had one chance, it was us getting that cure, and soon. But if we couldn't get Jacob to protect Rocky while we were doing it, he'd be killed by the pirates before the Bloody Death had a chance to finish him.

I took off toward Jacob's cabin as if the devil himself had just started the stopwatch.

***

Jacob's door was already open, and I could hear them talking before I stepped inside the cabin. Stinky and Murrell were standing beside Jacob's desk, where the man himself was seated. They all turned and looked at me.

"Go," Jacob said to them. "And shut the door on your way out."

They both gave me a wide berth as they left, I'm sure having witnessed how close I'd been to Rocky on deck.

Jacob got up from his desk and walked over to the porthole, looking out and shaking his head as I walked over. I didn't bother sitting this time, as I wouldn't be staying long.

I had one shot at saving Rocky, and the window to do it in was seventy-two hours, at most.

There was no time to

explain what I knew the pirates had already told him, so I cut to the point quickly. "Can he stay here?" I wasn't sure what I was going to do if Jacob said no, or to what lengths I'd force the issue.

His hand was fisted on his hip. "Dammit. This is why I don't let just anyone on my ships."

I knew he wasn't speaking to me, but I didn't have time to wait for him to come to grips with the realization that he and all his pirates might already be exposed.

"I have one shot of getting the cure. If I have to take Rocky with me, I'll be that much slower. And when I get the cure, I might not make it back if I have no reason to return. He's already been in contact with enough of your crew that you want me to have a reason to come back. None of us have time to waste."

He looked at me like I'd personally spread the disease myself, but nodded. My feelings about Jacob ran the gamut, but the one thing I was sure of was that he was a pragmatist.

"I want what you have left of the cure the Skinners gave you before you leave."

And now I was going to find out how much I wanted to save Rocky. "They said it didn't work. That it made them sick."

"I'll keep him on the ship, but I want it," he said, and I wondered if he thought I was trying to save it for Dax. He didn't know Dax couldn't get sick. If I left it with Jacob, he might take it.

But I'd warned him. My code, normally so crystal clear, suddenly looked a bit grey around the edges.

Then I heard myself say, "You can have it, but I don't want Rocky's body thrown overboard, even if he dies before I get back." Or he died because they thought it was the best way to handle the disease and decided to change the circumstances of his death in their explanations.

"I'll give you four days. I won't have someone decaying from the Bloody Death on my ship."

"I won't need four days." If I didn't get back in less than three, he'd be dead anyway.

"You better not. I'll get a boat ready to take you to the mainland."

I didn't wait for him to say anything else and rushed to the cabin to find Dax. He was tucking a couple of jars of water beside Rocky, along with some jerky. It was as good as it was going to get. I didn't have the option of staying behind and nursing him, and I knew from firsthand experience that I wouldn't be of much use anyway. I hadn't been to Bookie. Once the disease took them, they didn't eat or drink.

Rocky was already breaking out in a sweat. I wasn't sure if it was from the pain setting in or the fever. I grabbed his hand. "We'll be back as soon as we can. Hold on."

He nodded, and I let go of him and grabbed my bag, which was always packed and ready.

Dax grabbed his and I watched as he reset my booby traps quickly before we walked out.

He shut the door to the cabin and I said, "Hang on. I've got to give Jacob the cure we got from the Skinners before we leave. That's the price to protect Rocky while we're gone."

"Does he know everything?" Dax asked.

"Yes," I said as I pictured Jacob when I'd told him. "But I don't think he believes me, and he's demanding it."

"Then there's nothing else you can do," Dax said, so matter of fact.

"No. I guess there isn't," I said, not having nearly the same confidence in my tone as I clutched what was left of the cure, possibly poison in my hand.

Chapter Thirty

Stinky couldn't get us to the shore quickly enough. Once we reached the beach, we wasted no time setting out. Even at a run most of the way, it took a good hour for Dax and me to get to Bitters. I almost wished I was still back at the Rock, and Dax and I were still fighting over afternoon activities and what Rocky wanted from me. If we were swapping verbal punches, my mind wouldn't have time to be running around Worst-case Scenario Land in the pitch dark without a map showing me how to get out of the emotional tornado that was my emotions.

Give me a monster and I could handle it. I knew how to fight them. That was a landscape I could find my way around. How did you fight a disease? No one to punch, no one to kill—you were a bystander and no one would let you get a blow in. This disease made me feel more helpless than I'd ever felt at the Cement Giant.

Bitters opened the door before we got to it. "You're early!" he yelled before ducking back in.

"We didn't have a choice," I said, not caring if he was annoyed. I was just happy he didn't have one of those pungent cigarettes out.

"It's like that, is it?" he said.

"Yeah," Dax said from where he walked in behind me.

Bitters shook his head and walked over to a line of steins sitting on his mantle. He grabbed the one on the end, hesitated, and put it back before picking up the one next to it. He gave it a sniff and turned his head quickly before he nodded to himself.

"It should be brewing some more, but it'll probably get the job done," he told us as he walked over.

"Drink half of this," Bitters said, handing the stein to Dax.

I knew it must have tasted as bad as it smelled from the expression on Dax's face as he tilted it and then chugged his portion. I already dreaded drinking the other half, which was most likely reserved for me.

Dax handed the stein to me, under the same assumption. I stalled for a second, waiting to make sure Dax didn't keel over dead or anything. Other than disliking the drink, Dax   didn't appear any worse off.

Bitters reached out and urged the stein to my lips. "Drink it!"

I nodded. The smell of rotten eggs was unavoidable, and I knew that my only shot of getting this down was to do it quickly. Stein tilted back, I chugged until I was nearly choking on the vile concoction.

"Don't throw it back up!" Bitters said, as if I wasn't fighting to keep it down.

I thought he was going to say something about it ruining the spell if I did, but then he continued, "I haven't had my lunch yet and I don't feel like making another batch."

I waved my hand in front of my face, like that was somehow going to keep the stuff down, until I finally won over my stomach's better instincts. I took a tentative breath, testing the passage before I said, "I'm good."

"Now hold hands and be quiet," Bitters said.

I could feel the roughness of Dax's hands and wondered if they'd always been like that or if helping out on the boat had changed their surface. They felt good, confident and strong, their grip sure, like if you were to shake hands with him, you would trust his word. And I did trust him. I'd better, since I still wasn't sure I trusted Bitters.

"One soul tied to another, bound to walk the Earth together. While one   remains, so does the other…"

The air in the room seemed to grow heavier, saturated, and the warmth in my chest grew hot, as if my own magic was waking up along with the spell. A tingling sensation was surging through Dax's fingers and spreading to mine.

I looked over at Bitters, wondering how much longer this would go on, and I saw the obvious discontent on his face as he continued. If I wasn't worried about ruining the spell by interrupting him, I would've asked what had him so pissed off.

He finally finished, and I didn't have to wait long to find long to find out. "Letting me know how much magic you both have would've been beneficial!"

"Sorry! I didn't know how much we had," I said. No one had given me a magic chart or said it was important information.

Dax, with the exact opposite approach, said, "You're the wizard. Shouldn't you know these things?"

"I don't go poking around in other people's mojo. It's rude!" Bitters took his stein back from me and placed it back on the mantel, and I had a sneaking suspicion that it wasn't going to be washed. It wasn't a good thought to dwell on, as the contents of my stomach could still come up.

"What's the problem with the magic?" I asked, preferring to hear that than to imagine how many uses the stein had before us.

"That spell isn't meant for folks with this much magic. All sorts of shit could've gone wrong."

"But it didn't, right?" I didn't feel any different. Dax looked pretty much the same. The place wasn't on fire from some strange fireball out of the sky.

"I don't think so, but who knows. Magic doesn't always show its cards right away. Sometimes it likes to sneak up on a person." Bitters waved his hands about and then took a swig from a bottle he had on the table that, even though was clear, I suspected wasn't water. "Either way, it's done now and it's not my problem."

"So it's finished?" I asked, not feeling any different. I'd never had a spell cast on me, but a logical person would assume they'd feel something, even if it were as small as a tingle in your belly.

"Yep. You're good to go."

"You're sure it's going to work?" Dax asked, and I guessed he was waiting for that special tingle, too.

"It'll work because all my magic works. How else do you think I got to be so damn old? If you like, I can stab her in the chest to demonstrate, but it might be a bit traumatic for her."

I thought he was jesting, until he made a move toward my knife on my hip.

I held up a hand to ward off a demonstrative attack and stepped well out of his reach. "That'll be quite all right."

"Good. Now get out.

283

It's going to take all damn day to clear this room of the magic you two let loose, and I've got other things I need to do." He opened the door, a clear indication that he meant *get out right now*, and we didn't hesitate. By my count, we had seventy hours, tops, left. "I'll send you my bill," he yelled after us, and I wondered where he thought he was sending it.

***

The moment we stepped out of Bitters', I hoped to hear the chimes, but of course I didn't. Why? Because that would've been too easy, of course, and my gut was telling me I was going to have to do a little finagling.

"I need a denser forest."

Dax nodded. "I know where we can go. Come on."

"Hang on," I said, pulling back when he would've urged me on. "I need to go alone. If you're there, what was the point of the spell?" I could see the hesitance, and spoke before he dug in. "They can't kill me if they can't get to you, right? Isn't that the whole point of this?"

"There's things that are worse than death, and I'm tough to kill, even if I'm there."

"You know I'm right. It's safer if you go somewhere they can't get to you, like on the beach, right smack near the salt water. They hate it there. You are my lifeline, and I'm the only hope of talking to them, which is the only possibility of getting the Dark Walker to help us to get a cure." It was all true. The only thing I didn't add was that if for some reason this spell didn't work and I was killed, he wouldn't be anywhere near them because I couldn't handle any more blood on my hands.

"You know I'm aware of all this. You couldn't have just said, 'I prefer you to leave'?"

"I could have, but I felt it lacked the same dramatic impact." Not like I needed more drama at the moment, but it was a hard habit to break.

"I think it would've been fine."

"Are you sure? I've never seen people go crazy over *your* stories."

"Because I don't tell any."

"Is it because you're bad at it?"

"You know what? I'm going to do what you want just to end this conversation."

"A win's a win." This was what I had missed. That even in the face of a disaster, he didn't panic. Dax never panicked, and somehow it calmed me down. Like yeah, things were tough right now, but we'd get through it and live another day because he wouldn't quit and neither would I. Some people are made up of hopes and dreams, rainbows and sunshine. Dax was made up of hard, solid truths and immoveable boulders. It might not seem as pretty as fluffy white clouds in the sky, but when you leaned against a boulder, it didn't shift out from underneath you.

He kicked the ground and made a smooth patch of earth and then grabbed a branch, drawing directions. "This is a straight shot to the densest forest in these parts. Meet me here afterward," he said, making an X due west of the spot. "You shouldn't need more than a few hours."

I nodded.

"You have both knives?" he asked, only seeing the one at my hip, and not the concealed one that was tucked into my boot and under my pants.

"Yes."

"Three hours."

"I got this."

His eyes went all sorts of soft before he said, "I know you do." His fingers grazed my cheek before he walked off.

He did? Okay, he did.

***

I was happy I was wearing my thickest pair of leather pants today, as the branches and brush were dense. As I made my way into the heart of the forest, I realized this place must have predated the Glory Years. Some of the trees looked to be twisted with age and at least a couple centuries old, and the air seemed almost drenched in ancient   magic.

As soon as I found a clearing that was big enough to stretch my arms out, I looked around. The entire way here, I'd waited to hear the chimes. I didn't, but I knew the Wood Mist were near. I felt them, like their magic was poking and prodding at me, looking for my soft spots. All it did was make me stoke up a fire of my own.

"You wanted to talk. Here I am. Let's hear it." I lifted my hands, in a *come and get me if you can* challenge, and waited for a sparkle in the air.

Silence. Okay, I'd expected they might play a little hard to get now after being rejected for weeks. I'd probably do the same, but they were here. They'd been dogging my steps for too long. I didn't believe for a moment they didn't know exactly where I was. I found a nearby log, figuring I might as well make myself comfortable while I waited for them to stop playing games and being stubborn.

"You know, you did try to kill me last time. Was I supposed to be tripping over myself for another go at it?" I asked. I crossed my ankles while I tried not to think of the time I was wasting on these things. I wondered if we were better off trying to force the information out of Croq without trying to convince the Wood Mist to reverse the curse. The only thing that kept me seated was remembering how well it hadn't worked with Dark Walkers in the past.

I forced myself to lean back on a tree trunk behind me and keep the tension from my face. If they knew how badly I needed them right now, it was all over.

I could feel them getting closer. Their magic pushed at me, trying to find a way in, but I was a lot stronger than the last time we'd met. And I'd been willing then. I wasn't ready to open the door and invite them in this time.

They probed, with considerably more strength each time, for a good fifteen minutes before a single robed, faceless body appeared before me. I could live with the robe, even though it was a touch dramatic, but I hated the no-face thing.

I stood. I didn't know why. Sitting or standing probably didn't change my odds much. This wouldn't be a knife fight or a battle of physical strength, but it felt better somehow. If I did die, I wanted to go down giving it everything I had.

When it didn't speak, I decided to plunge in and get the negotiations rolling. I didn't have time to work things out on their schedule.

"The Dark Walkers say you cursed them."

It wasn't a question, but I still waited for a denial. When one didn't come, I continued. "They're the cause of the Bloody Death, but I'm guessing you already know that." No reply. Thing couldn't at least nod or something? "I need you to fix one of their people so that I can get the information I need."

"What do we get in   exchange?"

288

"What do you want?" I asked, knowing they wouldn't have even shown if they didn't already need me for something.

"We want your dead removed."

"All of them?" I tried to think of how many bodies I'd buried. This might take a while.

"Only the human. We want him removed."

Of all the bodies I might have had to dig up, there was only one human. "Why?"

"We don't want him there."

Forgive me, Bookie, if you're hearing this right now. It's a bluff. I promise. I'll never let it happen. "You're all powerful. Dig him up if you don't want him there." Even having apologized to Bookie in advance, I wanted to shake at the notion of these things touching him—not that I'd ever let it happen.

"No. It has to be you."

"Why?" Something stank, but I wasn't sure what it was, and I doubted they were going to tell me if they hadn't already.

"You put him there. You take him out."

Bookie, I'm sorry, but if moving you will stop anyone else from dying, it's the right thing and I know that's what you'd want. "Fix the Dark Walker of whatever you did to him and I will."

"Move the body first."

"No."

I stood there facing

289

down the faceless. Talk about a good poker face. How was I supposed to read expressions on a thing that had no features?

"Bring him here. We'll reverse what we can and you will remove your dead."

"Agreed."

The faceless creature was gone, but I still felt them around me, could feel the probing the whole walk out of the forest. I didn't feel safe until I hit the beach where Dax was waiting.

He was already walking toward me when I saw him. He didn't ask if I was okay, but it felt like his eyes had taken in every hair on my head. I saw a flash of heat cross his expression that made me think of flesh on flesh.

Then I thought of what lay ahead. I crossed my arms, feeling a chill that I wasn't sure was from the ocean, as the heat his look had generated faded. "It's on like Donkey Kong."

"What the hell is Donkey Kong?"

"I don't know. I read it in one of those books that came from the Glory Years library. I thought maybe it was just me."

"But they made a deal?"

I nodded. "We've got to go get the monster and bring him back to the Wood Mist, and they'll undo whatever they did."

"What did they want   in return?"

"I'll tell you on the way."

He must have read the unease that was steeped into me so deeply it oozed from my pores. This was going to be a rough one.

Chapter Thirty-One

We were getting close to Croq's cave when I finally spoke about what I'd agreed to do for the Wood Mist in exchange for them healing Croq. "They want me to dig up Bookie's body and move him somewhere else. I told them I would."

"Did they say why they wanted that?" Dax asked, his voice calm, even though I knew it had to bother him as much as me. He'd known Bookie his whole life. They might not have had the same type of relationship as we did, but Dax had watched out for him since he was a kid.

These were the times I could appreciate the glacier he tucked unwanted feelings behind. I had enough of my own volcano of emotions ready to rupture given the right catalyst. I needed him to be cold and analytical about the subject, and he was doing it without me asking.

"No. I can't see any reason for it to be a problem. But it doesn't matter what I think. I've got to do it if they hold up to their end."

We'd taken quite a few more steps before he said, "It's only his body. It's not Bookie."

"I know." It was what I'd been telling myself since I agreed. Funny how it didn't seem to matter. "I swore I'd kill every Dark Walker I met and now I'm trying to save this one and negotiating with the Wood Mist who tried to kill me. I gave Jacob the stuff that might kill him. I don't know who's good and who's bad anymore."

"You warned Jacob. He insisted anyway. That's on him." His conviction was so clear that I envied him.

A smile cracked my face. "I forgot to mention we're also indebted to a crackpot wizard," I added, and I didn't know why that seemed so funny to me at the moment. Maybe I was cracking up. "You don't think anything bad will come out of the Grounding Spell, do you? He seemed a little concerned about the effect our magic might have on the spell."

"Little late to worry about that now," he said as we stepped onto the beach and walked toward Croq's cave.

"Croq?" I called as we entered the dark interior. The bottle from Bitters sat almost empty on his stone table. There was the sound of feet dragging along the cave floor heading toward us. As he came into view, I could see the black spots had progressed. "The Wood Mist are going to fix you."

"Why would they do this?" he asked, making his way toward us.

"It doesn't matter. But I want assurances that you'll do what you say. I want answers now," I said. "I want to know what the cure is before we take you to them."

"If I tell you what the cure is, they'll fix me?"

He was looking at us like we were rattlesnakes, trying to draw him in before we stuck. Couldn't say I blamed him. I certainly wouldn't trust us, and he didn't even know how many Dark Walkers I'd already killed. "Yes."

His eyes bounced between Dax and me for a moment and then he spoke. "The cure is our flesh, our *real* flesh—not what's covered in borrowed skin, but what's underneath. After a month it's useless. But it has to be from a Dark Walker that is healthy, not how most of us are."

No wonder he was willing to speak. It only firmed up his position. Even if he reneged, we had to try.

"Let's go," Dax said.

"Can you make the trip? It's a few hours away," I said, looking at how he was staggering, even now. The thought of having to touch him entered my mind, and it was about as attractive as walking into a swarm of bees.

"Yes," he said, moving even slower than he had been. Dax stepped forward, looking like he was about to throw the creature over   his shoulder.

"No," Croq protested. "I can make it!"

Dax let out a very loud sigh, shook his head, and stepped away, and I realized Croq didn't want us to touch him any more than we wanted to lay hands on him.

"I don't believe he can handle the trip," I said to Dax.

"I'll make it," Croq said. "I'm not having a beast touch me." He looked over at Dax. "That's right. I know what you are."

"How?" Dax asked.

"Her," Croq said, and nodded toward me. "I can smell your magic when you get close to her. I know the scent of a beast."

"You just overplayed your hand." My hand instinctively went to my knife, and I realized the price had just gotten too high. Not Dax. I wouldn't have him hunted the way I was. We healed this monster and they'd have someone who knew exactly who Dax was. I'd always suspected the reason Dax's brother had died in beast form was because he'd been protecting his twin. It was the only thing that made sense. If he'd turned human, he would've been able to get help. He also would've possibly led the Dark Walkers right to his brother. I wouldn't undo his sacrifice.

My knife was out of its holster and I was less than a second from killing this monster when Dax spoke. "Dal." Him simply uttering my name stayed my hand. "Don't kill him. This is what you wanted."

"The cost is too high," I said, my hand held in check but knife poised to strike. This was a line I wasn't willing to cross. I couldn't do it to him. Not Dax.

"Is it?" he asked. "You were willing to give your life."

"I won't help him so that you end up being hunted the way I was. I won't do it." I could see Dax still waiting for something else, something from me. The woman in me understood what it was, and it scared me worse than the Dark Walkers.

"I won't have more blood on my hands," I said, and I could see something shuttering in his eyes, but not before I caught a glimpse of disappointment.

"I have to kill him," I said, trying to change the subject back to the threat at hand.

"He's your best bet. Are you sure you want to do that?"

"I have to," I said as I replayed his sentence in my mind and realized he'd said "your," not "our."

"This is your crusade. I won't try and stop you either way, but think about what you're doing."

"I am." It was all I could think about at that moment.

"I won't tell anyone," the Dark Walker promised. "I can prove that you can trust me with my magic."

"How?" I snapped, pushing Dax's "your" from my mind. This was exactly why I shouldn't be involved with anyone. It was already clouding my mind.

"If I share some of my magic with you, I won't be able to do anything that would intentionally harm you, including hurting him," Croq said.

I felt like I was swimming in dark magic these days, and I didn't even know how to tread water. I turned to Dax, wondering if he had any idea of what he was talking about. "Dax—"

"Never heard of it." Damn, it annoyed me when we were on the same page like this.

"You can test it," Croq said.

"How do I know it won't kill me?"

"Because I want to be cured of this curse and you're the only chance I have of that happening."

I looked at Dax. As long as I was the only one who did it, I'd be fine. This Grounding Spell was going to come in handy. Then Dax shook his head. Keeping Croq in my sights, I moved closer to Dax so only he could hear me whisper, "Why not?"

"I knew what Bitters was doing, but you don't know what his magic will do to you."

"It's not going to kill me."

He leaned closer, taking up some of my personal space. "You keep thinking that's the worst thing that can happen. It's not."

"I know myself. If my heart is beating, I'll be fine."

Dax shook his head.

"I'm not sure you fully appreciate the restraint I'm showing."

"What?" I asked Dax.

"Nothing. Might as well see this out now," he said as he stood back.

The Dark Walker was waiting for an answer when I looked back to him. "Okay. So, how do you go about sharing this magic?"

The Dark Walker looked at Dax and then me, as if he knew he was missing some piece of this situation. I wasn't certain I was the one who had the answers to his questions.

"I need you to bring your face close to mine," Croq said.

I did as he asked, hoping this wasn't going to be as bad as Bitters' potion.

His mouth opened and I could see it: a thin mist of vapor left his lips and then traveled the couple of inches to mine.

I steeled myself to act as if this were nothing, even as I wondered what it was going to do to me. I could feel it entering, this strange magic, as if it had a life force of its own. It was thick and cloying and I could feel the panic starting to take control of me. I tried to breathe through the sensation…until I couldn't, and I gripped my throat.

"What did you do to her?" Dax asked, as I felt his presence nearby and the sensation of my air being cut off. I reminded myself I had that grounding spell. I would make it out of this. I'd be okay. I would. The Grounding Spell would protect me.

"It'll pass soon. It's just settling into her," Croq said, his voice raspier now than it had been.

I felt my throat clearing as the magic moved deeper, air slowly coming back into my lungs.

Croq rested a hand against the table as he slumped forward. All I could think was that this bastard wasn't going to die before I got my cure, if I had to hog-tie him and drag him to the Wood Mist.

"Try and cut me with one of your knives," Croq said.

"What?"

"You won't be able to do it because you have part of me now." He drew a few ragged breaths before he continued, "And I can't hurt you because of that same part."

I pulled my knife out and tried to aim for a target on him.

Dax stared at me, waiting for an answer, and I nodded. "He's right. I can't get an aim."

Dax walked over to Croq and hoisted him up, the creature not having enough life in him left to complain.

Chapter Thirty-Two

We entered the clearing, all three of us, as the sky was tinged with the first light of dawn. Any thought of Dax staying by the coast was destroyed by the need to get a barely alive Croq here. I had one whopper of an imagination cultivated after years of being in the Cement Giant, but this? I'd never imagined a situation where I'd be trying to heal a Dark Walker.

I turned to Croq where Dax placed him on the ground beside me. "The minute you're healed, I want a piece of your flesh."

He nodded.

"Hey? Wood Mist? Let's get this show on the road?" I yelled out, knowing they were near. I'd felt them close by for the last fifteen minutes but hadn't seen a thing.

"You didn't remove it." The voice was strong but there was no golden mist or faceless body.

"It's too far away, but I will as soon as this is done. I will do as I promised."

"Make sure you hold up to your bargain. You don't want us as enemies."

I nodded. They'd already tried to kill me. If they considered our past relationship friendly, then I didn't know what would happen if we were enemies. I looked down at Croq beside me, literally rotting away. Maybe I did know what that looked like.

"I will."

"Move away from him," they said, and I couldn't have stepped back quicker.

Dax and I moved a good twenty feet back as the faceless started to appear. They circled around Croq, and for the first time, I could see what it must have looked like when they'd done this to me. From the outside, the air glittered and lit the invisible dome they created.

Croq's body, which had been almost lifeless, contorted with pain as he curled into a ball.

"What if they're killing him?" I said to Dax.

Dax shrugged. "Then he's dead."

The golden mist grew stronger and I saw Croq's form at the center, lighter than the dome. He was being completely covered by the shimmering gold. As we watched, his form uncurled and then rose to its feet. The gold started to peel away, leaving a man with golden brown hair and perfect flesh to emerge.

"Are you seeing this?" I asked, knowing Dax was, but too shocked to come up with anything more original.

"Yes, I am."

The charred and rotten skin of the Dark Walker was gone. The only things left from the creature before were the rags he was wearing, the ones that had looked so fitting on the pathetic creature and now marred the skin of the beautiful being in front of us.

He could pass for human—if you didn't look too closely. There were clues there if you looked close enough: a slight luminescence to his bronze-tinted skin, a strange sheen to his hair. But there was nothing so glaring you couldn't ignore it if you chose to.

As he stood in the circle, a new kind of fear gripped me. Right or wrong, when you saw Croq before, you knew he was a monster. No one would see this coming. Not even me. He looked closer to an angel, and there wasn't a trace of the smoky mist I was familiar with.

How many Dark Walkers had I missed?

The Wood Mist disintegrated into the air and the only ones left were Dax, Croq, and me. It took a moment for our small group to adjust to the changes, and then with a nod and nothing else, we all started walking toward the shore and closer to the salt water and air, and hopefully out of reach of the Wood Mist, because as it stood right now, I was more comfortable in the Dark Walker's company than theirs.

We walked the entire distance to the shore without speaking. We didn't stop until we stood on sand and the water lapped just shy of our feet.

"Give me your knife," Croq said.

I pulled it from my holster and handed it over willingly, knowing what he was going to do. He took it, and I watched him slice off the padded part of his pinky finger.

"Here," he said.

I dug through my bag until I found the map Bitters had given us, and used that to take the flesh from him and wrap it. By time I was taking it from him, his finger was healed.

"Dice that into tiny pieces and feed it to a sick person. It'll cure them within an hour," Croq said.

I thought back to how large a dose was and did the math. There might be more sick people than there were Dark Walkers that existed. Another huge problem: the Dark Walkers I needed were much harder to spot.

But it was enough to heal Rocky, and right now that was the most pressing need.

"You said if we helped you, we wouldn't need a cure," Dax demanded.

Croq hesitated long enough to make me worried he'd bluffed.

"You'll never be

able to cure them all completely with one Dark Walker, but you might be able to stop it from spreading."

"How is it being spread?"

"The cure turns into the disease itself after a month, but the disease's virulence depends on the initial host. It's limited in its damage unless it's a piece of one of our strongest. That's why there are only small outbreaks most of the time. The smaller outbreaks are usually when a group of us mine the population for Plaguers. Plaguers have the best skin. They last longer.

"A bigger outbreak like what's spreading now needs a Dark Walker who is healthy and strong among our kind. Most of us are dying. There's only one of us I know of who could spread the disease this far and wide."

"Who?" Dax asked, more interested in the information than I'd seen so far, but that made sense, since I had a feeling where this was about to lead.

Croq stared at us, but especially intent on Dax, as if trying to decide how much of a threat he was. "I told you how it works. Names aren't part of the deal," he said, testing the waters.

"She might not be able to hurt you, but I can," Dax said, and he stepped forward as if he were going to demonstrate it shortly.

Croq stepped back, but not as quickly as some might. "What did you promise the Wood Mist to obtain a cure for me?" Croq asked. "If you share with me, I'll tell you what I know."

I weighed the damage of telling him anything and then thought of the vaguest explanation. "I have to go retrieve the body of my friend where I buried him." I left out the details of who or where.

The creature threw back its head, laughing heartily, making me wonder if he was all there.

"His name is Zarrod. He's our leader. I don't know where he is now, but I'd assume he's still in Newco. Last time I saw him, he was missing the tips of two fingers, but now I'd imagine after this last outbreak it would be three." Croq bowed slightly, smiling the whole time, and took off down the beach.

Dax watched him walk off and I rested a hand on his chest even though he didn't do anything to follow Croq. "We can't. We made a deal and he honored his part."

"This code of yours is mighty annoying at times."

"Yeah, tell me about it."

I waited until Croq was completely out of sight, and we were halfway back to the port, before I spoke. "We've got another problem."

"What is it?" Dax asked, just as I was figuring out how to tell him.

"Once the Wood Mist fixed him, he didn't have the dark mist around him anymore." Not a smidge of it—not even in the brightest sunlight.

"Would you have known he was a Dark Walker if you'd seen him somewhere else?" he asked. It was bad news, but we couldn't forget that we were still on the clock and were Rocky's only hope.

"Yes, but not until I was close to him. He still smelled different, but you didn't see the unusual sheen of skin and hair?"

"No. Fuck."

I didn't ask how that could be, but I wondered it.

Chapter Thirty-Three

It was late morning by time we got back to the dock and I could see the ship, far off in the distance. But whoever was supposed to watch for us coming back to port wasn't sending out a boat to get us.

"If they're playing poker or so drunk they forgot…" Those were actually our best-case scenarios, and somehow I feared they were unlikely.

"I don't think so," Dax said.

"Can you see anything?" I asked as he stared intently at the ship, squinting.

"No one is stirring on deck. I can't see any motion."

I squinted too, but it didn't help. I realized that even if his eyes weren't quite as amazing as his ears, they were still much better than mine.

He turned to me and I knew I wasn't going to like what he said. "There might be nothing but dead people on that ship."

He might be right, but it didn't matter. "I can't leave. What if Rocky is still on board and I'm the only person in the world who has a cure? He came here to help me. I need to know for sure."

Dax nodded. "Hey! You!" Dax yelled to some guy farther down on the beach about to push his boat into the water. "How much to row us out there?"

Dax brokered a deal, and we got in his boat and rowed out toward the ship.

Then we rowed past a dead body, bobbing in the ocean. I checked to make sure it wasn't Rocky, and then spent the rest of the trip hoping not to see another one.

I'd never felt such relief as when a rope ladder was thrown down from the deck.

I knew before I cleared the rail that something was definitely wrong. When you live in a place for a while, you come to know the sounds. The men moving about on deck, crates being slid across wood, hollers to one another—all the noises I'd come to know were gone. I climbed over the railing and Marty was the only one on deck to greet us.

"Where is everybody?" I asked as Dax climbed over and stood beside me.

"Most of the ones that didn't die abandoned ship. Only a handful of us left now. Bloody Death hit hard right after you left. Jacob came down with it a little after that friend of yours. It came so quick, we think there must have been some carriers on that ship we boarded." Marty's eyes were a little glazed, as if he was still coming to terms with what had just happened and how quickly.

"Is Rocky still alive?" I asked as I started making my way across the deck, knowing I didn't have time for too many details if he was.

"Yes. Rocky is in your cabin, still hanging on. Jacob is still alive as well." Marty's eyes went as round as two full moons before he added, "But barely."

I ran my hand over my bag as I headed below deck, Dax behind me.

"There isn't enough for both," Dax reminded me.

"I know," I said as I stopped in front of my cabin, looking down at Jacob's door.

"I'll go check in on Jacob, see if there's anything that can be done."

I nodded, but we both knew there wasn't.

"Go," he said. "You might not have much time." Dax opened the door for me and then walked down toward the captain's quarters.

"Rocky?" I called as I walked into the cabin.

He didn't answer, and one look at his ashen face told me he was barely holding on. I ran to him, pulling my knife out as I went and dicing up the small piece of flesh, hoping the whole   time it wasn't a

309

complete scam.

I pushed the small pieces into his mouth and forced him to swallow, hoping he had enough life left in him to come back from this.

He didn't speak, but as I massaged his throat, he swallowed the pieces down until I had nothing but bloody residue left on my hands. I wiped my hands on the piece of paper that had held the flesh and then ran a hand through his hair.

"Rocky, I'm telling you right now, I can't handle another death on my hands, so you better snap out of this."

When I heard the door open, I knew it was Dax before I looked up.

"He doesn't look good," he said as he came to look over Rocky's still form.

"No, but I got the stuff down him, so we'll see."

"I'll keep an eye on him. Jacob's conscious and wants to speak to you. From the looks of him, I don't think he's got much time."

I nodded and left Dax with Rocky, knowing there wasn't much I could do for him now anyway.

***

Jacob's quarters were dark and smelled like the sickness that was claiming him. I didn't want to see another person die, not even him with my mixed feelings, but I felt a debt to him.

His head turned to me, and I hadn't realized how alive his eyes had always been before until his dull gaze landed on me. The fact that he was conscious at all was a testament to the strength he had, but I could see the blood at the corner of his mouth and his nose and knew he didn't have much longer.

He waved me forward, and this time I went and kneeled by his bunk. His hand took mine and I realized it was the first time he'd ever touched me.

"I need to tell someone what happened with her."

His grip was weak on mine, but I didn't try to pretend ignorance or pull my hand back. I knew he was talking about his wife, could still see the image of her dead in my mind.

"I killed her and it was the biggest regret of my life. Part of me is grateful to die, because maybe I'll see her again or go to hell and pay for my crime. Either way, I won't have to live with it anymore."

I nodded, realizing he must believe in something similar to Fudge's faith.

"I need to tell someone why."

I knew it was wrong, but it was hard to think for a second, *You couldn't have unloaded on Dax?* I already saw what he'd done. I didn't need the details.

"She'd tried to stage a revolt on my ships. I barely escaped death. She'd betrayed me, but I didn't blame her for doing it. She loved me once. I'd taken her for granted, abused it like it was a weakness until I turned it to hate. They say love and hate are closely related, and they're right. No one can hate you as much as the ones that once loved you.

"If I hadn't killed her, I would've lost control of my ship. At the time, I was young and stupid enough to believe that was a good enough reason. Not a day goes by that I don't miss her."

"Why are you telling me this now?"

"Because I'm going to die and I can't leave this world without at least one other soul knowing the truth. If there isn't anything after this life, I need someone to know how wrong I was. That I still love her even now. How I'd give anything to have her back."

Jacob's eyes had closed halfway through the telling, and his hand fell limp. His chest was still moving slightly, but it seemed like he'd used the last of his energy to get the past off his conscience.

Chapter Thirty-Four

I woke up alone on the floor of my cabin, the sun coming through the porthole to hit the empty bunk. Rocky was gone. Was he dead? I jumped up and ran to the deck only to find him looking out at the coast, standing tall and whole.

I sagged beside him, resting my arms on the railing and trying to catch my breath. "I thought you were dead," I said. "I thought I was going to find you being tossed overboard."

He smiled, looking no worse for the days he'd spent clinging to life. "Feel good as new, thanks to you and Dax."

"Jacob?" I asked, knowing he probably hadn't been as lucky.

He nodded. "Passed in the night. Dax told me you didn't have enough to help him."

I shook my head, looking down as the waves beat against the wood of the ship. "We only got one dose. But we know where to look for more now," I said, trying to put a positive spin on it for Rocky before switching subjects altogether. "So, my fellow Plaguer, the memories freaking you out yet?" I asked, knowing he would've picked up something from one of the crew. Not that there were many left—I looked about the deck and only spotted two.

Rocky shook his head. "I haven't gotten any."

"Nothing?"

It had to be the cure. Rocky would've died otherwise. He wasn't a true Plaguer, then.

I looked out at the coast, trying not to think of how many others might be dying right now, and realized we'd moved. "Where the hell are we?" There was nothing but forest and a small port up ahead, Sling City gone.

"Dax had the pirates turn the ship and get us farther north. It'll be a straighter shot to the Rock from here. We'll be close to port in under an hour."

It would be easier to get to Bookie's grave, as well. There was my promise to the Wood Mist to fulfill.

Rocky leaned on the railing beside me. "I want to know what your plans are."

"I have to go visit a

314

friend," was all I said, not wanting to talk of it yet, maybe not wanting to talk of it ever. I'd move him to a safe place while I tried not to think of what I was doing.

"I'm going back to the Rock. I want to know if you'll come with me."

"Rocky, you know it wasn't good there when I left," I said, hoping he'd leave it at that.

"Don't worry about any of that. I'll fix things. If you come back to the Rock, I'll protect you."

The Rock, a community of people who had run me out, nearly by torch and pitchfork. But what if he could fix things? They were his people. They listened to him. What if after the Bloody Death passed them, their fears had calmed down? Maybe I could have the life I'd always dreamed of?

Everything I'd ever wanted was being dangled in front of me...

Except it wasn't really what I wanted anymore. Dax and I had a different road we needed to take. We both had a reason to go to Newco, and I felt it in my gut that that was where I should be heading.

"I know that you think it's all about using you, but it's not," Rocky said, as if he could sense my decision before I spoke.

"I believe you. That's not the reason I'm not coming."

"Then why?"

"The cure I gave

you—I can't tell you what it is, but I know what's causing the sickness. If I go back to the Rock, I'll be turning my back on ever eliminating the disease. Do you realize how many lives can be saved?"

"What about your life? Don't you deserve one? You keep going and you might never find a cure. You'll probably end up dead."

"Going with you would be the easiest choice, and I'd regret it for however long I live."

He straightened. "It's Dax."

"No. I mean yes, I'll be going with him, but it's only because he needs to go to the same place."

He took a couple of steps away and shook his head. "I should've known that night. Dax showed me but I didn't want to see it. After you left, I talked myself out of it."

"See what?"

"The way you were with him. I told myself it was just your inexperience, but it wasn't. You're in love with him."

"No. I'm not. We just have a similar goal at the moment. It's a strange situation, is all."

"You don't get it yet, but I hope you do. That compulsion you feel, that's love. It isn't easy. Sometimes it burns you down and other times it builds you up, sets you free, higher than you ever thought you could go. There's nothing else like it in the world, and I wish I was the one you   felt like that about, but

316

I'm not."

"I told you. I don't love him. It's not love…it's convenience and…it's complicated."

"Then I wish I was the one you felt complicated by."

He raised his hand and trailed a couple fingers down my cheek before he turned.

I wrapped my arms around myself as I watched him walk away.

Chapter Thirty-Five

I made my way back to the cabin and opened the door to find Dax there, putting the last of his things into his bag.

He looked up as I walked in, and I expected him to ask me if I was ready. Then he kept packing.

I asked, "What are you doing?"

"I'm leaving. Jacob is dead. The cure isn't here. No reason to stay. Rocky is going back to the Rock. He'll help you move Bookie. I already talked to him about it. You can go there and be safe."

"But what about your revenge? You're going to Newco without me?"

"I think I've got enough information to do this without you."

"But I have to go there too. Why would you go without me?"

He shook his head. "You don't. I'll find this guy on my own and take him out. I won't be gone forever. I'll come back after it's done. I think maybe it's better this way. Less dangerous for you, and you'll have time to—"

"Absolutely not. You can't do it without me."

"Dal—"

A knock at the door preceded a call from one of the pirates. "The boat to take you ashore is ready."

"I'll be right there," Dax said, as he grabbed his bag.

"No. It's crazy. You'll never know for sure if it's even a Dark Walker you're killing. Bullshit. You aren't leaving without me. You can't." I grabbed my bag, shoved the few things that were out in the cabin into it quickly, and slung it on my shoulder. "This is just some test to see if I'll leave again."

"No. It's not. You didn't want any more blood on your hands. The Rock is the best place for you. It's going to be tough there, Dal. Maybe tougher than it's been so far."

"Sure, you'll just let me go now. No, I'll save us both the aggravation of doing that and just come with you," I said as I walked out the door, gripping my bag tightly and forcing myself to breathe evenly as I waited for him to tell me to leave again but hoping he wouldn't. I didn't know what this was between me and Dax, but I knew I couldn't walk away from it and I hoped he wouldn't make me.

We walked up to the deck and then I threw my bag over the side to the guy waiting in the smaller boat below, still waiting for Dax to tell me he didn't want me to come.

I was just about to climb over the rail and climb down the rope ladder when I heard him say, "Dal…"

Here it was. He was going to tell me I couldn't come. I gripped the railing while I waited for the words to come. When he didn't speak, I forced myself to turn around, fighting the burning in my eyes.

"What?" I asked, even though I knew what was coming. I looked at him, knowing that if he was done with me there would be no stopping him. I waited, afraid to speak, to breathe, even, waiting for him to say that he didn't want me to come with him.

As I waited, I didn't know what I'd do. I'd want to rage against him for shoving me aside, but I'd already taken the first step myself when I came here. Would I beg him to reconsider? Maybe…possibly—definitely. I didn't know what this gaping hole in my chest was right now, but I knew it would eat me alive if I left him.

The worst was, I had no idea what he was going to say. His face was blank as he stared at me without speaking.

His eyes softened first. "I really hope there's a brush in that bag, because your hair might be the worst I've ever seen it."

"No. Actually, there isn't. I lost it overboard a week ago." It hadn't been funny at the time, but we both laughed. We were back. It had been close, but turned out there was yet another reset button left for us.

I was starting to realize that for better or worse, I wasn't sure I could live without this man. I wouldn't go as crazy as saying it was love. I wasn't sure I knew what that even was, but something in me died when he wasn't around and didn't come back until he was beside me again. And I hoped whatever this emoiton was, he was feeling it too, because if he wasn't, I needed to get away from him now before it got worse, and I had a suspicion it would. I needed to limit the damage and move on.

That connection, that strange bond that was growing between us, was almost palpable as we stood a few feet apart, but instead of feeling miles away like I had in the past, I could feel his energy wrapping around me.

It was something so strong it still scared me, and yes, he was right, I'd been running before. But now I knew what it felt like without him, and I knew real fear. I didn't know if this was what they called love, like Rocky said, but I wasn't sure I could go on without it.

"I can't believe you thought you were going to be able to do this without me," I said, as I picked up the rope ladder and dropped it down the side of the ship.

"I know. It's not like I'm Moobie or anything," he said as I started climbing down.

A minute later, as he

321

settled into the boat beside me, I said, "Exactly my point. You need me. You can't be running around the Wilds alone."

Dax laughed as the pirate rowing the boat raised his eyebrows.

Chapter Thirty-Six

After buying the only bike in existence in a ten-mile radius, we rode for nearly a day and a half straight until we finally got to the place I'd buried Bookie.

My legs were already weak from all the riding as I walked over to the place I'd buried him and fell to my knees beside the grave. "He's here." I ran my fingers over the stones I'd covered his grave with, as if I could touch Bookie somehow.

Dax looked about for a stick, but I pointed to nearby shrubs. "There's a shovel there."

"Why did you leave a shovel here?" he asked as he dug around and found the spot it was hidden.

"So I could bring him new books when I visited."

Dax grabbed the shovel from where I'd left it and

walked over to where I was. "You don't need to stay. Go take a walk. I'll handle it."

I shook my head, refusing to sit there and cry while Dax did all the work, or worse, run away and hide from the ugliness of Bookie's death. "No. I put him here and I made the deal. I need to stay with him." I moved some of the stones aside.

He didn't argue with me as he started digging.

"How far down did you bury him?" Dax asked after he'd been digging for a little while.

"About three feet or so," I said, and leaned over, looking down into the grave like I'd avoided doing until now.

"He's not here," Dax said as he jumped out of the grave.

I didn't think of what I was doing, but I climbed into the spot he'd vacated. I dropped down and dug with my fingers for his body under the dirt. "How could he be gone?"

"Dal."

They'd taken Bookie. "Who would take him? Why would they do this?"

"Come on," Dax said, a hand reached down toward me.

"Why would they do this?" I asked again, ignoring his hand and feeling like I was back in the house when Bookie had just died. When I buried Bookie here, I knew I'd always be able   to visit him. Now he was gone.

"Dal, give me your hand," he said.

"I have to find him."

"There's nothing there but dirt, and I don't think I can handle watching you look for him for another second."

Ignoring him, I continued to dig, my nails breaking and the skin on my hands getting cut up by rocks.

Then Dax was in the hole with me and pulling me upward as I fought against him.

"No, I have to find him."

"Dal, he's not here," he said, wrapping his arms around me. "Stop. He's not here."

The strength left me, my hands no longer pushing against his chest but just resting there.

"You don't understand. He was my best friend. He didn't care who I could be or what I could do for him. He liked me."

Dax's arms were warm around me and I felt his hand stroking my back. "I'll be your best friend," he said softly.

"You don't even like me most of the time," I said on a half sob at the notion.

"That's not true. Just some of the time." It was the most idiotic thing to say, and the most perfect, because instead of crying, I started to laugh.

A couple minutes passed before he climbed out of the grave and gave me a   hand up.

325

"This is bad. I made a promise to the Wood Mist. Who would've taken him?" I looked at the empty grave, with only the books I'd buried there now.

"I don't know, but I'm thinking we'll find out. Come on. Let's get going." He tugged me away, and I let him.

He got on the bike and I remembered the Rock was only a few minutes ride from here. "Dax, I'm not going back to the Rock. Not even for the night. It's a safe place for Tiffy, Tank, and Fudge, but it's not the place for me."

"That isn't where I meant."

"Then where?" I asked, knowing we'd have to stop somewhere to rest up and plan. He appeared as fresh as someone who'd just slept a solid eight hours, but I didn't need a mirror to know how I appeared.

"The farm."

It was too good to be possible. "But I thought it wasn't safe?"

"I heard from Lucy before I left. A couple search parties stopped by but haven't been there for a while. They're probably watching the place, but they won't be watching the way we come, and it's closer to Newco."

"What about Tiffy, Tank, and Fudge?"

"They're better off staying there—for now, anyway. We'll figure it out after we get there if it's safe," he said.

I climbed back onto the bike and then couldn't stop myself from mouthing, *We're going back, Bookie. We're finally going back home.*

I told you it would be okay.

You were right, I said as I wrapped my arms around Dax.

***

We rode through a cave that led out of the stone wall that protected the backside of the farm. I couldn't believe I'd never noticed the entrance before.

I watched Dax cover the opening. "How come we didn't take this way when we left?"

"Too short for Fudge's horse."

I got off the bike and couldn't believe I was stepping back onto the farm's rich soil, breathing the crisp air and smells that were uniquely this place's. I stepped around the trees that hid the cave completely to see the yellow farmhouse standing there, and then checked immediately to see if they'd been tending my garden.

It was almost surreal, as we approached and heads turned in our direction. It wasn't the smiling faces that I'd gotten at the Rock, but I wouldn't get that reception there either—not anymore.

I spotted one person smiling and standing on the back porch. Lucy walked toward us, and it was the last person I'd ever expected to get a warm welcome from.

"I hope you're back for a while," she said to both of us. "This *being in charge* shit ain't what it's cracked up to be." She looked around at the crowd gathering as she said it, and I could see the disgruntled expressions on both sides.

Dax started making the rounds with his people as Lucy fell into step beside me.

"Was it bad?" I asked, not having to specify that I meant the Newco force coming through.

"Nah. They'd show up and leave as soon as they poked their noses around. Haven't seen them for a while now."

I headed in the house, but not before I saw a bike with a *grey* gas tank sitting beside the house.

"Is that Dax's bike?" I asked.

"Yeah, he sent us word to get it from the Rock and bring it back here."

Blue tank my ass. He'd tricked me!

"Your room is still free, as commanded," Lucy said, oblivious to my annoyance over the bike.

Dax had told her to keep everyone out of my room? Okay, maybe not an ass, but we'd be having a word. I looked to where Dax had stopped to talk to a group of his people. I should've been mad, but I wasn't. His head turned in my direction and suddenly it was just the two of us there. I knew he'd do a perimeter run—he did it at every new place—but I wondered what bed he'd be climbing into after that, and found I hoped it was mine.

"You slept with him, didn't you? I know there's something there."

Maybe I hadn't   given Lucy enough

credit.

"I'm super tired. Going to bed!" I said as I half ran up the stairs and locked the door before collapsing on the soft coverlet and perfect bed. It was going to be hard to leave this place again.

***

I snapped upright, drenched in sweat, but at least I hadn't screamed.

I looked out at the night sky through the bay window, back in my old room at the farm, the one I thought I'd never see again, and this time I didn't need inventory. I knew Dax was probably out there, patrolling for threats.

And then I felt the presence there, and it didn't feel like Dax. I froze, not sure whether I should turn toward it or not, and trying to remember where I put my knives when I'd crashed.

"Dal?" a familiar voice said.

I turned and saw Bookie standing on the other side of my bed, clear in the light of the moon.

"Bookie?"

He nodded, but not in a smooth movement, as if he wasn't completely sure himself.

"Bookie, you died. I buried you." My eyes scanned him. It was a trick, some sort of ploy by the Wood Mist or the Dark Walkers,   something.

"I know."

He was terrified. I could hear the tremble in his voice. Every logical thought told me not to trust the creature in front of me, that there was no way it was Bookie.

But it was Bookie's big hazel eyes, his mouth. It stood like Bookie, and even had the small line that cut through his eyebrow that he told me he got when a horse had kicked him and almost taken his eye.

I should've headed the warnings my mind was telling me—that he was dead and buried—but it was hard to hear them when my heart was screaming so loudly. I leapt from bed, my arms going around him tightly and almost knocking him off his feet as we stumbled back together. I locked my hands together behind his back as he returned the embrace.

"Dal, some crazy shit happened. I'm really freaked out," he said as his arms tightened around me.

"It's okay, Bookie," I said, not caring what it was. "I've got you back and I'm going to protect you this time."

The Wilds Book Four Coming in September of 2016!

For more information on Donna Augustine and her books, go to www.donnaaugustine.com.

21772388R00188

Made in the USA
San Bernardino, CA
06 January 2019